Never Giving Up

By Anie Michaels

Edited by

Krysta Drechsler

To Kamryn and Noah,

Without you this book wouldn't even exist.

Never Giving Up
© *Copyright Anie Michaels 2014*

Chapter One

Ella

"Ella, I swear to God, if you pick up that box you're going to find yourself strapped to a chair and not in the sexy way."

I huffed out a breath laced with frustration. This was a battle I'd been fighting for weeks unnecessarily. Every time I bent over, tried to lift anything, or Heaven forbid, I opened a door for myself, he barked at me. I tried to always remember that he was just being himself, just being *Porter*, the protective and possessive man I loved, but one can only take so much.

"And I swear to God, if you don't lay off, I'm going to call your mother and tell her she'll never get any grandchildren because I've sworn off men. You've got to cut me some slack here." He must have picked up on the fact that I was one raised eyebrow away from losing my mind because he walked over to me and pulled me into his chest, his arms wrapping around my shoulders. We stood there for a moment, him trying to take my stress away and me letting him.

"Hey," he said, pulling away from me enough so I could look up at him. "I'm sorry. You know I'm not trying to upset you. I'm just worried."

"I know. But you have to understand that I'm not even pregnant –"

"Yet," he interrupted. I resisted the urge to roll my eyes at him.

"I'm not pregnant. There is no baby in my womb, ergo, no reason for you to put lifting restrictions on me."

"You could be pregnant. You could be two weeks pregnant. There could be a little Porter right in here," he said, laying a hand over the flat, soft part of my stomach. "You don't know."

"You don't know either and there's no such thing as two weeks pregnant. You have to be four weeks pregnant for it to count for anything, so please, lay off a little. It's not like I'm over here trying to lift boulders. This is a box of scarves. I think I can manage. I'm not putting myself, or the baby you think could possibly be in my uterus, in jeopardy." A smile danced across his beautiful face and it was hard not to smile back at him.

"I think there's a baby in there, Ella. I think my boys managed a honeymoon baby." His nose came down and nuzzled into my neck, his breath flitting across my skin making goose bumps appear. "I think that night we were on the beach, in that cabana, with only the moonlight surrounding us…" My mind wrapped around the words he was saying and I was transported back on the beaches of Bora Bora where we'd spent our honeymoon. He was talking about one night in particular and I remembered it well. I would always remember that night.

I had instructed him to wait in the cabana for me and told him I would be out in a minute. It was one of the bravest moments of my life when I walked out of our private bungalow and tried to casually yet seductively make it to him without tripping over sand. I had purchased a special piece of lingerie especially for this occasion, for my husband.

I felt the breeze swirl through the lace that flowed down from the tiny bow made from ribbon that was nestled between my breasts. The sheer lace covered my breasts, barely, then flowed out, open in the front, all leading down to the tiniest pair of white, lacey, thong underwear I'd ever seen. Obviously, the lace was just a pretense, because every part of me was on display. I took in a few deep breaths, trying to calm myself as I walked towards him.

The sand had cooled considerably since the sun was no longer beating down on the beach. The small particles slipped through my toes as I made my way towards the little hut that held my husband.

My heart fluttered at the thought of Porter being my husband. We'd known each other less than a year, been swept away in a sea of unimaginable love, faced seemingly insurmountable obstacles, and still managed to end up here, at the ocean, where everything had begun. He was my calm and steady surf when storms and winds had raged around me. When everything in my life had been confusing and tortuous, Porter had been the one who always brought me back around to my center. He was the only thing I had ever *needed*.

I came around the side of the cabana to find him lounging back, hands behind his head, biceps deliciously taut, legs crossed at the ankles, admiring the ocean that was every shade of blue imaginable, including the midnight blue it became after dark. Say what you like about how we met, how fast it all happened, but when his body was on display for me like this, I welcomed every hurdle we'd ever jumped over to be together. He was made for me, exclusively. He was breathtakingly beautiful and just seeing him like that, relaxed and unburdened, only made my insides melt into a hot puddle of lust.

"You're beautiful." I thought I'd spoken my thoughts aloud but then realized I hadn't said them at all, but he had said the same thing about me. I hadn't noticed when his eyes found me because I'd been preoccupied with him. My eyes finally met his and the tether that tied us together, something that held me to him, tugged at my center and pulled me towards him.

His white swimming shorts matched the lingerie I was wearing and as I straddled his waist, our centers melded into one another. I ran my hands up along his chest, my fingers grazing through the soft smattering of hair and my eyes caught his.

"Hello, Wife," he said with the most loving smile upon his face, his eyes sparkling up at me.

"Hello, my husband," I whispered back. His hands came to my hips, fingering the single string that held on the triangle of lace. I felt the roughness of his hands continue down my thighs and circle back to grab my ass. His grip forced me forward and I pressed my chest to his, resting atop him, his hands still running over my sensitive skin, my hands finding their way to run through his dark hair. "I love you, you know." Our faces were just inches from each other, my voice a quiet whisper caught in the breeze that feathered over us, gently moving the curtains of the cabana. His response was simply to lift his head and softly bump the tip of his nose against mine...

"Ella?"

I snapped out of my daydream to see the same sparkling eyes still staring back at me. I smiled and tipped up to kiss him.

"Sorry. I was thinking about Bora Bora." I smiled knowingly at him. His eyes widened in recognition.

"I miss Bora Bora," he said quietly.

"Well, I could have recreated the experience for you, but you ripped off my pretty bridal lingerie," I said with mock irritation. I loved it when he ripped things off my body. It was an expensive habit, but I wouldn't make him change it for anything.

"I'll have plenty of chances to ruin more pretty things as long as we're making babies."

"And even if we're not, I hope."

He smiled and nodded. "But since we *are*, no lifting. Honestly Ella, you've got to take care of yourself."

I chose to remain quiet and not argue. Instead, I kissed him gently and moved on to hang garments on hangers, a task he couldn't possibly find fault in. After a few minutes of working quietly together, I heard the door to the shop open and looked up. Kalli walked in, smiling broadly, looking fantastic.

"Kal! What are you doing here? I thought you were in Seattle for a few weeks." I walked quickly over to her and wrapped her in a hug, thankful to have my friend back unexpectedly.

"Megan wanted me to come and try on bridesmaid dresses, so I decided to make a weekend of it. Aren't you coming?"

"She hasn't said anything to me, but that doesn't mean I'm not going. It's probably on my calendar and I didn't pay attention. I'm so excited to see you!" I hugged her again. Besides Porter, Kalli was one of the things brought into my life in the last year that I was so thankful for. In the most tumultuous time of my life, Kalli offered an instant friendship that grounded me when I couldn't remember a part of my life. She listened to my worries and concerns and *believed* me. She was the one person in my life who I knew was being completely honest with me and didn't have any ulterior motives.

"Hello, Porter," Kalli said, walking towards him. He gave her a hug and smiled at her.

"Hey, Kalli. So what do you think of the new place?" He asked. Kalli's eyes floated around the store, taking everything in.

"This place looks awesome, you guys. You've been working hard. How long until you think you can open up?" She looked at me expectantly.

"I am hoping to open up next month. I still have to put out all the merchandise and work on hiring. Megan is putting together interviews for early next week."

"You're still planning on spending the majority of your time here and not at Poppy, right?"

"Yes, Megan and Brittany are doing a fantastic job running Poppy so I am going to focus on this store until it is up and running one hundred percent."

"Have you decided on a name yet?"

"Yes! I'm going with Dahlia. You like?"

"I love! So pretty."

Porter walked over to us and placed his hand on my waist. "I'm going to head out, Babe. I've got to go check on the worksite over on Miller Street." He pressed a kiss against my temple and I felt his breath on my ear sending chills throughout my body. "Remember what we spoke about," he whispered. "Be safe." My eyes closed involuntarily and I leaned into him.

"Always," I sighed. He kissed my cheek and patted my bottom then walked towards the door.

"It was good to see you, Kalli. I'm sure I'll be seeing you again before you head back to Seattle?" He asked, pausing at the door.

"It'll be hard to get rid of me," she said with a smile.

"Good," he said, then he winked at her before walking out.

"Your husband is so ridiculously attractive," Kalli said wistfully. I noticed the blush on her face and smiled to myself.

"Yes, I'm aware and so is he. I think he tries to make you blush."

"Mission accomplished," she says quietly, making me laugh. "Can I help you with anything?"

"No, you cannot. In fact, I was about to break for lunch. Want to join me?"

"Definitely."

Thirty minutes later, we were seated at one of my favorite lunch spots, a little delicatessen in downtown Salem.

"So, I haven't heard much from you since the honeymoon. How was it?" Kalli asked, raising her eyebrows at me, a sly grin on her face.

"Oh my goodness, Kal, it was wonderful. You *have* to go to Bora Bora sometime. It's the most beautiful place I've ever seen." Kalli took a stab at her salad.

"I don't think it's a place for single people, Ella. Bora Bora is a place for couples."

I looked at my friend and knew what she was thinking. I reached out and placed a hand over hers. "You'll find someone, Kalli. You're a great girl and any guy would be lucky to have you." She inhaled deeply and nodded.

"I know, I know." She shook her head, seemingly trying to erase the thoughts she harbored there. "I've just never had a good track record with guys, and the whole thing with Kyle just really put a nail in that coffin."

I grimaced at her words. I knew she felt guilty about Kyle and I didn't know how to help her let those feelings go. I had explained, time and time again, that she couldn't be responsible for his vile and ultimately psychotic behavior, but she harbored those feelings of guilt deep and I couldn't reach them. Honestly, we'd all been affected by Kyle and what transpired, but Kalli seemed to be the only one who didn't have someone to help her move past it.

"Don't let Kyle and what he did make you miserable, Kalli. Don't give him that kind of control. He doesn't deserve it," I stated, wishing she'd do more than listen, wishing she'd *hear* me. She nodded her head and let out a sigh. Then I watched as she plastered on a fake smile for my benefit.

"How's Megan holding up? Only four months until the wedding. Has she become a bridezilla yet?"

"No, I think she is starting to see the appeal of doing it the way Porter and I did though."

"You mean eloping?"

I nodded. "Yeah, I think she's getting bogged down by details and just wants to be married." I shrugged. "It'll be beautiful and over before she knows it."

"Why *did* you and Porter elope?"

I thought about the question, trying to put together a good answer for her. "I guess, after everything that happened, we just wanted to be together. After a few months of trying to plan a traditional wedding, thinking about guest lists and table settings, all stuff that didn't really matter to either of us, we just wanted to skip the planning and start the marriage."

"Well, that's the most romantic thing I've ever heard," she said with a grin. "Married life suits you."

"Porter suits me." I couldn't help but smile. I remember what life was like without him and I never wanted to be that person again. The idea that I could have gone my whole life without experiencing the way he made me feel was depressing. Everyone deserved to have someone love them the way Porter loved me. His love was transcendent. It lifted me up in so many ways. I would gladly spend the rest of my life trying to make him feel even a small semblance of how he made me feel. It was the least I could do.

"So, you'll be there tomorrow to try on dresses?" Kalli asked hopefully.

"I'll be there. It'll be fantastic."

That evening when I walked into our rental house in Salem, I didn't see Porter in the living room so I called out to him, "Babe, you home?"

"I'm in the bedroom," he responded. I set my purse and bags down on the kitchen table and walked back to the bedroom.

The house was small. Much smaller than I would have ever wanted, but it was only a rental while our house was being completed, so I knew I could deal with it in the meantime. It had been a struggle to find another house that was available so quickly. I never could return to the first house we rented in Salem, never could bring myself to walk back into the house where Kyle abducted me. No one blamed me and Porter didn't want to go in that house either. We found another house to rent, albeit smaller, until ours was built and move-in ready.

"Hey, you," I said as I leaned up against the doorframe of the bedroom. I wanted to take a picture of him as he was sprawled out on the bed in my most favorite of Porter pastimes: lying in bed, in his pajamas, reading. Nothing sexier than a relaxed Porter reading a book. Well, there were a few sexier sides of Porter.

"Hey, Babe. How was the rest of your day?" He asked as he laid the book down on his chest, pages opened up against him, saving his place.

"It was good. I had lunch with Kalli and then just worked on the merchandise at the store for a little while. By the way," I said as I walked to the dresser in the corner of the room, unbuttoning my jeans as I walked. "I'll probably be a little late tomorrow evening. I am going to Portland to do some dress shopping." I watched his eyes follow my movements as I pushed the pants down my legs, taking care to bend at the waist, carefully aiming my bottom at him, knowing he'd enjoy it.

"I was planning on working in Lincoln City tomorrow, so maybe I'll stay a little later and have dinner with my mom."

I smiled at him. Not only did I love his mother, Tilly, but the idea that he thought of her and went out of his way to spend time with her made my heart melt a little. I grabbed the hem of my shirt and slowly pulled it over my head. I watched as he swallowed hard, his eyes raking me over as I stood at the foot of our bed in just my bra and panties. He picked his book up and closed it, laying it on his bedside table.

"Good book?" I asked him innocently.

"Huh?" He asked, confused.

"The book you just put down, is it a good book?"

He looked over at the nightstand and then back to me. "I don't want to talk about books right now," he said, his voice becoming low and sexy. He crawled forward on the bed towards me, making me giggle. When he reached the edge of the bed, he sat up on his knees and I reached forward, pulling his tee shirt up. He had to help me by pulling it over his head, but that gave me the opportunity to place my hands on his fantastic body.

"I should have held out for a sexier husband," I said, trying to keep a straight face as I splayed my hands over his pectoral muscles, sliding them up and over his glorious shoulders and biceps.

"Oh, you've got jokes, Mrs. Masters?" Hearing him use my married name did more for me sexually than I thought he could ever comprehend. I loved that our name bound us together, that he gave me something so sacred to him – the name his father gave him. I took his name willingly and thankfully. I loved being Mrs. Masters. "Jokes on you, I think. I got the better end of this deal," he said as he grabbed my ass. He pulled my body into his as he peered into my eyes, our foreheads gently meeting. I felt his erection pressing into my belly, his obvious need for me making my own insides burn intensely.

"Do you ever think we'll tire of each other? I can't imagine keeping up with this level of sexual appetite forever," I said as his mouth came down to nibble on my collar bone. I felt his tongue flash over my skin and the goose bumps raised all over my body.

"I'll never get tired of being with you, Ella. But eventually, at some point," he said placing more kisses up my neck, "there will come a time when we'll have to remember our passion, and bring it back to life." I knew he was right. All marriages went through troubles and dry spells. I wasn't living in a fantasy and I was well aware that marriages took work.

"Promise you'll remind me?" I whispered. His face appeared in front of mine and his eyes looked lovingly at me.

"I've done a pretty good job so far, haven't I?" He said with a grin.

"Yes, my love, you have."

Chapter Two

Ella

I saw Kalli's expression in the mirror reflecting back at me and I tried hard to stifle a giggle. Megan couldn't see her face because she was focused on the embellishments along the hem of the dress Kalli was currently wearing, but I could see and it was hard not to laugh.

"What do we think, girls?" The very eager, yet nice, saleswoman gave me an expectant look.

"Uh, it's…" I stammered.

"It's not bad," Megan offered.

"What about all this *stuff*?" Kalli motioned to the bottom of the dress.

"The rhinestone detailing?" The saleswoman clarified.

"Yeah. Does it, maybe, look a little cheap?" Kalli wrinkled her nose, but said the words softly as if not to offend anyone.

"You think it looks cheap?" Megan whispered. If there was anyone in the room to trust about this, it was Kalli. She was a big-time Hollywood costume designer. Kalli opened her eyes wider at Megan pleading silently not to make her utter the words. Megan's head whipped around to me. "What do you think, Ella?"

"I think we can find something more perfect." That was my attempt to soften the blow. We didn't need rhinestones or sequin distractions on our dresses. We needed a good fabric, a pretty color, a nice design, and then we needed to fade into the background. Megan was the focus of the wedding, after all. "Do you have any catalogues we could look at?" I asked the saleswoman. She huffed a little at my request but promptly walked away saying she'd bring us some magazines. "Kalli, please take that dress off," I laughed.

Megan sat down in the chair next to me and exhaled loudly. "It shouldn't be this difficult." She sounded defeated and we'd only just started.

"Megs, everything will be just fine. We'll look through the catalogues and get some ideas. Do you think you want Kalli and me to wear the same dress or different ones?"

"I don't care. I just want them the same color. You guys can pick different ones. I want everything to look cohesive."

I placed a hand on her shoulder and squeezed gently. "Everything is going to turn out fine. We've got plenty of time." She turned and smiled at me.

"Thanks, Fella." Just then, the saleswoman brought us some catalogues and we spent a few minutes flipping through them. Kalli seemed to gravitate towards the dresses that were corseted and fitted through the torso and I hoped for something a little looser, an empire waist perhaps.

The saleswoman brought us some dresses similar to what we were drawn to. I slipped on a strapless, empire waist gown that flowed down around my ankles. The fabric was light and airy. I loved it. I walked out of the dressing room and waited for Megan's scrutiny.

"Ella, it's a pretty dress, but it doesn't do anything for your figure. You look like a fancy peasant."

"Ok, well, first, that's an oxymoron. Second, I don't need anything done for my figure so I'm not worried about that."

"It's true, Megan. Ella is already married to the most handsome man we've ever met. She's officially the Matron of Honor. She's not looking for any single men to hook up with at your wedding."

"Patrick is the most handsome man I've ever seen," Megan stated, confident in her fiancé's good looks. "But come on, Ella. You don't want to wear a loose fitting drape to my wedding, do you?"

I sighed loudly and decided that it was impossible to keep our situation a secret any longer. "Listen, Megs. The truth is, I'm going to need to order a dress like this in case my body is different in four months." I tried to imply meaning without blatantly stating that Porter and I were trying to have a baby. Kalli's head poked out around from the doorway of her dressing room, eyes wide, mouth open into a big "O". Megan was looking at me like I'd asked her a calculous question.

"Shut. Up." Kalli whisper-yelled.

"Shhh! It's not really a secret but we haven't told anyone yet. I don't want to jinx it. Let's just order me a frumpy dress and be done with it."

"Are you already…" Kalli's eyebrows rose up and she eyed my midsection.

"No, I'm not pregnant yet, but we're trying."

"What?!" Megan yelled, finally catching on. "You're having a baby?"

"We're *trying* to have a baby. Nothing is growing yet," I said as I waved a hand around in front of my belly.

"So you're saying you didn't have a shotgun elopement because you're pregnant?" Megan said, shooting me an expectant glare.

"No, we did not elope because I was pregnant. I am not pregnant. Like I said, we're trying. We've been trying."

"I'm sure you have," Kalli said with a snicker as she went back into her dressing room. I grinned too, realizing that once you announced that you were trying to have a baby, everyone automatically knew you're having a lot of sex. I blushed and turned away from my sister.

"In light of recent information, I approve of the baggy peasant dress. Just make sure you put a baby in your belly to make it worth it."

"I'll, uh, do my best."

Kalli and I successfully picked out dresses in a very pretty, soft lilac color. Kalli's dress would be sure to snag her any single guy at the wedding if she wanted one. Neither of us, though, would hold a candle to my sister. I couldn't wait to see Patrick's face as she walked down the aisle.

It was seven o'clock before we were done and after I said goodbye to Kalli and Megan, I sat in my car and called Porter.

"Hey, Babe," he said as he answered.

"Hey, yourself. I'm done dress shopping. Just calling to see what you're up to."

"I'm sitting here at the restaurant with my mom, just chatting."

"Oh, great. How is she?"

"She's good. She misses you. Speaking of which, I am going to have to come back to Lincoln City tomorrow to work on some issues happening at the job site here, so I was wondering if you wanted to drive out for the night. I can come back to Salem, no problem, but I thought a night at the beach house could be good, too."

My heart fluttered at the thought of the beach house. Porter's house. The house where we fell in love.

"I don't mind driving out. It's only seven. I can be there by nine."

"Perfect," he said softly, as if he were imagining us at the beach house just like I was.

"Yes. And then tomorrow I can have breakfast with your mom," I added, excited about the idea. We said our goodbyes as Porter always insisted that I not talk on the phone and drive at the same time.

Being used to the drive from so many trips back and forth over the months, I found my mind wandering as I made my way through the dusk. The trees whisked by helping my mind relax and thoughts seeped in, welcomed or not. I thought about the wedding, that wonderful week we spent on white sands and in blue waters so crystal clear you could see straight down to the ocean floor.

I remembered laying in a hammock with Porter, gently swinging in the shade, napping, and reading. I remembered dancing slowly with him to tropical music, feeling his hands wandering across the skin bared by my sundress. I smiled widely when my mind recalled the nights spent together, loving each other, worshipping each other, celebrating the obstacles we overcame to get to that moment.

I drove into Lincoln City proper and, as always, tried to ignore the tightening in my chest and the way my heart sped up as my car neared the street which held the house I rented so many months ago. It was in that house where I forged this soul-altering relationship with my husband, but it was also the house where I had done the unthinkable. I always told myself that I wasn't going to look down the street. I wasn't going to turn my head and try to see the house. I knew I couldn't see it from the street. I knew it was dark and nothing could be seen anyhow. But every time – my head turned, my breath caught, and my heart pounded.

I don't know if I expected to see Kyle standing there, or if I expected the feelings of guilt and regret to go away, but every time I passed that street my panic returned. Porter and I had discussed whether Lincoln City was a good place for me to be after all that had happened. My therapist had convinced him, with my help, that as long as I was using my tools to deal with the panic, and wasn't holding it all in, I could be fine here. I wanted to be fine here. This was where everything started, and beyond all the bad that happened, our everything was beautiful.

I made it to Porter's house and again was hit with the absolute beauty of what he created. He would never call himself creative or an artist, but that's exactly what he was. Anyone who saw the houses he built would agree; the man was gifted. The beauty of the house was instantly magnified when I saw his gorgeous frame step out onto the wrap-around porch. He waited for me and I appreciated that so much. I knew, deep in my core, that he felt my absence. I knew it to be true because I felt it as well. Months ago we'd made an agreement to never spend a night apart and we hadn't since. It was important to our relationship that we fed our need to be near one another. It meant a lot of driving sometimes, and getting up earlier than I would have liked on some days to make a longer commute to work, but the benefits to *us* were hardly comparable to the costs.

To feel him next to me every night, to know that I would wake every morning with his arms wrapped around me, was a kind of serenity I'd never experienced before and I was glad to make the sacrifices needed to give him the same feeling of security it gave me.

"Hey, Babe," he said with a smile as I got out of my car. "Good drive?" He asked because he knew how hard it was for me to drive past that street.

"It was the same. It wasn't harder, so that's good, but still difficult." I made my way up the steps and walked right into his waiting arms. I rested my cheek against his chest and felt his hands spread over my back, one coming to rest at the base of my neck, the other landing possessively on the curve of my rear.

"I have some dinner for you if you're hungry," he mumbled against my hair.

"You cooked?" I asked, surprised, cocking an eyebrow at him.

"My mom sent me home with something for you," he admitted.

"Ah," I said, laughing. "That makes more sense." He kissed my temple then took my hand and led me into the house. We never bothered to pack when we left one city for another, we kept everything we needed at both houses to avoid it. And when we weren't in town, either his mother or his friends, Matt and Brook, kept an eye on the house for us.

"Why don't you eat and I will go draw us a bath?"

"That sounds perfect. A bath sounds wonderful." He led me into the kitchen and I sat at the barstool at the island. I smiled watching him bring a plate out of the microwave. He couldn't cook anything and his mother knew this. I loved that she thought of me and knew us well enough to know what we needed. I was blessed with the best mother-in-law.

He set the plate down in front of me and I smiled at the lasagna knowing his mother had made it herself.

"I love your mom's lasagna," I moaned, the scent of it wafting towards me.

"And she loves you," he said as he kissed the top of my head. "Eat, then come upstairs."

I watched him disappear up the stairs, not at all bothered by the sight of his backside as he climbed each one.

Porter

I knew when she arrived she'd be upset. I also knew she'd be more upset than she would let on. It was one of the traits of hers I loved – her strength and her need to handle things on her own. I also knew that she would let me help her, as long as I was subtle about it. Dinner was easy; it wasn't even my idea. I had my mother to thank for that. Ella and I both knew I couldn't cook, but I could offer her a little peace and comfort with a bath.

All those years ago when I'd built this house, designed it from the ground up, I never knew I'd been building it for her. What did I need a giant jetted tub for? Nothing. I hadn't even necessarily wanted one, but somewhere inside me I guess I knew that someday she'd like to have one. It was moments like this I was glad I'd listened to that little voice in my heart that whispered *someday*, even when my mind said *never*.

I placed candles around the ledge of the window that was dark now, but usually had a breathtaking view of the Pacific Ocean. I placed candles on the counter and a few in the bedroom as well, then I lit them all and began to fill the tub. I found her favorite bubble bath that smelled of vanilla and poured it in, watching the froth of the soap build, smelling the scent that always brought me back to her. When the tub was filled with hot water and bubbles, I turned the faucet off.

In the bedroom I turned on some low music, just wanting to fill the silence. I knew it was in the silence where her mind took her away to the places that troubled her. I didn't want to overwhelm her, but the distraction of the soft piano music would hopefully be enough to keep her away from the darkness.

After a few minutes, I heard her coming up the stairs and watched as she walked into the bedroom, a smile gracing her face. Her resiliency took my breath away. There were so many times I wanted to wrap her in my arms and make all her fears disappear, but I knew that wasn't what she needed. She needed me to support her, to love her, and to be present – to listen when she wanted to talk and to hold her when she needed comfort. But she didn't need saving, even if I longed to do just that. Together we'd been through enough, but on her own she'd battled the worst demons and won every fight. I was so proud that she was mine and that she fought so hard to come back to me.

"Feeling better?"

"Your mother's cooking always makes me feel better," she said with a sleepy grin.

"Come here," I motioned for her to stand in front of me as I sat on the bed. When she made it to me, I reached out and started unbuttoning her jeans. She toed off her shoes and kicked them to the side, her eyes never leaving mine. I slid her pants down her legs, my hands grazing over the smooth skin of her thighs. She stepped out of them while placing her hands on my shoulders for balance. I grabbed the bottom of her sweater and pulled it over her head, her blonde hair falling softly back to her shoulders, mussed in the sexiest of ways. She stood before me in just her bra and panties, looking so much like an angel, her blue eyes sparkling at me. I leaned forward and placed a small kiss on her stomach.

"You really think there's a baby in there?" She whispered, sounding hopeful.

"I think there's a good chance."

She smiled at me, her eyes even brighter.

"Let's get in the bath," I said, standing and reaching behind her to unclasp her bra.

"You're coming with me?" She asked as she piled her hair on top of her head and secured it with a hair tie.

"If that's ok." I pulled the straps off her shoulders, the bra falling away to the floor leaving her bare to me. She placed her hands on my chest and pressed a kiss to my chin.

"Of course it's ok." Her hands found her panties and she slipped them over her bottom and walked towards the bathroom, leaving me to watch her beautiful, naked silhouette. I quickly shed my clothes and followed her. She sat in the middle of the tub, her knees drawn up to her chest, her hair piled on top of her head in a messy knot, waiting for me. I climbed in behind her and stretched my legs on either side of her, sighing as she leaned back into me.

The water sloshed around us until we settled, her head resting back against my shoulder, the steaming water coming up just far enough to cover her pretty, pink nipples. I saw flashes of them peeking through the bubbles and had to remind myself why we were here; to help her, not to seduce her – yet.

"How was the drive?" I asked her again, looking for a different answer this time and she knew it.

"Same as before. I panicked as I got closer to the street. I kept telling myself I wasn't going to look, but then, of course, I did."

"Did you have to pull over?" She had to in the past. She panicked so much that she wasn't able to drive, nearly fainting. Thankfully, she never wrecked.

She shook her head. "It wasn't too bad, but still made me anxious."

"What were you thinking about?" I knew the answer to this question, but I always asked because it helped her get her thoughts out of her head; if kept inside they festered. If I could get her to talk about it, she had an easier time letting it go. She shrugged her shoulders.

"The same thoughts I always have – wishing I had handled the situation better, wishing I hadn't killed him. I think about everything, every move, trying to figure out a way where in the end he wasn't dead and I hadn't taken his life."

This was the hardest part for me, hearing her guilt for killing Kyle. It had been one hundred percent self-defense. If she hadn't killed him, he surely would have killed her. Yet, she still felt the ache of guilt for taking his life, wishing things could have ended without his death.

"You did nothing wrong, Babe." I whispered into her ear, hoping that this time she not only listened to me, but that she *heard* me. "You were protecting yourself. He made all the decisions that led to that situation. He kidnapped you, drugged you, and you were only trying to get away alive." She nodded in recognition, but I felt her body tense. I reached up and started rubbing her shoulders.

"Hey," I whispered even softer. "I'm sorry, Ella. I don't want to make you upset." Her hands fell to my thighs, the water rippling with our movement.

"I know, Porter. There's a very big part of my brain that knows I had no choice but to pull the trigger. But I just can't get over the fact that I ended a life. I took his life. Who am I to take that from anyone? Sometimes I feel like that doesn't make me any better than him."

It was my turn to tense at her words. I never heard this from her before. My hands stilled on her shoulders, my heart thudded in my chest.

"You are nothing like him, Ella. He was a coward. A thief. A low-life asshole who took advantage of you, tried to have you killed, and then lost when he went up against you." I wrapped my arms around her body, trying to keep her as close to me as possible. "You are nothing like him." I didn't know how else to say it, what other words I could use to convince her. I felt her start to shutter, her breathing sped up, and I knew she was crying. I released her and gripped her hips to turn her to face me, not caring about the water spilling over the sides of the tub.

Her legs wrapped around my waist and her arms wound around my neck. She buried her face in my chest and I listened to her cry, gently rubbing my hands up her back, bringing the warm water with them, aiming to soothe her, trying anything I could think of to comfort her.

"I never wanted to kill him," she said into my chest. "I tried to run away first. I tried to get away."

"Shhh. I know, Babe. I know." She cried for what seemed like hours and if I didn't feel an overwhelming urge to simply be strong for her, I would have cried along with her. I hated him even more in death for making her feel this way, for causing the guilt she was carrying around unnecessarily. Finally, she quieted, breathing evenly against my skin. The water was colder so I used my foot to push up the lever, adding more hot water.

Ella pulled her face away from me, looking me in the eyes. "How many of my breakdowns are you going to hold me through?" She asked, dejectedly.

"All of them," I said. Her eyes misted up again at my words and she pressed her lips into mine. The kiss tasted of salty tears, soapy water, and Ella; nothing tasted sweeter than her. Her legs were already wrapped around me, but I felt her press closer, grinding into me. "Ella, you can't do that right now," I growled. She moved to kiss down my neck.

"Please, Porter," she whispered against the damp skin of my shoulder, slowly pressing her center right into me. I was already straining and hard. I never wanted to deny her, but I didn't want to mess with her head either. She was in a vulnerable place and I didn't want to distract her from dealing with her feelings. "I just want to feel something else besides this."

"Besides what?" I wiped away the hair that came loose from her bun, the fallen strands hiding her eyes from me. "What are you feeling?"

She paused, her breaths coming hard and fast, fighting tears again. "It was either going to be him or me. And somehow I lived. I lived, Porter. Why? How can I ever make myself worthy of being saved in that way? How can I ever make up for taking his life and saving my own?"

I pressed my palms against either side of her face and forced her to look at me.

"Listen to me, Ella. You lived because you fought to live. You lived because you *deserved* to live. He had his death coming to him, Ella. If he had somehow made it through that night alive, I would have killed him myself. You're supposed to be here, with me. We're bigger than all of this. You and me."

"Show me," she whispered.

I was done holding back, done treating her as though she might break. I gripped her around the waist and held onto her tightly as I stood up, water cascading off our bodies, the air chilling my skin. I grabbed a towel hanging from the door as I walked into the bedroom. I put the towel down on the bed and laid her over it. She leaned up on her elbows, looking at me expectantly. Using both hands I grabbed the towel and started drying off her belly. I hoped to God she was pregnant. I wanted her full of me in every way. I wanted her round and soft and beautifully carrying a piece of me.

I rubbed the towel along her stomach, down her thighs, up and over her mound. She gasped at the contact and I knew she was wired and receptive – electric. I moved the towel up and dried both of her breasts and watched as her back arched farther off the bed. I moved to my knees, still palming her breasts through the towel, and kissed my way up one of her legs, from knee to hip. I splayed wet and open-mouth kisses right over her heat, slowly licking up her center, just trying to taste her.

My hands abandoned her breasts and came to hold her thighs open, making it easier for me to get to all of her. I heard her whimper and it made my blood pump faster, knowing I was succeeding in helping her feel something other than lost. I was harder than ever, blood pumping, pulsing through me.

Fueled with the sounds of her arousal and the throbbing in my cock, I quickly moved up over her. She anticipated me and moved backwards on the bed, crawling towards the headboard, her eyes blazing at me, challenging me to show her. I ripped the towel out from under her as she moved and threw it to the floor. My bare hands grazed over her breasts, sliding all the way up her arms and stopping at her wrists. I grabbed them both and pinned them to the bed above her head. Our faces now even, I breathed hard looking into her eyes.

"You're mine. I need you here, with me, understand?" She nodded and I dipped down, kissing her roughly. She responded with fire, meeting me lick for lick. Her legs came to wrap around my waist and I felt her heat running along me. That was one thing I loved about Ella; when it came to sex, to us connecting and bringing each other and ourselves gratification, she'd always been shameless. She took what she needed unabashedly and without reservation, and gave me everything I could ever hope for. Our bodies were made for each other and it was never difficult to lose myself in her.

"I need you. Now, Porter." She whispered softly, looking straight into my eyes, asking me to help her, to give her what she needed. Without breaking our gaze, I slowly pushed into her and watched as her eyelids fluttered, mouth opened, and hips moved into me. I kept one hand on her wrists as the other moved down to grab her ass and brought her even closer, to get even deeper. I slowly moved in and out of her, each thrust pushing me just a little bit closer to her. Our bodies were intertwined, one seeping into the other, no beginning and no ending – just us.

My mouth found her breast and I lived for the gasps she made as I pulled on her nipple with my teeth, gently urging her towards her peak. Her hands wiggled and I freed her, bringing my other hand to the small of her back. Her hands gripped my shoulder blades and I felt her heels dig into my ass, bringing her core up to me, enveloping every inch of my shaft. She ground her hips into me, circling me, finding her rhythm. I pushed into her farther, knowing it was pressure and contact she was looking for.

I knew she was close when she held her breath and bit her lip, eyes closed, head back. I loved to watch her fall apart. I gripped her firmly, pulled her into me as hard as I could, matched her rhythm, using my hands to grind her into me. Her eyes shot open wide, looking at me with surprise.

"Don't stop," she cried. I didn't. I worked her until I felt her walls pulse around me, until I heard her cry out my name, until I felt her relax and fall limp back onto the bed. My mouth found her neck, kissing her slowly in the spot I knew she liked, until I knew she had come down from her orgasm.

"How do you do that?" She asked breathlessly as I resumed pumping in and out of her slowly.

"Do what?" I asked, smiling against the skin of her neck.

"Read me like that? Know exactly what I want? What I need?"

"Ah, that's simple, Ella," I said, taking one long and thorough stroke into her, her mouth opening at the feeling.

"I need and want the exact same thing. I'm not reading you. I *am* you. And you're me." She turned her head and her lips found mine. Her hands came to the sides of my face and I wrapped my arms around her tightly.

"I love you," she whispered against my lips.

"And I love you." Her hands moved through my hair, gripping it gently.

"Now, take me however you want me." My pulse thundered through my veins at her words. I didn't think it were possible, but I grew harder.

"Fuck," I growled into her mouth. She surrendered to me, gave herself over to me, and I loved her even more for it. "Flip over, Babe." She smiled at me as I pulled out of her and rolled onto her stomach. She knew what I wanted and brought herself up on her knees, pushing her perfectly round ass into the air for me. My hands smoothed over her cheeks and then continued up her back. I could stare at her forever, but she had other ideas. She spread her knees wider and then bent down so her forearms rested on the mattress, giving me a gorgeous view of all of her.

I slid slowly into her wet heat, groaning at the feeling. "You feel fantastic, Babe. So hot. So soft." She made her whimpering noise as she met me with a quick thrust backwards onto my cock, making my heart rate spike again. I couldn't be slow anymore, couldn't be gentle. I pumped in and pulled back, each time increasing the force. I was rewarded by hearing her groaning and moaning each time I hit that spot inside of her.

"More," she cried out. That was all I needed to lose myself in her. One of my hands found her shoulder, pulling her back onto me while the other sought out her clit, helping her feel as good as I did. My head rested on her back as I felt her come again, the tightening around me signaling she'd found her release. "I want you to come inside of me," she said breathily, spurring me on, bringing me closer. I continued to pump into her, holding off as long as I could, relishing in the feeling of her tight, wet heat enveloping me. Eventually it was too much and I found my release, groaning as I came, needing to brace myself with a hand on the mattress as my orgasm rocketed through me.

After a moment she fell forward, relaxing on the bed, and I shivered as my cock pulled out of her. I flopped onto the bed next to her, trying to reign in my breathing, waiting for my brain to turn back on. Eventually she turned over to look at me, a smile shimmering over her face, lighting up the dim room.

"We're good at making babies," she said coyly. I had to smile at her, still a little out of breath. Usually, under previous circumstances, she would have gotten out of bed and gone to clean up, but lately she'd been staying in bed after we made love, obviously the protocol altered by trying to get pregnant. I couldn't lie; the thought of her spending the whole night with my cum inside of her was a huge turn on. There've been a few times when we had a quickie in the morning and she left the house for the day with me inside of her, smelling of me, and my reaction was primitive. Positively primal. She was mine and I marked her to prove it. I laughed at myself. I knew I was having caveman thoughts, liking the idea of my seed inside of her, but I would challenge any man in love to argue with me. Having her full of me was an intensely gratifying feeling.

"I'll add it to my resume. Hopefully it works, but I love perfecting our technique." I made it out of bed, bringing her a glass of water.

"Thank you," she said before taking a sip. I put the water on her nightstand and then flipped off the lights and climbed into bed, bringing her close to me, twining our fingers together.

"Do you want a boy or a girl first?" She whispered. I rubbed my thumb along the palm of her hand. We had this discussion before, but I loved talking about our future child with her, so I answered.

"I don't care as long as it's healthy, but I think deep down I'd like a boy." Ella brought my hand to her mouth and kissed it softly right over my knuckles.

"Your father would be very proud of you, Porter." Of course she'd hear what I hadn't said. I longed for a son in a way that defied logic to me. I would love a daughter. I would spoil her and protect her and provide for her, but my soul needed a son. I wanted to feel that connection a father had with his boy.

"He would have loved you," I whispered into her hair.

"I know," she said sleepily, making me smile.

"I love you," I said against her ear.

"Mmm. I love you too."

Chapter Three

Ella

It has been five weeks since my last period. That morning, after Porter left, I readied myself for work and was surprised to find myself leaning over the toilet when brushing my teeth triggered some weird gag reflex. I heaved my breakfast into the toilet and then wiped my mouth with the back of my hand, smiling as I pressed my other hand against my belly. I had never been so excited to throw up in my life.

Porter and I both knew that I was late – he watched the calendar even more carefully than I did. But neither of us had mentioned it. I assumed his reasoning was the same as mine; we didn't want to jinx it. But the barfing clenched it for me. Morning sickness? Yes. I *had* to be pregnant. I could feel the straining in my cheeks from the biggest smile I'd ever worn, only to be out done, I imagined, by the smile I would wear watching Porter come to the realization he was going to be a father.

I got up and nearly ran to my phone, dialing Megan's number as quickly as I could.

"Hey, Fella," she said cheerily as she answered her phone.

"Megs, do you have any free time today? Can you come to Salem?"

"I think so. I've got all three girls in Poppy today so getting away shouldn't be a big deal. What do you need?"

"It's not work related. I need a sister favor today."

"Oh! Well then I can definitely fit you in. What's up?" Her voice was still calm, but she sounded concerned.

"I just need you to come to Dahlia, but I need you to bring me something."

"Ok... you're being cryptic."

"Can you bring a pregnancy test with you?"

"Are you serious?"

"Serious as a pregnancy test."

"Holy shit, Ella."

"Holy shit is right. Will you come see me? I could use a little sisterly support."

"Um, yeah. Just let me call Brittany and let her know I won't be in this morning. Oh my God, Ella. You think you're pregnant?" She sounded wistful and far away, like she was lost in her own mind. I felt the stinging and prickling of tears coming on but I didn't want to cry so I stood up and moved into the bathroom, turning on the shower.

"Yeah, I think I am," was all I could manage without losing my composure.

"Ok, I'll be at Dahlia in about two hours, with a pregnancy test. No big deal. I'll just walk in with a brown paper sack that will change your life forever. No pressure."

I had to laugh at her dramatics. "Megan, it will all be ok. Just buy a test and meet me there. You won't change the outcome of the test by worrying about it."

I heard her exhale loudly. "Ok. See you there." She hung up and I got in the shower. My mind was so frazzled I couldn't remember if I washed my hair or not so I ended up doing it again, just to be sure. I found myself smiling as I drove to the store, my mind clouded with images of Porter pushing a stroller, holding a newborn baby, tossing a baseball to a little blonde boy. I kept reminding myself that I still had to take the test and even then, still had months of waiting to do beyond that.

The waiting wasn't any better at the store either. I found myself folding shirts, then refolding them, walking to the window to look for Megan, then finding something else to fold. I finally couldn't take my own inability to sit still and decided to walk down the street to the coffee shop I went to every once in a while.

"Hi, what can I get started for you?" Asked the pretty brunette girl behind the counter. She smiled and was friendly, causing me to smile back at her.

"Hi, can I get a medium iced mocha?"

"Iced, huh?" She said as she scribbled on the plastic cup with her marker. "It's pretty cold for iced drinks."

"Oh, yeah," I said as I dug through my purse for my wallet. "I don't like hot drinks. Doesn't really matter how cold it is." I reached out to hand her my credit card and then a thought shot right to the front of my brain, making my heart falter. "Is it too late to make it decaf?"

She shook her head, "Of course not." I breathed a sigh of relief. I'm sure one cup of coffee wasn't going to hurt, but I wanted to do everything by the book. I couldn't go screwing up this baby before I even was sure it was in there.

"Thank you."

I walked back to the store really feeling the cold now that I was holding a cup of ice in my hand. I spotted Megan's car parked on the street in front of Dahlia and a little jolt of anticipation shot through my system and my steps quickened. I unlocked the front doors and walked in, my eyes scanning for her.

"Oh my God, Fella, you're glowing." Megan stood behind the counter where a cash register would eventually be, smirking at me.

I narrowed my eyes at her. "Ha ha ha."

"I'm just kidding. You look great."

"Did you bring it?"

"Of course I did. Do you know how many choices you have when purchasing a pregnancy test? There are, like, twelve options. It took me a while to compare and contrast."

"Ok, well, let me see it."

She reached into her purse and pulled out a box that was mostly blue. "I chose the one that had actual words. I didn't think you wanted any room for confusion."

"No, I think if there's any time in a woman's life when she wants clarity, it's while taking a pregnancy test," I said, holding the box in my hands, looking it over, reading the instructions.

"Ella," Megan said.

"Yeah?" I didn't look at her, still focused on the box.

"Pee on the freaking stick."

My eyes snapped up to her and my heart rate picked up with the expectant look on her face. This was it. I was going to take a pregnancy test. I couldn't help but laugh at how, for so many of my younger years, the idea of taking a pregnancy test held a scary connotation. Being pregnant would have been terrifying, something that interrupted my life. But now, with Porter, a baby would even everything out, bring us closer, and ultimately make us that much happier. Now, instead of hoping it was negative, I would be praying and wishing for it to be positive.

I went into the small employee restroom, followed the instructions, and checked my watch to make sure I waited the appropriate three minutes. I walked back out to where Megan was waiting anxiously, tapping her fingers against the countertop.

"Well?" She asked excitedly as soon as she saw me.

"One more minute." Officially the longest minute ever. When the second hand of my watch reached its mark, I closed my eyes, took a deep breath, and felt Megan come to stand right beside me, her arm wrapping around my waist, leaning in trying to peek at the test. I exhaled slowly and flipped it over.

Pregnant.

One word.

One perfect word.

I gasped and my hand came up to cover my mouth and I had to remind myself to breathe after a moment.

Everything went a little blurry and as I blinked, I realized tears were filling my eyes.

"Oh my God," I whispered.

"You made a baby," Megan said, just as quiet as me, as if speaking loudly would disrupt what was happening. "That's the coolest thing you've ever done." She sounded like she was in awe of me.

"Oh my God."

"Fella, you ok? Do you need to sit down? I could grab that step ladder."

"I can't believe it worked."

"What? All the sex?"

I looked at her and I could feel how big my eyes were, my eyebrows stretching up to my hairline. "Yes. All the sex. It worked. It made a baby."

Megan giggled a little and pushed me towards the step ladder by the counter. "Take a seat, Momma. Let the news soak in a little. Do you want me to call Porter?"

"No! I can't tell him over the phone!"

"Ok, calm down. Just relax. This can't be good for the baby," she said, winking at me and smiling. I smiled back at her.

"You're going to be an auntie." Megan's face lit up and she gave me the biggest smile that probably only rivaled my own.

"I'm going to be an auntie? Oh my God." She plopped down on the step ladder next to me, both of our rears hanging off the side for both of us to fit. Her head fell gently to my shoulder as my hand floated to my belly. We sat like that for a few minutes and then my phone started ringing, pulling us from our baby trance. I grabbed my phone and saw it was Porter calling.

"Here Megan, tell him I'm in the bathroom." I tossed my phone at her and, luckily, she caught it. She answered it and from her end of the conversation I could tell he was just calling to confirm that our night would be spent in Salem. Megan told him she'd relay the message and hung up, turning to me.

"What the heck?"

"I can't talk to him on the phone. He would be able to tell something was going on. I'm just not ready to tell him yet." I reached up and readjusted the messy bun of blonde hair that sat atop my head, trying to think of how I would tell my husband that he did, in fact, have excellent swimmers.

Later that evening, after Megan helped me plot and plan, I had what I considered a sweet and sexy way to tell Porter he was going to be a daddy. It had taken a little bit of effort, but I managed to get everything arranged in time before he came home from work.

The house in Salem wasn't optimal. It wasn't my dream home – Porter was building that for us on a plot of land right outside the city limits – a house without close neighbors, with land to grow on, a place where we could have privacy and house a growing family if that's where we chose to be. But tonight, the house was perfect. Lit with the soft glow of candles, it felt like home because this was where my husband was. Where ever he was would be home to me.

I heard the front door close and my pulse thumped in my chest, anticipation making room for nerves and excitement.

"Babe?" He called out to me. He knew something was going on, made obvious by all the candles.

"I'm in the bedroom," I called out.

"Ah, my favorite four words." I smiled at that. I made sure I was positioned in a way that was alluring without being distasteful. I was on my back, leaning up on my elbows, my blonde hair flowing over my shoulders. I had one knee bent and pulled up, with both legs twisted to the side a bit. I hoped I looked sexy and not ridiculous. My fears were abated when Porter walked in and I watched his face change from happy and expectant to dark and dangerous. His eyes darkened as they roamed over my form, his hands clenching into tight fists at his sides. "Holy hell, Ella."

"I've been waiting for you," I said, loving the way his throat moved as he swallowed, feeling the slow burn of his eyes as they traveled from the very top of my head all the way down to my bare feet. He ran his hand through his hair and I watched his biceps flex as his hand slid through his silky locks, making my stomach flip. I was here for a reason. I had a mission, but my body was very quickly hijacking my big reveal, opting, instead, for the sex I was trying to lure him in with.

"You have no idea how long I've been waiting for you," he said quietly, stalking towards me. He wasted no time pulling his shirt over his head, revealing the very hard and chiseled chest I was so in love with. He climbed over me in the bed, forcing my back flat against the mattress with his weight. His jeans felt rough against me, but I welcomed the friction. His hands slid up and down my sides. "This is very sexy. Is it new?" His hands bunched up the black fabric over my ribs and his mouth found my neck.

"I bought it just for you. I know you have a thing for lingerie." Perhaps it was because we were still in the honeymoon phase of our relationship and marriage, but Porter always responded to lingerie, so I was constantly buying new pieces to keep him interested and satisfied. I knew he would take me wearing anything and I would still feel like the sexiest woman alive. He had that keen ability to worship me and turn my body into his temple. I chose this particular piece, however, because it served my purpose.

It was all black silk; a strappy tank top that flared out a little at the hem and tiny black shorts that barely covered anything. It was soft and solid, covering my skin without giving anything away.

"You're wearing too many clothes still, Babe," I whispered into his ear as his mouth worked my neck.

"Hmm..." He grumbled against my skin. I felt him pull away from me and I missed his weight. He stood at the foot of the bed, giving me a grin that dared me to come and help him remove the clothing I was opposed to. I scooted down to him, never breaking eye contact, and kept looking straight at him as I reached for the button on his jeans. Once unfastened, my hands glided just into the waistband

and I smoothed them around his hips until I felt the swell of his ass. He smirked as I gave his ass a firm squeeze on both cheeks, then slid my hands down over the perfect globes, pushing his pants and boxers down as I went. He kicked them off the rest of the way along with his shoes and socks. Again, he climbed over me. His face hovered over mine for just a moment, our breaths mingling with each other's. Slowly, his nose flipped the end of mine and just that touch could have sent me over the edge. It wasn't overtly sexual, but it was Porter. And it was me.

His mouth found its place on mine, where it belonged, and I felt him gently lick the seam of my lips. I opened for him and met him and sighed as our tongues slowly danced with each other. This was all very good, everything was going according to plan, but I couldn't afford to lose sight of the main objective. I gasped when his hand found my breast. The roughness of his calloused hands coupled with the cool crispness of the silk sliding over my nipple nearly derailed the entire plan. My breasts felt overly sensitive and this new sensation was a little overwhelming. But even through the haze of arousal I saw my opportunity.

I twisted my mouth away from him, moving kisses down his throat, scruffed up by a day's worth of stubble. "That feels so good. I want your mouth on me," I rasped. He moved lower and pulled down on my top, exposing the breast he was currently focused on, his mouth finding the taut peak, sucking it in and tonguing it. I felt the urge to roll my eyes, cursing him for taking the easy route instead of pulling my top off, but I was lost in the sensation – drowning in the feeling of the chord strung from my nipple to my core being strummed by his tongue. He wound me up, slowly and steadily building the pressure that would eventually explode around me.

"Porter," I said, again, trying to redirect his attention.

"Hmm…" he hummed against the tender flesh of my breast, slowly moving over to capture my other nipple in his mouth.

"Now, oh God…" I breathed in and out, trying to maintain composure. "Now I'm wearing too many clothes." His head lifted and I saw the smile that I loved grace his face.

"Well, let's get rid of them then." He sat up a little farther, lifting himself off of me, his eyes raking over my body. He pulled down on my shorts and I lifted my hips so he could get them off. And then, to my delight, his mouth landed right above my mound. I smiled, my heart fluttering, knowing that in just moments his life would change.

His hands slowly pushed up the hem of my tank, and his mouth followed, trailing kisses up my belly. I closed my eyes, partly because it felt too good, but also because I couldn't take the anticipation any longer. When I felt his mouth stop, when I felt the cool air hit the warm wetness his mouth left behind, I knew he saw it.

"Babe," he said, softly. "What is this?"

I grinned and opened my eyes to find him staring at my belly, just as I'd imagined it. His hands, splayed over my hips, my top pushed up around my breasts, and his eyes, glued to the words written across my skin:

Hi, Daddy.

"Ella?" He asked, his eyes darting up to find mine.

"That's a note from your baby."

"My baby?" His eyes fell back to my belly, then found mine again.

"Yes. Our baby."

"You're pregnant?"

I nodded, smiling, tears falling down my temples, disappearing into my hair – small, happy tears. His hands came to cup the softness of my stomach, his thumbs moving over the words written there. Suddenly, he was on top of me, his arms wrapped around me, pulling me to him. His face found the space between my shoulder and neck, our legs intertwined. I snuggled in, letting him hold me, my hands running through his hair, letting him have his moment of realization.

I felt his shoulders begin to shudder and new tears prickled in my eyes. I continued to let my hands run over him, hoping I was helping him. After a few moments I felt his lips on my skin again, kissing up my neck and moving to my mouth. He captured me in the softest, most gentle and loving kiss I'd ever been a part of. His hands were on the sides of my face, angling my mouth to fit his perfectly, and he kissed me. I'd kissed him before, we'd kissed each other, but never could I recall a moment where I felt like he was giving me something in a kiss, exclusively from him to me.

"I love you," he whispered, not breaking our contact, vowing his love against my lips. "Thank you."

"I love you too, Porter. So much." Our foreheads rested against each other and we breathed together, tasting the salt of our happy tears. I would never forget this moment and I knew he wouldn't either. I would only get this one chance to tell Porter he was going to be a daddy for the first time and I couldn't imagine anything more beautiful than what we'd just experienced together.

"I'm going to make love to you now," he said and I could hear the smile in his voice.

"I wouldn't expect anything less."

Chapter Four

Ella

A few weeks passed and in those weeks I discovered a new side of Protective Porter. He meant it before when he told me not to lift anything, and he was serious when he now told me to rest at night. If I'd tried to do so much as a load of laundry, I was promptly deposited in bed. No amount of arguing could persuade him.

We had our very first doctor appointment today with my OBGYN, and Porter prepared for it as if it were a merger. He had an envelope with articles printed off the internet he wanted to discuss, a list of questions he wanted to ask, and of course, he insisted on driving me there. We were only eight weeks in and I was already getting a little irritated by his overbearing demeanor. Most of the time it was cute and I understood it to be a manifestation of his love for the baby and me, but sometime a pregnancy rage would come over me and I felt like I was going to punch him right in his tight abs.

We decided to see a doctor in Salem. Being at the beach was nice and all, but I didn't have faith in the hospital there. Salem was where I felt safer, not to mention that Porter would have shackled me to the bed in Salem had I mentioned having the baby in Lincoln City.

We arrived at the medical office and were sitting in the waiting room when a woman who was obviously uncomfortably pregnant waddled past us to check in with the receptionist. She stood at the little window, one hand on her giant belly and one hand rubbing her lower back, seemingly unconsciously. I watched her move, the pain etched across her face with every step, and started having very legitimate concerns about the whole pregnancy thing. This woman looked miserable. As if he read my thoughts, Porter's hand came to gently rub across my still very flat belly. He leaned in and kissed my forehead.

"It's going to be ok, Babe. Maybe she's pregnant with triplets."

Oh God. Multiples. I hadn't even thought of that. I swallowed hard, a wave of nausea coming over me. Just then a door opened and a younger woman with colorful scrubs on called my name, leading Porter and me back to an exam room. She made me pee in a cup, which I learned would happen every visit. Great. Just one more thing to not look forward to. She left me to change into a gown and then came back to take my vitals and was very chipper. Eventually she left us to peruse the graphic pictures that hung on the walls of the exam room.

One poster in particular caught my attention; it showed the progression of a dilating cervix, from closed to 10 centimeters. My eyes grew wide and my heart rate picked up. How in the holy hell was that supposed to happen? Porter must have noticed my panicked expression because his hand was on my arm, rubbing gently.

"Ella, what is it?"

I pointed to the poster and looked at him, my mouth agape. "Do you see this?" I swallowed and tried to tamp down the fear running through me. "I don't think I can handle this." I sat down on the exam bed, my hand running over my forehead. I felt him at my side and leaned into him.

"It'll all be ok. Women have been doing this since the beginning of time."

"Yeah, but *I've* never done this. I guess it just never occurred to me that now, since it's already in there," I said, gesturing to my stomach, "it has to come out." I started to feel ill just thinking about it. "I can't do this."

"Babe, I hate to break it to you, but it's too late to back out now. Everything will be ok, I promise. I'm sure this little freak out is totally normal."

I kind of wanted to smack him. It was not normal to stretch out one's vagina that big, not at all. Before I could tell him how I felt about it, the door opened. A woman of about fifty walked in, all smiles, and moved to shake my hand. I took hers, but immediately felt bad that mine was all clammy from my panic.

"Hi, I'm Dr. Bronson. You must be Ella Masters."

"Hi, nice to meet you," I said softly as we shook hands.

"And is this Daddy?" Dr. Bronson asked, looking in Porter's direction.

"Yes. This is my husband, Porter." They shook hands, exchanging smiles.

"Ok, well, let's get this party started," she said with way too much enthusiasm for my current mental state. "Go ahead and lay down and place your feet in the stirrups."

As I followed her instructions she wheeled over a machine with a screen attached to it.

"I'm going to use this machine to take a look at baby," she said as she removed something that looked like a wand with a cord attached to it. She produced a condom, as if from nowhere, and after opening it, started rolling it down the wand.

"Wait a minute, where's *that* going to go?" Porter said, speaking my words for me. The doctor didn't even bat an eyelash as she replied.

"Ella is not far enough along to do a regular ultrasound. I wouldn't be able to see the baby yet. So, we are going to do a vaginal ultrasound. Don't worry. It's virtually painless and over very quickly. It's important that we check on the baby and the pregnancy to make sure everything is progressing well." Porter looked as though he wanted to protest or argue with her, but she'd so soundly put him in his place that he looked a little dumbfounded. I couldn't come up with anything to say, either, but the wand looked intimidating. "Don't worry, Ella. It will be over before you know it, and in just a few seconds we can see the baby. Trust me. Now lie back and open up your knees for me nice and wide."

Well, ok, since she asked nicely. I tried to act like I didn't feel violated as the wand was inserted, but all my uncomfortableness was forgotten when my eyes found a little round blob on the screen. The doctor stilled the wand and used some buttons on the machine to zoom in and she tapped away on some keys. I was lost though, eyes glued to the fuzzy, quarter-sized, picture on the screen.

"There we are. That's your baby right there," she said, pointing to the area of the screen that I already knew was my child. I felt Porter take my hand, but my eyes could not leave the screen. "It looks like you are at eight weeks and three days, putting conception around the last week of

November." That information was enough to bring my eyes to Porter, thinking that he was right, a honeymoon baby. But my breath caught when my eyes landed on him. He looked at the screen, looked at the first sight of our baby, tears welling around his red eyes, in total awe of everything. I fell in love with him a little more in that moment.

"Are you ready to hear the heartbeat?" The doctor asked, as if we weren't having the most wonderful and intimate moment we've ever had. Before I had a chance to look at the screen the room was filled with the weirdest and most wonderful sound I had ever heard. It was a rhythmical *swoosh swoosh*, which sounded a lot like water. The doctor pointed to the screen and right above her finger there was a little fluttering. "That's the baby's heart, and it's working perfectly, a steady 160 beats per minute."

"That's so fast," Porter said, his voice sounding thick with emotion.

"Babies' hearts beat very fast in utero. It's completely normal and healthy. Everything looks very healthy."

My throat began to close up and the familiar prickling behind my eyes triggered my inability to keep my emotions in check. I let out a sob, staring at the screen, watching my baby's heart fluttering away. I felt Porter's head rest on my temple and my hand came up to cradle his cheek. We stayed like that for a moment, just listening to our baby's heart. After a minute I felt Porter's head lift and his hand moved my face to look at him. Our eyes met and he pressed his lips to mine, whispering "I love you" into our kiss.

"I can print off a few pictures for you, for scrapbooks and such," Dr. Bronson said, probably used to couples having breakdowns while seeing their baby for the first time.

"Thank you," I said, wiping tears from my eyes. When she was done messing with the machine, she removed the wand and told me I was free to sit up.

"Your baby is due on August 15th, a summer baby. Congratulations."

"Thank you," I sniffled. She handed me a tissue.

"Now, you'll need to take folic acid and prenatal vitamins every day. Stay away from tuna and other raw fish, and everything else can be explained in these pamphlets." She handed me a prescription and a few thick pamphlets. We had some reading to do apparently. "Now, what questions do you have for me that I can answer?" She sat on a little rolling stool and looked at us expectantly.

Porter immediately reached into his back pocket and produced his list of questions.

"I have a few," he said, unfolding his paper. Dr. Bronson didn't bat an eyelash. She was obviously used to people asking her questions. We must be typical first-time parents. "Should Ella cut back on work?"

"No. There's no need to cut back on work at this stage. Ella's healthy. The pregnancy is healthy. Life goes on as normal."

"Yeah, but she tends to lift up boxes and bends down a lot."

"She's pregnant, not crippled," Dr. Bronson said with a smile. I wanted to kiss her. "You shouldn't lift anything over twenty pounds and if you get tired you should rest, but there's no reason you shouldn't be able to work up until delivery. However, we can always assess the pregnancy as the weeks progress and make adjustments. But for now it's life as usual. Your body will tell you what you're capable of better than I can."

"I've read that pregnant women shouldn't eat processed meats or soft cheeses. And what about coffee?" Porter asked, sounding a little irritated.

"Those are valid concerns. I would always advise a pregnant woman to eat as if she were feeding her child. So, the more organic and less processed the better. However, anything in moderation is fine, even coffee."

"I can drink coffee?" I asked excitedly.

"Yes, but try for only one cup a day. Plenty of women drink tons of coffee throughout pregnancy and have perfectly healthy babies."

"Sex?" Porter asked.

"Porter!" I exclaimed.

"Perfectly safe," Dr. Bronson replied without even a moment's hesitation. "Sex is normal and healthy during pregnancy. In the later stages of pregnancy, intercourse can become difficult logistically, but there are pamphlets for that too. Some women find sex during pregnancy to be very pleasurable and find themselves with a high libido. Other women don't like to partake in sexual activity. Both extremes and everything in between are normal." Both Porter and I were a little dumbfounded by her response, but I was glad she put him in his place. "Any other questions?"

I looked over at Porter and he folded up his paper and put it back in his pocket.

"No, I think that covers it," he said sheepishly.

I almost laughed at his uncomfortable expression. The doctor turned back to me and smiled.

"Ella, we'll be getting to know each other very well over the next several months. There are no dumb questions and no concern too small. You have the office's phone number and you should never hesitate to call if you have even the tiniest concern. There is an after hour's number as well. Please," she said with the most sincere sounding voice, "call us anytime for any reason."

What she said eased my mind a little and released some tension I didn't realize I was keeping inside.

"Thank you, Dr. Bronson. I appreciate that."

"Check in with the receptionist on your way out to make your twelve week appointment. And Mr. Masters, be sure you take good care of her, the first twenty weeks can be pretty brutal for new mommies." She gave him a warm smile and then left the room.

"I like her," I said as I turned to Porter.

"Me too," he laughed.

After I'd dressed again and we'd left the office, I sat in the passenger seat of Porter's truck staring down at the black and white pictures of our little baby.

"This is surreal, isn't it?" I couldn't tear my eyes from the fuzzy little blob on the piece of paper.

"What is?"

"I don't know. The fact that we decided to try to have a baby and then it just happened. Like, right now, there's a baby, in my body. I'm *building* a human *inside* my body." I shook my head, still trying to wrap my mind around everything that was happening. "That's so weird to think about." I laughed a little, my shoulders jumping up and down with my slight laughter. "It was so easy, getting pregnant. I'm so surprised it never happened before." Truly, birth control pills worked wonders. I never really gave it much thought, taking the little pills every day, but they really did their job well. I could have had a dozen children by now if it weren't for those little pills.

"Perhaps," he said as he reached over and took my hand, "you never got pregnant before because, in the grand scheme of things, you're only meant to have *my* children." He brought my hand up to his mouth and placed a kiss on the back of it.

"Well, you're probably right about that. I'm so glad you're the father of my child." I don't think I'd ever spoken truer words. We sat in a warm silence surrounded by an unspeakable happiness.

After a few minutes Porter spoke up. "When do you think we should start telling people about the baby? I don't think Megan is going to hold up much longer."

I giggled because he was right. I'd sworn her to secrecy and she nearly killed me with a death glare. The last time I made her keep a secret from our parents, everything went to hell in a hand basket. "I guess if it's just close family we could tell them any time. Now that we know the baby is healthy and progressing normally, I think it would be fine.

But we should wait until the second trimester to tell anyone else."

"Do we call them or tell them face to face?"

"I think we tell them in person. I want to see your mom's face when she hears she's going to be a grandma." It nearly brought me to tears just thinking about it.

"Ok, so maybe we go to your parent's house tonight and then go to Lincoln City this weekend?"

I smiled at him. "Sounds perfect."

After making dinner plans with my parents, Porter and I found a baby boutique and perused for a little while. I watched him as he picked up a onesie and his eyes grew wide as he inspected it, turning it around in his hands.

"I can't believe babies are ever this small. How can anything ever be this small?"

"Says the man who doesn't have to push it out of his body," I smirked.

"You know what I mean. This is tiny."

"Yeah, I know what you mean," I said softly, smiling at his amazement.

We picked out a few things and then headed to Portland, our heads still spinning with all the information fluttering around in our heads. We stopped first at Poppy. I always tried to stop in when I was in Portland just to see how things were going, and also to see the girls.

The anxiety that was associated with Poppy never eased completely. I was usually fine and able to spend time there, working and keeping myself busy, but sometimes I had weird flashbacks, or a loud noise would startle me. Luckily, in the past months I had learned a few ways to cope with the panic that would come over me, and sometimes the biggest way to ease the fear was just to leave. I loved Poppy, but I also understood that there would be days when I just couldn't be there. Today, however, I was too happy to let bad memories ruin anything for me.

Megan spotted us as we walked in and gave me a big smile.

"Hey, Fella. Hi, Porter. I didn't know you were going to be in Portland today."

"Yeah, it's kind of a last minute trip. We're going to have dinner with Mom and Dad." I raised my eyebrows at her, trying to clue her in to our plans to tell them.

"Oh!" Megan said, recognition coming across her face. "Is this an *important* dinner?" I nodded my head, smiling. She exhaled loudly. "Oh good, cause I'm tired of this whole thing already."

"But you're an expert secret keeper," Porter said quietly.

"You guys are the worst with all the secrets."

"You should feel privileged to be in on this one. It's kind of a big deal." I smiled at her.

"Or a tiny deal, depending on your point of view." Porter stated. I laughed at his joke, but Megan just looked at him with confusion.

"We just wanted to stop by to tell you that after tonight Mom and Dad will know, so you can tell Patrick. But we aren't telling Tilly until this weekend or anyone else for a few more weeks. So don't go crazy telling everyone," I said, eyeing Brittany on the other side of the store.

"I should be ok if I can tell Patrick. He knows something is up but has given up on trying to get it out of me."

"Besides keeping secrets, how's everything else going? How is my first store doing?"

"Everything's great here. Sales are still strong even though the foot traffic is slow, what with it being cold as balls outside. Speaking of balls," she said with a grin, "you and Kalli need to get to work planning my bachelorette party." I rolled my eyes.

"There will be no balls present," Porter interjected before I had a chance to say the exact same thing.

"Hey, no husbands or fiancés allowed. And if I want to see some balls, I will see some balls."

"Really, Megan? Of the entire male form, balls are what you're focused on?"

"Good point. You know what I want – a stereotypical, over-the-top, full-of-naked-men, bachelorette party."

"And you're ok if I bring Patrick to a strip club and buy him a bunch of lap dances?" Porter asked, clearly not ok with the picture Megan was painting.

"Of course! That's what I'd expect from anyone throwing him a bachelor party. Let him live it up. It's the last time he can let a woman, besides me, fondle him guilt-free. What else would you do for a bachelor party? Smoke cigars and play cards? Yuck. That's what you do *after* you're married."

Porter just shook his head at her. "Well, I've never been happier that we eloped than in this very moment." Megan shot him her brilliant smile. "You're a piece of work, Megan, and Patrick is lucky to have you." He leaned over and kissed her cheek, which nearly made my heart melt right in my chest. "I'm going to go get some coffee down the street and read the paper. Will you be ok?" He said, whispering in my ear.

"Yeah, I'll be fine. Thank you. Will you bring me a hot chocolate when you come back? No hurry."

"Anything for you, Baby Momma," he said with a sly smile.

"Ok, you never get to call me that again."

"Deal, but it was fun just the one time." He lightly patted my rear as he headed out the door.

"I think we both really lucked out in the man department, Fella," Megan said, watching Porter leave the store.

"We sure did," I sighed. "I'm gonna go take a look at the sales reports in the back, cool?"

"Sure, everything is saved on the computer and I think the hard copies are in the filing cabinet if you'd rather see those."

"Ok, thanks, Megs." Megan was doing a fabulous job running this store for me, and every day I was more and more impressed by her drive and savvy business sense. I rarely worried about Poppy anymore knowing she was here and making it thrive. "You're really doing a great job here,

Megan. I hope you understand that I really appreciate everything you do for this store."

A slight blush spread over her face. "Thanks, Sis. I love this store and I love the girls. I'm so glad you gave me this opportunity."

I winked at her and headed to the back room. I grabbed some of the paper files and then settled onto the love seat to look them over. Megan was right, the sales at Poppy were strong, stronger than they had been at that time last year. I tried not to think about how last year's numbers could have been tainted by Kyle's embezzlement. Again, I tried to push those thoughts out of my head. Poppy was doing well all on its own, with Megan, Brittany, and Sarah supporting it. They were working hard and it was paying off.

I yawned, realizing all at once that I was exhausted. I flipped through a few more reports, but felt my eyelids drooping, feeling very heavy. Suddenly, I was alone in the dark, laying still on the couch. I must have fallen asleep, but I was confused as to why Porter hadn't come back for me.

I jumped when I heard a loud knocking coming from the front of the store, as if someone was banging on the glass. My heart stuttered and my pulse thundered through my veins. Without my permission, my body stood and started walking towards the front of the store. Inside, my mind yelled not to go out there, but my legs weren't listening; they carried me out. There wasn't anything I could do about it.

When I came around the corner, out of the backroom, I saw him standing there – the man in the black hoodie. This time he wasn't outside, he waited for me in the store. Head down, face hidden, he raised one arm towards me and I screamed the instant I saw the gun. My mouth opened and I heard my shattered cries echo off the walls.

I jumped, gasping for air at the sound of the gun firing, but when my eyes opened I wasn't looking at the shooter, I was looking at Porter.

"Ella, hey, what's happening? Is everything ok?" He knelt on the floor next to the couch I was sprawled out on. I blinked a few times, trying to focus on him and not the pounding of my heart or the incessant pulsing in my ears. I was sweaty and hot.

"He was here. I saw him," I mumbled, trying to put into words the thoughts running through my mind.

"Babe, no one is here. It's just me. Take some deep breaths for me." I gripped his arm needing something to anchor myself. His hand came up and gently caressed the side of my face and I leaned into him. "Just breathe, Ella." I took his advice and let the air pass through me, trying to release the tension with every exhale. "You don't have to be afraid. I'm here. I won't let anything happen to you."

"I must have fallen asleep," I whispered. "I was just looking over the sales reports and I think I dozed off."

"Were you dreaming about Kyle?"

I shook my head. "No, it was the shooter, the guy in the hoodie." I let out one last breath and I felt exhausted. "He was in the store this time, not outside." Porter's brow furrowed and I knew he was upset by the situation. When Kyle died, most of the threat went away, but there was still one last loose end just floating around – the shooter. According to Kyle, he was just some kid he'd hired, so chances were that he wasn't really after me, just doing a job. The police urged us not to be afraid. The shooter didn't have an agenda against me, and since Kyle was dead, he didn't have any reason to come back to finish at what he'd failed at – killing me. But, understandably, I was having a hard time *not* fearing the man who shot me that was still free.

Also understandably, Porter was not happy the shooter was roaming around Portland a free man. There was nothing either of us could do about it. I lived every day trying not to think about it, because I could drive myself crazy. But being here, in this store, on this couch, was obviously too much for my mind.

"What time is it?"

"Nearly five. I was just coming to get you to go to your parents' house. Are you still feeling up to it?" The back of his hand was still running along my cheek.

"Yeah, I'm ok."

"Ella, it's ok if you're not. We can just go home and tell them another day."

I shook my head. "No, I want to tell them tonight. I'm fine." I wasn't fine, but I would be. I wouldn't let this control me. I couldn't.

Chapter Five

Porter

The past few days were a roller coaster. Ella was up and down. She was constantly trying to pretend like she was ok, but I knew she wasn't. The dream she'd had at Poppy really dragged her down and she struggled. I could feel it.

She'd put on a brave face for her parents that evening, and I loved her even more for it. Watching her mom and dad realize they were going to be grandparents was an awesome moment. She held my hand and slid the ultrasound picture across the table to her mother over dessert. Her mom looked at the picture, then looked up at Ella, and must have looked back and forth a hundred times before she finally muttered a frantic, "Is this what I think it is?" Tears were in Susan's eyes as well as Ella's and all Ella could do was nod her head, lip trembling, chin quivering. I looked at her dad and he looked like someone had told him he'd won a million dollars – pure joy and elation.

Her parents stood and hugged us both, her dad holding on to her for so long I wondered if he'd ever let her go.

It was perfect.

Then her mom took her into the office and they started looking at nursery decoration ideas on some website about thumbtacks or some such nonsense. It was a distraction for Ella – one that, at that moment, she'd desperately needed.

We both arrived in Lincoln City late the night before and went straight to bed. When I woke it was to sunlight streaming into the large windows that faced the ocean. The room was bathed in soft white light, but even the sunshine couldn't remove the dark circles that were painted under Ella's eyes. She looked exhausted even as she slept. She hadn't mentioned having any more nightmares, but it was obvious the sleep she was getting wasn't doing her much good.

I rolled towards her, completely satisfied to just take her in, to watch her in a state a peacefulness. To see her relaxed was something of a rare occurrence these days. My eyes moved over the blonde hair fanned out across her pillow, the way her hands were tightly tucked in under her cheek, the way her shoulders moved with every breath she took in.

I must have dozed off because I startled when I felt something move against my face. I opened my eyes and met her dazzling blue ones. Her hand ran along my jaw, smoothing over the roughness of my skin, unshaved for a few days now.

"Did you wake up to watch me sleep?" She asked, a knowing smile on her face.

"How did you know?"

"You usually sleep facing the window." She shrugged. "Just a good guess." She moved towards me and I opened my arms for her, breathing in her vanilla scent as she pressed her body into my chest. My arms wrapped around her, pulling her in even closer. "You're worried about me, aren't you?" She said after a few moments of warm silence.

"I always worry about you," I said as I smoothed my hand over her golden hair. "But yes, I'm worried about you. And about the baby." I felt her press her face into the space between my shoulder and neck, her breath moving over my skin sent goose bumps along my arms. "Will you talk to me? Are you having more nightmares?" I felt her mumble something into my neck, making me chuckle at her playfulness. "I'm sorry, what was that?"

She moved away slightly and I heard her take in a breath. "I've had one or two nightmares in the last couple days, but I'm not sure it's the nightmares that are taking the biggest toll on me." She paused and moved back even farther, her eyes finding mine. "All day long I find myself thinking about the shooter, wondering where he is, worrying that he's going to come back or somehow find me." She rolled farther from me and her hands came to rub up and down her face. I sat quietly and waited for more from her. I knew she wasn't finished. Her hands finally came to rest above her head on her pillow and she looked over at me.

"How long will this last? How long will I have to spend my days fearing someone I can't even remember fully? It doesn't seem fair. I've had my life turned upside down because of this man: *we've* had our lives turned upside down, I've lost my memory, been hospitalized, and dealt with so much emotional baggage due to him, and yet he still haunts me. He was in front of me for all of forty-five seconds but he altered my life in an immeasurable way." Her hand came up to wipe away one single tear. My girl was trying so hard to be strong. I saw her strength every day and knew she didn't give herself enough credit.

"Hey, Babe," I said, pulling her back into me, her face just inches from mine. "He's got absolutely no reason to come back for you, none. He was more than likely just some homeless kid who wanted to make a buck. He doesn't know who you are. He doesn't care. You've got every right to be angry, but every reason to try and take back your life."

"What if the nightmares never go away? What if I have to spend the rest of my life battling someone who isn't even here?"

I could hear her voice edging on the precipice of panic. I would always do everything I could to make her feel safe, but I couldn't be inside of her head, as much as I'd like to be sometimes. Even if she looked fine on the outside, she could be waging a war on the inside and no one would ever be the wiser.

"I think you're doing a fantastic job, Ella. I can't imagine the stress you're under, but you have to understand that you are safe. I will never let anything happen to you. What else can I do to make you feel more secure? We can leave. We can up and move to another state, another country even. Anything, if it makes you feel safer." I felt her head shake in my hands, her no immediate and forceful.

"I won't let him run me away from my home or my family."

And that's how I knew, in the end, Ella would always be stronger than anything she battled against in her mind. She was a warrior, fierce and brave. She just never gave herself enough credit.

"And I won't let you put yourself through anymore torture. You need to talk to me more, talk to somebody, when you're feeling this way. Talking helps, yes?" She nodded. I kissed her forehead. "Good. Promise me."

"I promise to talk to someone when I'm feeling anxious," she said, humoring me.

I pressed a soft kiss against her lips, silently thanking her for appeasing me.

"Are you ready to go see my mom, or would you like to sleep a little more?" My hand wandered down and my finger feathered across her soft stomach, something I did now without even thinking about it.

"We might as well go now. I don't think I could get back to sleep if I tried."

"Will you shower with me?" I asked, my hand moving from her belly, over her waist, coming to rest on the swell of her ass. I was instantly glad she only wore a tee shirt and panties to bed as my hand had free reign over her smooth skin. I tugged her towards me, her hips fitting perfectly against mine, relishing in the way her eyes widened and mouth parted with a small gasp.

"Something tells me showering isn't the only thing you have in mind," her voice thick and low.

"I just want to make you feel better," I replied, dragging my lips across hers, purposefully teasing.

"You're on the right track."

"Mmm…" I gave in and took her mouth fully against mine. She had the most perfect lips: full, thick, and pink. They always molded perfectly to mine and that always reminded me that she was, undoubtedly, made for me. My lips parted hers and her tongue fluttered out, mingling with mine. I couldn't help the groan that found its way out of me and loved the whimper she met it with. The sounds she made when we were connected were, without a doubt, the sexiest sounds I had ever heard. Hearing her moan sent more hot blood through my veins, concentrating in my dick. I pulled back and she let out a startled complaint. "We need to get in the shower now, or it will take us an hour to make it there."

She pushed my shoulders down so I was lying flat on my back and crawled over me. She came to straddle my hips, her sex lining up perfectly with my erection, only two thin layers of cotton separated her heat from mine. Her hair came to rest around her shoulders, her blue eyes bright with arousal, and her hands splayed out around my ribs. I froze watching her, taking in her beauty, struck motionless by the love I felt for her.

Then, much to my pleasure, she ground her hips down on me. My eyes closed, my head fell back against the pillow, and I think I growled. Some animalistic sound came from me and she answered with a low moan. She alternated between rocking back and forth and moving her hips in tight little circles over my dick. It was the most wonderful form of torture. Suddenly, though, the wonderful, soft heat was gone and so was she.

I opened my eyes just in time to see her pulling her tee shirt over her head as she went into the bathroom, left only in her panties. She turned her gorgeous face over her shoulder and gave me the smile that would always and forever make my heart stop.

"Coming?" She asked sweetly.

Her eyes widened as I climbed out of the bed and stalked towards her. "Most definitely. And so are you."

We eventually made it to my mom's restaurant. When we entered, it was easy to find my mother. Her laugh was like a beacon and could be heard from anywhere in the building. Infectious, loud, and contagious, she laughed like she lived – without reservation.

She spotted us and I could see her whole face light up with happiness and love. It was nearly impossible not to mirror her expression. My mother was truly a wonderful woman and until I met Ella, I didn't think there would ever be another woman who mattered to me on the level she did. I could feel my stomach tightening with nerves, excitement bubbling over with the idea of telling her that, finally, she was going to be a grandmother.

She politely finished up the conversation she was having with the two older men at their usual table, always coming in to flirt with my mother, and walked towards us. She went to Ella, wrapping her in a tight hug. I was almost jealous that my mother didn't hug me first, but knew that no one could resist Ella. Also, it warmed my heart witnessing how much my mother loved her. She pulled away and then moved to give me a hug as well. I bent down and wrapped my arms around her waist.

My mother always smelled the same. It was a combination of baby powder and her favorite perfume, Chanel Number Five. She got her very first bottle from my father when they had started dating and every year on their anniversary he gave her another bottle. Eventually she had enough to last her a while, but he still bought her a new bottle every year. After he passed away, on their first anniversary she had to spend alone, I wrapped up one of her older bottles that hadn't been used yet and gave it to her.

At first, when my mother broke into sobs, I thought I made a terrible mistake. I only wanted her not to feel sad, I wanted to give her what my dad couldn't be there to give. I apologized and tried to explain how sorry I was, that I hadn't wanted to upset her. She quieted me, telling me it was all right. She hugged me and I held her while her cries slowed.

"It's ok," she said to me, still working through a few tears. "I'm just so happy."

"Happy?" I asked, confused as to how she could be happy without my father.

"I'm so happy that even though I lost your father, I still have the best part of him in you."

After that, every year I wrapped up the same bottle and gave it to her. Until, of course, I grew up and got a job and could afford to buy her a new one. It was still a tradition I cherished and I think she did too.

I pushed aside the memory and pulled back from my mother.

"I didn't know you two were in town today. Would you like some breakfast?" She looked at the watch on her wrist. "Or lunch?"

My eyes flickered over to Ella and I enjoyed the flush that played over her face, knowing she was thinking about why we hadn't made it for breakfast.

"Do you have time to sit with us?" I asked.

"I think I could make some time for my favorite son and daughter." Not once since our wedding had she called Ella her "in-law" and I knew it made both of them so happy.

We followed her to a booth and after we gave our order to the waitress I reached under the table, found Ella's thigh, and gave it a squeeze.

"Mom, we came here today with a purpose."

Her eyebrows rose in surprise. "Oh, you did?"

"Yes," Ella said, bringing up the gift bag she brought in with her and placing it on the table. She looked over at me and gave me a sweet smile, obviously getting just as excited as I was. She slid the bag to my mother across the table. "This is for you."

She took the bag with a confused look on her face. "It's not my birthday," she said, obviously trying to work out in her mind why we were bringing her presents.

"Just open it, Mom."

She shook her head and opened the bag, bringing out a box one might use to wrap a sweater in for Christmas. She took the lid off and I saw her eyes grow wide with surprise. I gripped Ella's thigh a little tighter and felt her hand come to rest over mine, showing me she realized how important this moment was for me. My mom reached into the box and pulled out a small pair of booties and a tiny hat, both were knitted with soft green yarn. She held one in each hand, looking back and forth between them and us.

"What is this?" She asked, her breath panting out as I could tell she was obviously holding back tears.

"There's one more thing in there," Ella said, her voice also rough with emotion.

My mom looked back into the box and placed the hat and booties on the table as she reached for the last item. She pulled out the ultrasound picture and held it up. I saw a tear fall down her cheek and tried to ignore the prickling behind my own, not wanting to cry in the middle of her restaurant.

"Does this mean what I think it means?"

Ella nodded her head and I moved my arm behind her back as she let out a sob, coupled with a very big smile.

"Oh my word…" My mother whispered. "You're having a baby?"

"Well, *I'm* having a baby," Ella said with a laugh. "But yes, you're going to be a grandmother."

I felt my smile widen and watched as my mother's world shifted. I couldn't imagine telling anyone *anything* and have them react with as much happiness as my mother was experiencing. She bounced in her seat, her hand covering her mouth, as she cried happy tears and squealed. She squealed so loudly that everyone in the restaurant turned to look at her. Then she let out another happy cry and started scooting out of the booth.

She held up the ultrasound picture over her head and shouted, "I'm going to be a grandma!" Everyone in the bar erupted into hoots and hollers, a round of applause rang through the building, and my mother did a happy little dance right next to our table. "Come give me a hug," she said to Ella when she'd finished dancing. She climbed out of the booth and my mother wrapped her in a tight hug.

"You've brought so much joy to our lives, Ella. I'm so thankful for you," my mother whispered in her ear, just loud enough for only her and me to hear.

"And you," she said, looking at me. "Get over here and give your mother a hug." I did as she said and brought my mother into me, placing my nose against the skin of her neck, breathing in her familiar scent. She was tiny, and I had to bend to reach her, but I still felt like a little boy sometimes when she hugged me. "Your father would have loved to be here to see you like this, Porter. Happy. Married. A father. I just know he is somewhere watching all of this and he is so proud of you, Son." I held on to her for a little longer, not wanting to pull away because I knew I'd lose my composure.

It was easy as the years passed to only think about my father on occasion. I buried myself in my work and didn't feel anything for so long. However, I found that as my life started happening around me, meeting Ella, fighting for our love together, marrying, and now getting pregnant, every time we hit a milestone or accomplished something, there was always a slight painful pang that came from missing my father. It was a double-edged sword; we missed him, but we also celebrated for him, knowing he'd be just as happy, if not more so, as we were.

"Thanks, Mom," I said as I pulled away. She lovingly patted my shoulder as we separated and her smile had never been so big or bright. It was simply awe-inspiring to witness.

"So, what names have you picked out?" Her eyes swung like a pendulum back and forth between Ella and me.

"We haven't really gotten that far yet," Ella said with a laugh.

"Well, you've got some time yet. When are you due?"

"The middle of August."

"A summer baby! How exciting! Oh! We'll have a baby here by Christmas!" She seemed to get lost in a flurry of thoughts all-things-baby. It was entertaining to watch. "Halloween, too! We could dress the baby up as a little pumpkin or a pea pod!" She went on and on like that for a few more minutes, but then, thankfully, our food arrived. We ate and talked about baby stuff, my mom asking Ella all about things like diapers, nursery décor, if Ella wanted to be a stay-at-home mom – all questions Ella had the perfect answers for.

When we left, Ella had plans with my mom for baby shopping the next week and I was exhausted. I had never seen my mother talk or smile so much. Not surprisingly, telling my mom she was going to be a grandma had been exactly as I would have imagined it. But all the excitement left me dragging.

"I think this momma needs a nap," I heard from Ella. I looked over at her, a little bemused that she'd read my mind and caught her running her hand lightly over her belly, gently breezing over a baby bump that hadn't quite formed yet. My heart caught in my throat, its pulse beating loudly in my ears. She looked so beautiful in that moment, the ocean behind her through the window, the hand with her wedding ring lovingly caressing our child's home for the next 7 months.

"I love you." The words came out of my mouth before I even realized I'd opened it.

Her gaze slowly shifted to me, her blonde hair falling over one shoulder to sway behind her back, her wedding ring still resting on her belly.

"I love you too." Smiling, she added, "but I still need a nap."

I laughed. "Good idea. I'll take one with you."

We made it home and she went straight up the stairs. She peeled her clothes off as she made her way across our bedroom, heading for the enormous king sized bed we shared. She crawled in, wearing only her panties, and pulled every blanket we owned up around her. She took my pillows, made a nest of sorts, and wiggled around until she finally turned to me and asked sweetly, "Do you think you could get me a glass of water?"

I smiled at her request. Surely, only a terrible man would make her unravel herself from her fortress to get her own glass of water. I walked towards the bathroom but was stopped by her voice again.

"Actually, Babe, would you mind getting it from the kitchen?"

I looked at her, a little puzzled. "Um, sure. No problem."

"Thanks. The bathroom water tastes different than the kitchen water." She turned back over, snuggling in again, and I started towards the door. "Oh! And could you make sure you put ice in the cup?"

I laughed. "Sure. Iced kitchen water. Coming right up." I went down the stairs and prepared her water, as requested, and grabbed a pillow off the couch on my way. In my head I thanked Ella for adding some feminine touches to my house when she'd moved in, otherwise I would have no pillow to nap with.

"One ice cold, kitchen water just for you," I said as I entered. Only, Ella didn't move. I walked around the bed and found her fast asleep. I placed the glass on her bedside table and then moved a lock of hair from her face and behind her ear. She didn't even budge at my touch, didn't stir, did nothing but sleep. So I walked to my side of the bed, laid down with my head on my pillow from the couch, and tried not to let the chill bother me because I didn't see a way to sneak any of the blankets away from her.

I fell asleep next to my wife, quite possibly the happiest I had ever been.

Chapter Six

Ella

"You're sure I don't look like a float in a parade?" I kept turning from side to side in front of the mirror, trying to see my body from all angles.

"I'm not really sure what you're asking me, but you look fine."

I shot my husband a 'you're not helping' glare. "Fine? I don't look fine. I look fat."

"There's no way anyone would look at you and think you're fat."

I was fifteen weeks pregnant and I was stuck in the Fat Zone. I didn't look pregnant. My belly hadn't taken on any particular roundness, but I definitely had a bulge. I loved my bump – Porter *really* loved my bump – but it didn't say "I'm pregnant!" Instead, it screamed "I ate an entire pizza by myself!" Tonight was Megan's bachelorette party and I had squeezed myself into one of my previously looser dresses, only to find that it had transformed into a sausage casing.

"I hate the way I look right now." I wasn't above whining. I watched in the mirror as he came up behind me. He placed his hands on my hips and rested his chin on my shoulder. His words tickled my ear and I took just a moment to breathe in the wonderful scent of wood and soap that lingered on his skin.

His hands slid over the fabric of my dress, slowly sliding to the front of me, running smoothly over the tiny hill on my belly that held our child.

"You look beautiful. Anyone who sees you will know you're pregnant. You're glowing. You've never been more beautiful."

His words went a little ways to making me feel better, but I was a little more focused on how much he *liked* me being pregnant. The moment my body started changing, from my bigger boobs to my swollen belly, he was extra attentive to it. I couldn't complain really – Porter could pay my body as much attention as he wanted and I'd always be more than ok with it. But as much as I loved his personal and private adoration of my new body, it didn't always make up for the fact that I wasn't used to having this much extra belly.

I took in a deep breath and tried to shake off the ugliness I could feel coming over me. I promised myself that tonight would be fun, drama free, and nothing but a good time. And here I was ruining it before it had even started. Besides, it really was only important that Porter liked the way I looked anyway.

"Thank you," I whispered as I pressed a kiss to his stubbled cheek. "Are you ready for tonight? How many lap dances are you going to buy Patrick?"

"As many as he wants, I suppose." He turned from me and left the bathroom, heading towards our fantastic closet that still made me smile every time I walked into it. I bit my lip to try and keep my thought in my head. I did not want to come across as the jealous wife. Who was I kidding? Porter, in a strip club? I decided to let my mouth open.

"And how many lap dances will *you* be getting?" I asked, really trying not to sound too needy or jealous. I was going for the relaxed wife who didn't care if some mostly naked woman rubbed her not-pregnant, flat-stomached, body all over my husband.

"I don't know," I heard him say from within the closet. "One, maybe two if I'm lucky."

And then my mouth *really* opened – in shock. I turned quickly towards the door to see him walking out of the closet, adjusting his outfit. He wore black suit pants with a white button up shirt and a black blazer. The top two buttons of his shirt were open, and the little V of skin that showed was just enough of a tease that my eyes were instantly drawn there.

I blinked at him a few times – the first few were to make sure that what I was seeing was real, that my husband was really that delectable. The last few were to emphasize my astonishment.

"*Two* lap dances? I'm sorry," I placed my hand on my hip and cocked it to the side, hoping I looked and sounded as annoyed as I felt.. "You're going to let *two* women grind up on you?"

"No, just one." He winked as he walked up to me and, without hesitation, took my mouth in a searing kiss. I opened for him instinctually, felt the heat of his mouth envelop mine, his hand reaching around my back, pulling me even closer to him. I moaned into his mouth and felt every part of my body flush when he growled in response.

His other hand reached around to the back of my neck and held me in place as his mouth assaulted mine. He kissed me, angling my face to fit his perfectly, until I was clawing at his blazer, trying to rip it off of him. When he pulled away, my bottom lip was caught between his teeth and he slowly released it, gently licking it afterwards, forcing all of my blood to flow to the ache between my legs.

He looked smooth and sexy, not one hair out of place or wrinkle in his outfit, and I was all loud breaths, chest quickly moving up and down, hair mangled, with lips swollen and sensitive.

"I was hoping when we got back tonight *you'd* give me a special show." His eyes twinkled, a smile breaking over his face.

"Oh," was all I could mumble in response.

"You don't think I'd let a stripper anywhere near me, do you?"

I shrugged.

"It's a guy thing," I said, still trying to recover from the world's most absolute hottest kiss ever.

"*You're* my thing."

"Ok."

He placed another kiss on my lips, but this one was small and sweet. It still made my knees shake, but gave my pulse a break. "You about ready?" He gave my butt a small tap as he left the room. I gave myself a look in the mirror and shook my head. He'd mussed up all my hard work.

"Give me fifteen minutes."

We arrived at our hotel in Portland in the evening. Everyone attending the parties had gotten a room for the night. Porter and I hadn't wanted to drive to Salem, and Kalli didn't want to make the drive to Seattle. Megan and Patrick just wanted an excuse to stay at a fancy hotel and take a limo. That was good enough for me; whatever Megan wanted, Megan would get. The guys and the girls said goodbye to each other that evening with plans to all meet back at the hotel.

Megan, Kalli, and I were all sitting in a stretch escalade limo, surrounded by a few of her friends from high school and college I was familiar with, along with a few I didn't know. We all did introductions and then I sat back to watch my baby sister in her element. Kalli hopped into the seat next to me.

"Feeling old?" She asked with a smile.

"Old and pregnant," I replied, refusing the urge to place my hand over my belly.

"Don't worry, us old ladies will stick together."

Kalli was my age and I was so glad that I wasn't the only person over thirty in the limo. We watched the girls laugh and take selfies, drinking, and making toasts. I glanced down at my bottle of water and sighed. When the limo came to a stop, it was outside of a small theatre not very far away from the west bank of the river.

"Here we go, ladies!" Megan hopped out of the limo first and we all filed out after her. We stood in line against the brick wall of the building, waiting for the doors to open.

Megan looked like the typical bachelorette. She wore a white halter-top dress that hugged every single curve the girl had. Her hair was styled and fell into perfect, dark brown curls down her back. She wore a pink tiara in her hair and a pink sash that draped from one shoulder proudly stating that she was the bride-to-be.

One of her friends walked up and down the line of us, handing out necklaces that had tiny replicas of penises dangling from them. All of Megan's friends giggled as they placed the necklaces over their heads. I held it in my hand and looked over at Kalli.

"Are we really going to wear a penis necklace?"

Kalli smiled at me. "Come on, big sis. She's only going to get married once. Don't be a stick in the mud."

"You're right," I said, placing the necklace over my head. I looked at my sister, talking with her friends, seemingly having the time of her life, and decided not to act like I felt: completely out of place and uncomfortable. I would do anything to make sure she had the best time.

A few minutes later a woman came out of the theatre and looked up and down the line of us. "Is there a Megan here? A Megan Sinclair? Celebrating her last night of freedom?" This woman, she had a very, *very* deep voice. I looked closer and realized that the woman was actually a man. I leaned over to Kalli very slowly.

"Kalli…" I whispered.

"Yes?"

"Are we here to see a drag show?"

"It would appear that way, wouldn't it?"

"I'm right here!" Megan's hand shot up into the air, waving around.

"Well come on, Momma!" The queen said loudly while waving her towards the door. "We've got your table all set up for you." Megan squealed and rushed in the door as we all followed.

The next two hours we spent watching very talented drag queens perform some of my very favorite songs from the eighties. I stayed in my seat, but many of the women in the audience made their way to the front to slip dollar bills in the queen's bras or panties. Megan got progressively drunker as the night wore on, and the drag queens loved her. They also loved all the money she shoved in their dresses. She was having a blast so none of us tried to reign her in.

When the lights came on, I stood up and grabbed my purse, ready to head to the door.

"Sit down, Sister!" Megan yelled from her chair.

I looked around, confused. "Aren't we leaving? The show's over."

"The *first* show is over. There's another one," she said with a grin. I looked at Kalli and she just shrugged her shoulders. I sat down again, still confused, but willing to do whatever Megan wanted.

The head queen came over to our table and Megan stood up and hugged her. The queen laughed and told her that our table had a round of drinks on the house in celebration of her bachelorette party. Shouts came from Megan and all her friends, and Kalli and I just laughed at them. A waiter came and took all of their drink orders and I ordered a cranberry juice.

When the waiter returned he was accompanied by one of the queens from the show. She was a small little thing with skin the color of caramel. She had on a long blonde wig and wore a short, black miniskirt with a matching halter top. The waiter delivered all our drinks and the blonde bombshell started addressing the audience, holding on to a microphone so all could hear her.

"Ladies," she said in a high feminine pitch, "and gentlemen". Gentlemen was said in a very burly, low, gravely tone, making the audience laugh. "Tonight is this woman's last hurrah as a single woman. She decided to come here to celebrate with a bunch of drag queens." She stopped talking for a moment and had a confused look on her face. "What the hell are you doing here with a bunch of drag queens?" The audience laughed again and Megan giggled in her chair.

"In any case, she's here to celebrate, and we are here to show her a good time." She snapped her fingers and the lights went out at the same time a spotlight appeared on her and Megan. Loud music rang throughout the auditorium and I instantly recognized Beyonce's "Single Ladies". The queen started grinding all over Megan's lap and Megan was laughing hysterically. My mouth gaped open watching the whole scene, and about thirty seconds into the song I came to my senses and pulled out my cell phone to take a video.

Halfway through the song more spotlights appeared behind Megan and four more queens showed up and executed the signature dance perfectly. We all laughed so hard, my phone was shaking and I knew the video wasn't going to be great, but I wanted to capture the moment. Megan's smile was so big and she was enjoying herself so much, I knew she'd like to watch the video some other time to remember how much fun she'd had.

The song ended, the lights came back on, and all the queens took turns kissing Megan on the cheek and wishing her good luck at the altar. The whole party giggled and sipped their drinks when a few minutes later the lights dimmed again. I prepped myself for another drag show, wondering if they did different numbers the second time around.

When the spotlight lit up the stage this time though, my mouth popped open again, but this time I was gawking at the half-naked, fully tanned, one hundred percent ripped, *man* on the stage. I looked over to Megan and she winked at me. The little slut had known all along.

For the next hour we watched a dozen men strip down to tiny little banana hammocks, bumping and grinding all over the stage, sometimes coming into the audience to tease the women. At one point, they pulled Megan on stage and gave her the lap dance of her life. Three very handsome male dancers took their turn rubbing up on her, shaking their barely clad asses in her face. She loved every minute of it too.

I'd be a liar if I said it wasn't entertaining and, ok, a little sexy. There were more than a few moments that I felt like fanning my face, but I contained myself and tried to seem like I wasn't affected. I was married after all. At one point I looked over at Kalli and she could have been watching a presentation on stock options and IRAs. I nudged her with my elbow and she looked over at me. I leaned towards her and put my hand up, cupping my mouth, aiming it towards her.

"These guys are pretty hot." I pointed towards the stage. She shrugged and turned back to watch the mail man deliver his "package". I poked her again and she looked over at me. "You ok?" She nodded and gave me a weak smile. I didn't believe her, but wasn't really in a good place to question her further about it. I turned back to the stage and SURPRISE! The package was his dick.

Again, Megan and her friends brought the house down with their screams and whistles and, while I enjoyed myself, I was very glad to be in my thirties, pregnant, and over the period in my life where male strippers were on my list of things to see. Eventually, after a very provocative finale, the men all took their scantily-clad bows, accepted the dollar bills being thrown up to the stage, and made their exit, bare asses in full view of everyone. The lights came up and I stood, not waiting to see if Megan had other plans. I'd spent many hours watching men, in various forms, shaking what their mommas gave them and I was ready to go to bed.

Once we had filed out of the auditorium and were back to standing on the street, Megan turned to her younger friends.

"Ok, ladies. Where are we headed next?"

"Kell's is just up the street. They've usually got some live music playing." This coming from Megan's friend, Beth, whose eyebrows went up, scrunching her forehead as she offered up the next activity.

"Oh! Irish Car Bombs! Let's go!" Megan started marching, albeit a little sideways down the street, but I managed to catch her elbow.

"Megan, I think I'm going to head back to the hotel. Is that ok? I don't want you to feel like I'm bailing on you, but, I'm bailing on you." Megan's arms came around me in a hug.

"Oh, Fella, I'm just glad you came out with us at all. I love you and I will see you tomorrow."

"I think I'm going to go too, Megan. I think I should make sure Ella gets to the hotel ok." Kalli's voice had the same soft tone mine did, not wanting to upset her.

"Sure, Kalli. Thank you both for coming. I had a great time."

"We did too, Megs. Make sure you don't drink too much and make sure you all take the limo back to the hotel. Don't get into cars with strange boys."

Megan waved her hand dismissively at me. "Ok, Mom. Thanks. Bye."

We watched her join her friends as they made their way down the street, the city lights illuminating the night, the tall buildings stretching up into the sky.

"You feel like walking or catching a cab?" Kalli asked.

"Cab. Definitely." We walked the opposite direction of Megan and the girls, waited at the corner for a minute until we flagged down an available cab. We told the driver which hotel to take us to and settled into the car for the ride.

"Hey, were you ok back there? For a single lady, you didn't seem to be enjoying the show very much." I tried to read Kalli's expression. When she was happy, it was really easy to see it on her face and in her eyes. But when she was emotionally closed down, I struggled to read her at all.

"Sure," she said as she patted my leg. "I've just got some things on my mind."

"Things?"

She shrugged, looking down at her hands that had found their way back to her lap. "I met somebody."

I tried to contain my excitement and shock at her words, allowing only my eyebrows to show any inkling of emotion, shooting straight up towards the roof. I knew Kalli had troubles trusting men since everything had happened with Kyle the spring before.

"Oh?" I could see her smile a little, even if she was trying to hide it from me. But the smile disappeared just as quickly as it appeared.

"Yeah, but he's gone. It wasn't a big deal."

"Wasn't it? You kind of seem like it was a big deal." I tried to nudge her gently, tried to get her to open up to me.

"I thought it was what I wanted. I told him that it had to be casual, like, a one-time thing. He was ok with it, at first, but then when it was time for him to go, it all just kind of blew up in my face."

"How?"

"He told me he wanted more. I told him I didn't." She sounded broken.

"But you did, didn't you?"

She nodded and wiped a tear that fell down her cheek.

"Oh, Kalli," I said as I pulled her closer to me, hugging her. "Who was it?"

"It doesn't matter."

"It kind of does," I countered.

"I can't tell you, though. I'm sorry. I worked with him and if it got out, it wouldn't be good for him."

Well, that was a surprise. If it was someone she worked with, I could probably do enough stalking on google to figure it out or at least narrow it down. "You know I'd never tell anyone, Kalli. You're my best friend. We should be able to tell each other these things." She leaned away from me, scooted back to her own seat, and I felt her close up on me again.

"It's ok. I'll be fine."

I didn't believe her and she didn't sound like she believed herself either. My heart hurt for her. I wanted nothing more than for her to be happy. Kalli was sometimes a conundrum to me. She just kind of showed up in our lives and wiggled her way in. I loved her and couldn't imagine my life now without her, but trying to get her to open up or talk about her past was a chore. It was as if she didn't want anyone to know who she was before we met her in Portland. She never invited us to Seattle where she lived. She never spoke about her family, never gave any insight into her world outside of our friendship. Did it matter to me? No. Not in the slightest. She had been there for me in the most emotionally tumultuous time of my life. She'd proven to be more loyal and loving towards me than I had ever imagined was possible. I loved her unconditionally, but I wanted her to trust me, to share things with me.

I placed my hand on her shoulder and gave it a squeeze.

"It's ok if you're not. You know that right? You don't have to be fine all the time." She didn't respond, but I knew she'd heard me and that was most important.

We made it to the hotel and when we split to head to our individual rooms, I made her hug me. I took her by the shoulders and brought her into me, wrapping my arms around her. She was stiff at first, but eventually relaxed into me.

"I love you, Kalli. You're like a sister to me. You can always count on me." I heard her sniffle and felt her head nod. She pulled away and gave me her signature weak smile and headed towards her room.

When I got to my room, I found it empty, but wasn't surprised by it. I expected Porter to have more stamina than me and to help Patrick have the time of his life. I decided that a hot bath sounded like the time of my life.

Soaking in the big tub was a luxury. The tub at the beach house was incredible, but not so much in Salem, where I spent most of my time, so I appreciated the tub and it's strategically placed jets that were currently working the knots out of my back. After my bath, Porter still hadn't returned and I was having a hard time keeping my eyes open. I turned on the TV, finding a movie I'd already seen, and laid down on the bed. I stretched out diagonally across the entire bed, my strategy to make sure Porter had to wake me to go to sleep.

My plan worked because I woke to the smell of my husband's soap and his warm hand rubbing soft circles on my back. I opened my eyes and saw my husband's face surrounded by just the soft light coming from the lamp by the bed.

"Hi," I smiled up at him sleepily. When my eyes focused, I saw his hair was wet. "Did you shower?"

"Yeah. I smelled like smoke and women." I cocked an eyebrow at him trying not to make it obvious that I had also noticed that he was naked.

"So you *did* go to a strip club."

"That we did," he said as he patted my butt, urging me to scoot onto my designated side of the bed. I slid over, rolling towards him, resting my head on my pillow, curling my knees up to my chest.

"Did Patrick have a good time?"

"If you're asking me if Patrick had nearly naked women rubbing up against him, the answer is a sacred secret I will take to the grave."

"So, what you're telling me is that he had a lot of lap dances."

"I've said no such thing." He laid his head down on his pillow, facing me, trying to hide a smirk.

I narrowed my eyes at him. "How many?"

"How many dollar bills did Megan shove into G-strings where you were?"

"None of them rubbed themselves all over her while they were alone in a dark room."

"How do you know lap dances happen in a dark room?"

"Don't change the subject, Porter. How many lap dances did he get?"

"We each bought him one," he finally conceded with a sigh.

"There were eight of you there! He had *eight* lap dances?"

"It's not a big deal, Ella. Megan wanted him to have fun and told him to go to a strip club."

"How many lap dances did *you* get?"

"None. I told you I wouldn't."

"How much money did you tuck into underwear?"

"None."

"None?" I repeated, not believing his story. Suddenly, I was below him and his arms were caging me in, his long, hard body draped over mine.

"You doubt me all of a sudden. Where is this coming from?" Before I could form an answer, or even open my mouth, his lips were on my ear. "Don't question my devotion, Ella. Don't think twice about the fact that every other woman pales in comparison to you." His hands found my wrists and slid them up, pinning them above my head. His thigh found its way in between my knees, spreading my legs underneath him and my breath caught in my throat. The panties I had put on before I fell asleep did nothing to hide the heat that was building, smoldering against his skin now as only a thin layer of cotton was between us.

"I don't doubt you," I managed to whisper.

"Oh, but you do." His mouth found my neck and instead of the kiss I was expecting, I felt his teeth bite into my flesh. I gasped, surprised by his sudden and unexpected fierceness. He soothed the tender skin by laying a wet, open-mouth kiss over the exact same spot he'd just assaulted. I couldn't help the moan that escaped at the feeling of his tongue on my throat or the wetness pooling between my legs. "When I see other women, the only thoughts that cross my mind center around how I still can't believe that I was lucky enough to find you, to make you mine, and to convince you to marry me." He continued to kiss his way down my throat, pulling not-so-gently on the neck of my nightgown. He growled when he realized he wasn't going to get to his destination without taking it off.

I was speechless. I knew how he felt about me – how he felt about us. And even though I never wanted to make it seem like I didn't feel his love or his need for me, lately with everything changing, inside my body and out, I found myself insecure. Obviously I'd let my insecurities into our relationship and he was having none of it.

His hands grabbed the bottom of the nightgown and pushed it up over my breasts and he wasted no time before taking one into his scorching mouth and palming the other, brushing his thumb over my hard, aching nipple. His hand and mouth did wonderfully terrible things to my breasts and I gasped for air, trying to wriggle free of the strong hold his other hand still hand on my wrists.

"Please… I need to touch you."

He pulled away from my breast to look me in the eye. "What more can I do to convince you? To show you that you're all I'll ever want, all I'll ever need?" As he said the words, his hips rolled into mine, igniting a whole new flame within me, sending a slow burn out through my veins. "I'm yours, Ella. I'll never be anyone else's and I'll never want anyone else. Tell me that I belong to you just as much as you belong to me."

Spurred on by his words, I felt a surge of possession rush through me. Of course he belonged to me and of course he wouldn't look at another woman, let alone touch one. We were the same, him and I, unimportant in life before we found each other. Worthwhile? Yes. Meaningful? Yes. But lacking still on a very base level. I was nothing until he found me and he had nothing before I found him. Together we were everything that mattered.

He loosened his grip on my wrist and I pried it free, using both of my hands to bring his mouth to mine in a kiss that had so much electricity I was sure we lit up the room. I saw lights – white, blinding lights. My body was drawn to his, my back arching, my hips searching for his, trying to take the edge off the lust. I needed the contact, craved it, so I pushed up and forced him to roll onto his back. Never breaking the contact of our kiss, I brought my leg over his waist and straddled him, still using my hands to keep his mouth on mine.

I could feel so much more of him this way, my body getting the rush of the contact it was longing for. My hands ran along the chiseled planes of his chest, my hips grinding onto his erection, my body came alive. He pushed my hair out of my face as he continued to kiss me, his hand finding the back of my neck, pulling me into him, pushing his cock against me, hot and hard; I knew he ached just like me.

I broke our kiss and reached to pull my nightgown over my head. Before I could even throw it on the floor, his hands were on me again, kneading and teasing. I placed my hands over his, loving the feeling of what he was doing to me, the way his hands felt on my breasts. I leaned down to place another small kiss on his lips and felt his hands glide down my sides, over my ribcage. I continued with my mouth down his chin, over his throat, and farther south down the center of his chest.

I found him hot and hard, the short hair around his cock still a little damp from his shower. I wrapped a hand around him and could feel him pulsing between my fingers, literally throbbing. I opened my mouth and licked the underside of his shaft from root to tip, swirling my tongue around the head a few times, finally making eye contact with him as I took him fully into my mouth. I watched his eyes disappear as his lids fluttered closed, and heard a strangled moan escape from his mouth as it gaped open.

He was such a strong and assertive man; it wasn't very often that I saw him give up his dominance. Knowing I was the one making him forget his need to be the aggressor only fueled the fire raging within me. My mouth took him in and the heat radiating off him simply warmed me. Everything combined – the heat, the throbbing, his relinquishment of control – it all boiled over and I felt myself start to claim him. Every bob of my head, every lick, every caress, it was all meant to convey one thing – that he was mine. Lost in the moment, living in the feeling of what passed between us, I hardly noticed he'd regained some attentiveness. I felt his hand move my hair from the side of my face, allowing him the pleasure of watching me love him. Our eyes met again and I watched as his hands came to grip me behind my neck, pulling me back up towards him.

He pulled my face within inches of his, both of his hands tangled in my hair, gently tugging. "Take me," he whispered. "I'm yours." We collided then, in every way possible. My mouth met his, my hands found his skin, and with one quick roll of my hips I captured him, felt him fill me completely. We were connected, emotionally and physically, and I couldn't help but think about how much deeper our connection was; I always had a piece of him in me, carrying his child, tying me to him irrevocably.

"If you're mine," I said against his mouth, "then I'm yours."

He growled and pulled down on my hips, burying himself deeper inside of me, causing me to gasp. I sat up, adjusting to being so incredibly full. My eyes closed and my head tipped back, my hands finding purchase behind me on his muscular thighs. I felt his hands roaming all over me, gliding over my skin, causing goose bumps to rise, blood to pulse. I rocked back and forth on him, mouth falling open at the instant pleasure coursing through me at the contact. I rode him, the head of his cock always managing to find that one spot, deep inside, that sent shockwaves and electricity straight to my core.

He let me continue to ride him, pulling my hips down onto him, adding beautiful pressure to my movement, allowing every feeling to be magnified. I spent most of my time working him over, making sure that he enjoyed it just as much as I did. I listened for his growls, taking note of what was turning him on, what was making him pulse within me. I started moving my hips in a small circle and heard him let out a gasp, followed by a low and slow, "fuck me." I smiled, because that was exactly what I intended to do.

"Porter, look at me," I rasped, still working my hips in slow and small circles over his cock, filled completely. I watched as his eyes opened and slowly focused on me. He looked magnificent. His biceps strained from their tight grasp on my waist. His eyes hooded with lust. His stone-like abs constricting from pleasure. "No one will ever get to rub themselves all over you like this but me." He bit his lip and groaned, pulling me down on him even more. "Now, touch me, Porter. Make me come."

He didn't need to be told twice. His hand came over my mound and his finger started its torturous rhythm over my engorged clit. The feeling of his cock stroking that perfect spot inside of me and his finger teasing that hot bundle of nerves sent me spiraling into an orgasm like none I'd ever had. Shock waves moved from my sex, down my legs, curling my toes. I felt my inner walls clenching around him, illuminating how incredibly hard he was. I cried out and was surprised at my volume; surely the people in the room next to us could hear me. I felt a warm wetness seep out of me, pooling where our bodies connected.

"Oh shit, Ella. You just came all over me." He sounded surprised. I continued to rock back and forth, trying to stretch the orgasm out as long as it would last, my over-sensitized clit aching and trembling.

"That," I panted, still gently rocking him in and out of me, "was possibly the best orgasm I have ever had."

"My turn," he said. In an instant he grabbed my waist and rolled me over. I was under him again, but this time he was still inside me. My legs instinctually wrapped around him, pulling him into me farther. He leaned down and brought one of my tight, pebbled nipples into his mouth. My back arched, offering him all of me, begging him to take. I willingly gave him everything, wanted to feel empty afterwards, needed him to take everything I had.

I whimpered as I felt him start to move in and out of me, starting with slow strokes, but gradually pumping faster and faster. He brought my leg over his shoulder, changing the angle, causing me to cry out as I gripped his bulging shoulders.

"Yes," I cried, dangerously close to another orgasm. "Please…"

"Hang on, Baby. Not yet. Wait for me." I looked up at him, wondering how in the world he thought I could hold off an orgasm. I was put in a trance as I watched a bead of sweat roll down his forehead, trail down the bridge of his nose, and drip off him, landing right in the middle of my chest. Then his eyes met mine and I felt so many emotions in his gaze. This man loved me more than any other single thing on the planet. He treasured me, coveted me, wanted me, above anything else, me and the baby we made together.

"I will always wait for you," I said as I brushed my hand through his hair, bringing his lips down to mine. He kissed me, his tongue brushing up against mine, like I was a breath of air given to a drowning man. And then he took. He took everything. I was lost in the feeling of his possession, swirling in the heat building between us, dangling off the edge of my world, hanging on by the connection between us, waiting for him.

"Now," he growled at me, as he seemed to lose his composure, pushing into me with new speed and fervor, gripping my hips harder, lifting me up to get to depths previously unknown to either of us. I cried out as I tumbled through my release and felt him tumble with me. We breathed in tandem, both of us slowly coming down from new heights. He rested over me, our sweaty bodies still entangled, his face nestled in the space between my neck and shoulder. I turned my head towards him slightly and placed a small, open-mouthed kiss on his cheek, loving the salty taste of his skin.

"All that baby-making practice really paid off," I whispered into his ear, hoping to see his beautiful deep brown eyes. I was rewarded when he lifted his head to look at me, and was gifted another surprise to see his smirk. Nothing was sexier than my man, sweaty from sex and smirking at me.

"You can't give all the praise to practice, Baby. There's something to be said for natural born talent. You've got it in spades," he said as he brushed the tip of his nose up against mine, making me smile in return. He gave me a quick kiss and then rolled off me. Immediately I was left cold, the frigid air turning my previously hot and sweaty body into a shivering mess.

"Hey," I said quietly. He turned his head to look at me, his hair all kinds of crazy, still sweat soaked. "I'm sorry. I shouldn't have questioned you or doubted you. You did nothing wrong." I let out a small sigh, taking just a moment to put my thoughts into words. "I think lately I'm just feeling really insecure and tonight it manifested itself in a jealous streak." He rolled closer to me, draping his arms around my waist, resting his forehead against mine.

"I can't imagine how you're feeling right now, with everything happening to you and your body. I get it. I really do. But you have to understand, and *believe me* when I tell you that seeing your body change, knowing it's my baby inside of you causing that change, it's the sexiest thing to witness. I see nothing but beauty when I look at you."

His words warmed me. I believed him and I trusted him, always and completely. But I also knew that there would be times down the road when I would forget this moment and give in to the demons in my mind out to sabotage me.

"I promise to try and remember that you're always on my team, but I might need a reminder every once in a while." I peeked out at him through my eyelashes.

"Oh trust me, Ella. If what we just did is the kind of reminder you need, I'll be more than willing to give you a refresher."

"Ok," I said shyly. He smiled at me and landed a loud smack on my naked ass. "Ow!" I exclaimed, caught off guard by his attack.

"Come on, let's take a shower and go to sleep."

I followed him to the bathroom and started to unwind under the hot water spraying down on us. I let Porter wash me, loving the gentle feeling of his hands on me, spreading silky soap over my skin, getting sleepier and more tired as he used his hands to knead out the tense muscles in my back.

I was hardly conscious when he pulled me from the shower, dried and dressed me, and put me in the king-sized bed. The last thing I remembered was feeling the comforter being pulled over me and his lips on my temple, telling me he loved me before I drifted into darkness.

Chapter Seven

Porter

Living with a pregnant woman was more challenging than I could have ever anticipated. Not only was I trying to deal with running, essentially, two businesses, I was constantly worried about Ella and the baby. When we were together, my focus was making sure she had anything and everything she needed. Most days she was happily content, if not stubbornly independent. Did I want her walking up the two flights of stairs to get her giant pillow from the bedroom? No. Did she want to get it herself because she was, as she so eloquently stated, "Pregnant, not immobile?" Yes. So, I found myself compromising a lot – picking my battles. I let her make her way up the stairs all she wanted, but I made sure to carry in all of the groceries, do all the laundry, and generally make life easier for her. Of course, I had to be sneaky about all of it so she didn't catch on. I figured eventually she'd tire of walking up stairs.

Today she was six months pregnant and her bulge from a few months ago blossomed into the most beautiful bump I'd ever seen. She was perfectly round in all the right places. My newest favorite activity was just sitting on the couch with my hands on her stomach, coaxing our baby into kicking so I could feel the most incredible thing in the world: my baby moving in her belly. The baby would kick, Ella would laugh, and I rode the wave of bliss that came over me every time.

Each day she grew more beautiful, more precious to me, and more impressive. Motherhood was something she was inherently good at. Our baby wasn't even born and yet, she already was a great mother. The fear in the beginning of pregnancy of the actual birth, transformed into a need to be educated and prepared. She took Lamaze classes, prenatal yoga classes, and read every book she could about childbirth. I did not envy the task and tried to hide the fear that slowly grew inside of me. The bigger her belly grew, the more I grasped the idea that she would, in fact, have to birth a baby. So, if I had to run to the grocery store for mint ice cream at three in the morning, so be it.

I stood next to Patrick, watching my gorgeous wife walk down the aisle, wearing a flowing dress that took my breath away. She eyed me as she walked towards the altar, smiling like she had a secret. I almost didn't notice when Megan started her walk down the aisle, I was so caught up in Ella. Then everyone stood and looked at Megan and my eyes were drawn to the bride making her way towards her groom.

Megan became one of my favorite people in the last year. She was still young and sometimes acted her age, but she was a great sister and simply fun to be around. She and Patrick were a phenomenal couple and I admired him for loving Megan as she was, never trying to reign her in. Her hand was threaded through her father's elbow as he walked her down the aisle, her eyes glistening with unshed tears, looking at Patrick with clear and obvious love.

The ceremony wasn't long, but filled with love and commitment. Traditional vows were made by both bride and groom and were spoken with such conviction I had no doubt they were making a conscious decision, not going into the marriage lightly. I was proud of both of them. I looked over at my own bride as she watched her little sister kiss her husband for the first time, wiping tears from her eyes. She looked over at me briefly and I winked at her, wanting to wipe the tears from her eyes myself.

I kissed her temple as she met me to walk back down the aisle, and felt my heart beat faster when she leaned into me, taking the comfort I was offering. She could be stubborn about a lot of things, but taking the love I offered her was never one of them.

Our duties in the wedding were over with the ceremony and I was very much looking forward to spending some time with my wife; she'd been noticeably absent the last couple of days, making sure everything with Megan's wedding was on track. Both Poppy and Dahlia were closed today so that all the girls could be here to celebrate, and that was a big deal in and of itself. The only time a store was closed in the past was just shortly after the shooting at Poppy. Megan was moved when Ella told her the stores would both be closed.

"You look beautiful," I whispered into Ella's ear as we danced. My hand was on the small of her back, pulling her close to me.

"Thank you. I paid someone a lot of money to make me look this way," she said with a laugh.

"You know that's not what I'm talking about."

She smiled at me, her blue eyes sparkling. "Thank you." Her voice was soft and light. We swayed back and forth to the music and we both had to laugh when a big thump was felt against my stomach, coming from hers. "Baby wants to dance too," she said as her hand came to the spot she'd just been kicked in.

"I still can't believe the two of you won't find out what you're having," Megan said as her and Patrick danced up next to us. We, all four, stopped dancing while Megan laid her hand on Ella's stomach, hoping to feel the baby move.

"We know what we're having, Megan – a baby."

"You know what I mean," Megan responded with a sigh.

"I'm really looking forward to the surprise," I said as I took my wife back into my arms, wanting her belly and baby kicks to be saved for me alone.

Megan looked over at her new groom. "Don't get any ideas. When we get pregnant, we're finding out if it's a boy or a girl."

Patrick held his hands up in surrender. "I wouldn't even dare to suggest otherwise."

Megan gave him a dreamy smile. "You're so perfect for me."

The two of them floated away on their newlywed cloud and I returned my attention to my wife. "Are you still ok with not knowing if it's a boy or girl?"

She shrugged. "I like not knowing." That was enough for me. If Ella was happy, I was happy.

The reception continued and we watched Robert give a heartfelt speech, singing Megan's praises and warning Patrick about what would happen to him if he ever hurt her. The cake was cut, the garter removed, and Megan tossed her bouquet. Kalli caught Megan's bouquet, but for some reason didn't look too happy about it. When I gave Ella a questioning look, worried about her friend, Ella waved it away and had her own sad look on her face. Something was going on there and later I would try to remember to ask her about it. For now, though, I wanted to spend some more time with my wife's belly pressed up against me as we danced.

"Honey," Ella said softly, her cheek resting gently against my shoulder. "Your pocket's vibrating."

"Huh?"

"Your phone in your pocket is vibrating," she laughed. I stepped away from her and reached into my pocket and pulled out my phone. I didn't recognize the number, but that wasn't really out of the ordinary – a lot of people called me for quotes on work and to make consultation appointments. I went to put it away but Ella stopped me. "Just answer it. You'll be thinking about it all night if you don't."

"Nope," I said, dropping the phone in my pocket. "They'll leave a message. It's a Saturday. I'll call them back on Monday." She rolled her eyes at me sweetly, trying to look annoyed but really not pulling it off.

We danced for a little while longer, but eventually I could tell Ella was losing steam.

"I think it's time we head home. These shoes were a big mistake." We both looked down at her feet and I couldn't believe how swollen they were.

"It's a good thing I have power tools. We'll need something heavy duty to cut you out of those shoes. Come on," I said as I placed a kiss on her forehead. "Let's tell everyone goodbye and head home."

After what seemed like an hour of goodbyes, we finally made it out to Ella's Toyota. She handed me the keys and I was glad we were in agreement over who should drive. Her feet were in no condition to be operating a vehicle.

"That was a really great wedding. Megan did a fantastic job," Ella said as she dug through her purse, pulling out her phone. "Huh. That's weird."

"What?"

"I got a phone call from a number I don't recognize." She stared at her phone, as if it would announce who had called her, answering all her questions. I pulled out my phone and pulled up my missed call log. I turned the screen towards her.

"Is this the same number as the one that called you?" She looked at my screen and then back to hers.

"Yeah. Weird. I wonder who it is."

"One way to find out." I pushed a button activating the Bluetooth and dialed the number from my phone. When the phone on the other end of the line picked up, it was a man's rough voice they heard.

"Dillard here," the voice said in the way of a greeting.

"Uh, hello. I missed a call from this number earlier this evening."

"And who am I speaking with?" The man asked, almost as if I were wasting his time.

"Porter Masters. Who am *I* speaking with?"

"My name is Detective Henry Dillard. I am investigating a crime and looking for a Ms. Ella Sinclair. This number was listed as a contact for her. Are you able to get ahold of her?"

"It's Ella Masters now, and yes, I can get ahold of her. She's my wife."

"Great. Is she available?"

"I'm here, Detective," Ella said, placing her hand on my thigh as we drove down the highway.

"Good evening, Mrs. Masters. Sorry for bothering you on a Saturday evening, but I was wondering if you could come down to the Portland police station. It's a matter involving your open case." My stomach tightened at the detective's words. The shooting. Ella's wide and worried eyes found mine and I knew I had to keep it together for her. She would feed off any panic I showed, so I took steady and calm breaths.

"Well, Detective Dillard, my husband and I were headed back to Salem for the evening. Can we make arrangements to meet tomorrow or even Monday perhaps?"

"I don't want to alarm you, Ma'am, but it's a matter of urgency for you to make it to the station as soon as possible." Ella looked at me, waiting for me to make the decision.

"We'll be there in fifteen minutes," I stated flatly.

"See you then." I heard his line go dead over our speakers and gave Ella's hand a squeeze. Neither one of us said a word as we made our way to the station.

Twenty minutes later, Ella and I were seated in a stale room that looked like it came straight out of a cop drama: large mirror (one way, I was sure), aluminum table, three chairs. Nothing else. It was cold and I felt goose bumps as I rubbed my hand up and down Ella's arm. The door opened and a tall, imposing man stepped in, looking us both over. Once the door was closed behind him, he reached his hand out to both Ella and me. We shook his hand and all three of us sat down.

"Thank you for meeting me on such short notice. As I alluded to over the phone, there have been some developments in your case."

"What does that mean?" Ella's voice shook as she asked the detective her question.

"Yesterday the Portland Swat Team took down a drug ring in the inner city. We took in a young man who is facing drug and weapon charges that are scaring him shitless. Pardon the language," he said quickly, looking at Ella. She didn't even blink at him so he continued on. "He's young and it's his first offense. Luckily for everyone involved, he's scared and looking for a way out. He offered up some information that could possibly lead us to an arrest in your case."

"What?" Ella said, disbelief and excitement evident in her voice.

"Yes. In exchange for information on a few cases we're working on, he will be getting a lesser charge and stay out of jail. He claims to know of a man who was involved in a shooting about a year ago, in the area of your store, and the suspect matches the description of the man who shot you."

"Oh my God," she whispered.

"So you have the bastard in custody?" My blood boiled at the thought of the person who shot Ella being in the same building as I was. I would rip him apart.

"Well, it's not that simple. We have a name and a general area he was last seen. But he could be anywhere. We've put out an APB, and we've got our eyes out for him, but it might be a while before we find him."

"So, what? You brought us here to tell us you kind of, sort of, have news about our case, maybe?" I was beginning to feel my rage take over. What were they playing at?

"Mr. Masters, listen, I'm trying to solve this case too. I want nothing more than to lock this guy up, but it's going to take some time. I brought you in here to bring you up to speed and give you information. It's very possible that this kid, and he is just a kid – nineteen-year-old boy – who shot you is long gone. He could be on the other side of the country by now. Or he could have gotten word of the arrests made today, that our suspect ratted him out, and he could be waiting outside to finish the job he messed up last year."

I stood up and the chair I sat in scratched across the floor behind me with force. I leaned over the table and pointed my finger in the detective's face. "You don't bring my wife in here to tell her some half-assed news about the man who shot her and then try to scare the daylights out of her. Cop or not, I will kick your ass if you talk to her like that again." Ella pulled on my arm, urging me to sit back down.

"Listen," Dillard said, raising his hands in the air, "we're all on the same page here. I want to catch this asshole just as much as you do. But if you threaten me again, you'll be locked up faster than you can blink and you won't do your wife any good behind bars." He kept his hands up and looked at me until I finally exhaled loudly and righted my chair, sitting again. Dillard turned to Ella. "Again, I'm not trying to scare you, I'm trying to help you."

"What's going to happen now?" She asked quietly.

"Well, like I said, we have no real idea of where this kid is. He could be in town or he could be in another state. But I wanted to give you a heads up and offer what help we could."

"What kind of help are you talking about?" I was still pissed and even I heard it in my voice.

"Well, we can put more patrols past the sight of the crime."

"It's a store. It's called Poppy," Ella said quietly.

"Right, we could have more cars making passes by the store, if you live inside the city limits we can have cars patrol by your house."

"You think he knows where we live?" Ella asked, sounding scared all over again.

"Chances are, no. Most likely, this kid doesn't even know your name. He was probably hired to show up at a spot and shoot a gun. He doesn't know who you are, but he does know where you were. So, the store really is a place of interest."

"We'll hire private security again," I said immediately. Ella looked at me with relief, no doubt worried about her sister and the girls who work there. "We live in Salem right now."

Dillard nodded. "We'll partner with the Salem PD and ask them to watch your house, just leave me your address."

"Will that start immediately? We're headed there tonight."

"Shouldn't be a problem. I'll call their captain myself."

"So, we're just supposed to sit here like ducks, waiting to be picked off?" I could hear the panic coming over her and it tore my heart open. I wasn't going to let anything happen to her. I took her hand in mine and held on tight, trying to remind her that I was here to protect her.

"No. You've got the police looking out for you, but you need to be careful. Don't go anywhere alone, report anything suspicious, and be smart. Trust your instincts. And call me whenever you think you have something to offer, anything at all. No piece of information is too small. And I'll be doing my best to catch this kid before anything can happen. Expect the best, prepare for the worst."

Ella's hand floated her belly and I saw the moment she really fell into the abyss of irrational thought. I turned to her, not a care in the world that the detective was with us, or who might be watching through the mirror, and pulled her forehead to meet mine.

"Breathe with me Ella, in and out, slowly." I took a few over-exaggerated breaths to get her to sync up with me. She shook, trembled, and I knew she was slipping away from me. "I'm not going to let anything happen to you or the baby. Do not give up on me now, Ella. Stay with me here, breathe." We sat there, breathing in each other's breaths for a few minutes until I felt like she wasn't going to hyperventilate or go into some sort of shock. When I finally looked over at Dillard, I saw sympathy in his eyes and that went a long way to make up for some of the shitty things he'd said since we got there. He was a hard ass, that was clear, but in that moment, when he looked at my wife like he wanted to help fix her, I felt confident that he would keep his word and protect her as best he could.

"Let's get your address to the Salem PD and get you home," Dillard said, handing me a pad of paper and a pen. He left to make the phone call and Ella's head found my shoulder. She was calm and quiet, both hands resting on her belly. Her silence was equally comforting as it was alarming. In the quiet, she found the terror. I put my hand over hers and tried to remind her that I was there.

"I don't want you to worry about this, Ella. I'm going to take care of everything." She didn't say anything in response. I would have preferred to hear her crying or yelling. The silence was killing me. "Babe, talk to me. Please."

"This is a hopeless situation." Her voice is calm, cold, and still – like stone.

"No it isn't."

"You can't protect me from a man with a gun, Porter."

"Yes, I can." I knew what she was saying. If he found her and got anywhere near her, it would be hard to stop a bullet from hurting her. But I wasn't going to let her out of my sight, wasn't going to let anyone near her, not until we knew for sure the police had him in custody. "Look at me, Ella." My hands found her face and I pulled her to look at me. "You've got to think positively. We will make it through this." My eyes searched hers, looking for a key to alleviating some of her anxiety. "What's going through your head?"

"I want to run."

Her words were like boulders settling in my stomach. Her flight instinct had kicked in. The danger was here so her mind told her to leave. I rubbed my thumbs across her cheeks.

"I know you do," I whispered. "I want so badly to make this go away for you, but we've got to stay. We've got to fight. I won't let him near you."

A new wave of panic flooded her eyes. "What if he gets to you first? Oh God. Porter, I can't lose you. Please…"

"Shh…" I pulled her back into my shoulder and smoothed down her hair. "It'll all be ok." I knew I couldn't promise her that, but it was all I could say in the moment. Dillard came back in the room and his eyes flickered to my wife crying into my neck. "You better find this guy, and fast. If I find him first I can guarantee you never will."

Dillard nodded. "I'd be thinking the same thing if it were my wife."

"Good. Then we're on the same page."

"The Salem PD are going to be making rounds past your house and for the next few nights a cruiser will be positioned on your block just until the dust settles."

"Thank you," I said, sincerely.

"Do you have a license to carry a concealed weapon?"

"Yes. We got one last year after her abduction."

"Good. Remember, if someone comes into your home, you have every legal right to shoot them. No questions asked. Take them out."

"You don't have to tell me twice, Detective."

"Ok. Well, I will keep you updated on our progress. This case is my first priority. If he's in the state, I will find him."

I believed him. I gently stood, trying not to jostle Ella too much. I shook his hand. "I appreciate it." I led Ella out to our car, flanked by two uniformed officers. They made sure we got into the car safely and I watched them disappear in the rear-view mirror as I drove away. Merging onto the freeway, my hand found Ella's knee.

"How are you holding up?" I asked softly.

"I just want to go to sleep."

I nodded, understanding she was tired, exhausted – both physically and emotionally. "I need you to promise me something, Ella." Her head turned and she looked at me, eyes half closed, near sleep already.

"Hmmm?"

"If you're going to run, you have to take me with you." I looked her in her hooded eyes, trying to be very clear, to make sure she understood me. "I want to stay here and see this guy captured, but if you're going to run, we run together."

"You're not safe with me," she whispered.

"I'm dead without you." She took in a deep breath and exhaled loudly. "Please, I need to hear you say it."

"If I feel the need to leave, I promise I'll tell you. I won't leave you behind."

"Promise me you won't give up the fight, Ella."

"That's just it, Porter; I'm not sure how much fight I have left in me."

We rode the rest of the way in silence, my hand wrapped around hers. When we pulled up onto our street, I spotted the cruiser a few houses down. I could see the outline of two officers in the car and admittedly was a little relieved to see them. I just hoped Ella would sleep better knowing they were out there.

We entered the house and Ella readied herself for bed, not saying one word. She was silent again and I felt myself settling into the same panic she often found herself in. I couldn't lose her.

That night, when I was finally sure she'd drifted off, I wrapped my arm around her waist and pushed my body close up to hers, wanting to follow her into sleep with her body safely pressed against mine.

Chapter Eight

Ella

It's amazing how a person can become accustomed to living in fear. The fear becomes normalized, something akin to the everyday. It was now normal to have a bodyguard in Dahlia with me every day. To see a police car drive by my house was relieving and to get a nod from the officers inside the car was calming.

Weeks passed and it didn't seem as if we were any closer to finding the man who shot me as we had been before we knew his identity.

Jason Ramie.

One name changed my whole universe. I couldn't find his face in my mind, but I could see him – his black hoodie, his slumped shoulders. I heard his voice, shouting through the glass he eventually shot me through, asking for food or money. So many things I could have done differently that night, but I still can't find myself regretful for the way anything happened. Anytime I started to feel the panic come over me, I placed my hand on my belly and remembered that through all the terrible and scary things I'd been through in the last year, I was still in the best place I could ever imagine: married to, undoubtedly, the most wonderful man ever in creation and carrying his child. Would I do it all over again to make sure I ended up right here, right now? Yes.

I went to the doctor a few times since we learned about Jason Ramie and it was obvious that the stress of the situation was taking a toll on me. My blood pressure was sky high and my energy low. But I wouldn't let him win.

It wasn't in my nature. Sure, I'd taken a few days to regroup. The stores had to remain closed for a few days to sort out security and I'd let Porter handle all of that – like he'd have it any other way. I took those days to allow myself to feel every emotion that came my way. Fear, pain, panic, guilt – it was all there and it tried to drag me down, tried to force me to throw in the towel.

But then I'd feel my baby move inside me, see my belly move and shift as the life inside me grew and changed, and I made a decision. I was never giving up. Never. I'd fight until there was no fight left in me. So, although I was afraid, I was brave. I went to work every day and distracted myself. Heck, I even found myself laughing eventually. Life went on as it had before, the only difference being that, every once in a while without warning, a flash of fear would shoot through me like lightening.

A man's voice, a dark shirt, even hearing the name Jason could send me into a momentary lack of composure. The people around me understood and helped me cope but, truth be told, it was getting old. I didn't want to live in this fear any more. So, when Detective Dillard called me one rainy morning, I was hopeful.

"Hi, Ella. It's Detective Dillard. Do you have a free moment?"

"Sure. What can I do for you?" I was filing some sales reports in the backroom of Dahlia, sitting at my desk. I felt my heart rate pick up speed, anticipating whatever it was he called to tell me.

"We picked up a man by the name of Jason Ramie last night in Portland. We are pretty confident he's the man who shot you, but we need you to come to the station to look at a line up. If you can ID him, it will help the case tremendously."

"You caught him?" I whispered, shocked. Those were words I had given up on hearing.

"We got him, Ella," he said softly.

"Like, right now? He's in custody this very moment?" I could hear my voice getting higher, tears stinging my eyes.

"I told you I'd get him. He's locked up this very moment, Ella, behind bars. He can't hurt you."

I exhaled. I let it out. So much more than air came out of me: fear, anxiety, sadness, guilt. It all came rushing out and when I breathed in, I felt lighter. I smiled and a happy tear slid down my face.

"Thank you," I managed to whimper into the phone.

"No thanks necessary. It's my job. But I do need you to make your way to the station as soon as possible. The line-up is important."

"But I don't remember what he looked like. I won't be able to identify him."

"Regardless, it's still important to try, Ella." He paused, giving me a moment to absorb everything. "Can you come to Portland today?"

"Yes. Yes, of course. I'll be there as soon as possible."

"See you then." He disconnected and I immediately dialed Porter.

"Hey, Babe," he said in greeting.

"Porter, Dillard just called me."

"And?" His voice immediately went from happy and light to tense and worried. I had spent a lot of time focused on keeping myself sane and hadn't paid enough attention to what this had done to my husband. Of course he was always strong and protective, but this had to have been eating away at him.

"He says they've caught him."

"What?" I laughed just a little at his surprise. Surely we'd been living with bad news for so long we'd only come to expect it. Hearing good news was so much of a shock, his first reaction was to assume he'd heard me wrong.

"Yes," another laugh breaking through. "He says they caught him last night and they want me to go to Portland and try to pick him out in a line up."

"They caught him?" I heard his emotion through the phone and wanted desperately to hold him in that moment.

"Yes, Baby. They got him." He took in some deep breaths and let them out, shuttering. Oh, how I wanted to be with him. "Porter, come and get me. Bring me to Portland," I whispered.

"I'll be there in forty-five minutes." I laughed because it was an hour's drive.

"Drive safely, Love."

True to his word, Porter showed up at Dahlia only fifty minutes later. He walked in, nodded at Chad, the security detail he'd hired, and came straight for me. The next instant I was in his arms, smelling the familiar scent of wood and soap, ready and willing to crawl right inside of him and live there forever.

"Are you ok?" He asked, stroking his hand down my hair.

"I am now."

"You ready to go?" I nodded and he turned to Chad. "You'll follow us to Portland?"

"Of course," Chad responded, moving from his posed position of feet spread shoulder-width apart and hands grasped behind his back. He held the front door open for us and we headed out, shouting a goodbye to the girls left at the store for the day. In the past weeks, Chad had become somewhat of a shadow. He drove me where I needed to go and went with me everywhere, unless I was with Porter. Megan had a similar guard at her shop, but he only stayed in the store. She didn't have the pleasure of having a quiet and seemingly grumpy man with her at all times.

Another development over the last few weeks was that Porter now carried a gun. It made me nervous to see the handle sticking out of his belt, or to see it holstered around his ribcage, but I knew there was no talking him out of it. And, really, I wanted him protected too, so I accepted it. I refused to carry a gun. I knew what it felt like to fire a gun into a person, what it was like to shoot someone and watch them die. Porter agreed that as long as I was with him or Chad, there was no need for me to carry a gun. It was one argument I was glad we avoided.

An hour later we pulled up to the police station and before I could even try to open my door, Chad was there, his eyes roaming around the parking lot, looking for any sort of trouble. Porter came to my side of the truck and took my hand, leading me into the station. My other hand instinctually found my belly, and I took a deep breath, trying not to freak out about what I was going to do.

Detective Dillard was waiting for us when we entered and he ushered us into another interrogation room. We sat down and Porter never let go of my hand.

"Thanks for coming in on such short notice."

"Do you really think it's him?" Porter's question was short and strained. I rubbed my thumb over the back of his hand, trying to calm him. I could only imagine what he was thinking, possibly being in the same building as the man who shot me. His protective instincts had to be tearing him apart.

Dillard took in a deep breath and seemed to hold it for a moment longer than normal. "I think it's him." I felt Porter's hand grip mine a little tighter at Dillard's statement. "But we really need Ella to try and ID him in a blind line-up." His eyes drifted over to me and I could feel my pulse beating in my temples.

I shook my head at him. "I don't remember his face. I never saw it." Dillard put his hands out like he was offering me something. I couldn't help but think he was trying to give me my life back, I just had to claim it.

"You're just going to go into a room, much like this one, only instead of a mirror there will be a window. On the other side there will be eight men, all with a number above their heads. You just take your time and look at each of them thoroughly. If one of them stands out to you, or even two of them, you let me know."

"You don't have to do this if you're not ready," Porter said as he pulled my chin to look at him.

"Don't I?" I whispered.

"No. If you're not ready we walk right out of here and go home. They can wait."

"No, we can't," Dillard interjected. "We can only hold him so long on a charge with no substantial evidence. If we don't ID someone, he'll be back on the street by morning. And if it's him in there, the man that shot you, he might get a crazy idea to go after you."

Porter nearly growled at the man. "Do not use *fear* to coerce her into doing something she isn't ready for." His voice was full of rage and I could feel his pulse pumping through the tanned skin of his wrist. It was my turn to comfort him. I placed my hand on his cheek and urged him to look back at me.

"Porter, it's going to be ok. I'm going to walk into a room and look at a bunch of strangers. I don't remember him."

"And if she doesn't remember him, but he's in that room, what then?" Porter was seething.

"I'll do everything I can between now and morning to get something out of him that can give us cause to hold him."

"There's nothing to lose by going in there, Porter. If I leave he gets off anyway." My hand slipped to the back of his neck and I pulled his forehead in to touch it to mine. "I'll be ok," I whispered.

"You ready?" Dillard asked. I turned to him and nodded. He stood up and started towards the door.

"Give me just one minute alone with her," Porter said without looking at Dillard, still fuming. He said nothing, but left Porter and I alone in the cold room. Before I could look towards him, I felt his hands on me, pulling me into him, and his mouth pressed against mine.

There was nothing soothing or calm about this kiss. His hands were in my hair, on my neck, holding me to him, as if he were afraid I was going to float away. I let him take me. It was obvious that was what he needed, to hold on to a piece of me while we were separated. He felt helpless that I was doing this alone and in turn, he felt alone.

When he finally pulled away from me, my bottom lip was trapped between his teeth, hanging on to the very last part of me he could. If we had been anywhere but this sterile room, I would have felt very differently about that kiss. It would have morphed into something so unbelievably hot, so ridiculously passionate, neither one of us would have been able to stop it from progressing. But we were here, and it wasn't hot. It was frantic and heartbreaking. I moved back from him, trying desperately to appear the strong and infallible person I wanted to be in that moment.

"I'll be ok. I'll be right back." My hand trailed across his cheek as I walked away from him, leaving the room, attempting to put on my mask of courage. I nodded at Dillard as I came upon him in the hallway.

"Listen, Ella, take as much time as you need in there. Don't just give up if you don't recognize any of them right away. There's no rush."

I nodded at him again, afraid that any words I tried to speak would defy my attempt at bravery. If I tried to speak right now, the words would come out shaky and filled with fear, so it was better I kept my mouth shut. I let him lead me through the building and when his hand stopped on a doorknob, I felt the panic start to take over.

"Wait! Wait.... I need a moment." I laid a hand over my chest and tried to even out my breaths. I wanted to be strong. I wanted to do this without difficulty. I knew the men behind the glass wouldn't be able to see me, but I didn't want to go in there and appear to be broken – not to anyone. I wanted to hold my head high, shoulders back, and to be brave. Dillard let me have my moment, and when I stood up straight I pushed my shoulders back and ran a hand through my hair. There were no tears in my eyes and my breathing was even. "Ok. I'm ready." He nodded and opened the door for me.

The room was exactly as he'd described it, only, my side of the room was dark. It seemed fitting that I was in the dark while the alleged criminals were in the light – a reversal, if you will. Let them sweat it out a little. Let them feel like all the eyes are on them, while I rest in the cold and calm dark, I could use a little peace and quiet. Perhaps this wasn't going to be as hard as I thought.

I took a few steps until I was only a breath away from the glass partition.

"You're sure they can't see me?" I turned to Dillard.

"Trust me. You're safe. They cannot see you. They see a mirror." I nodded and my eyes returned to the men.

At first, my eyes fluttered all over the place, latching on to tiny, insignificant things about the men. One had blue eyes, one was wearing a beanie, one had on orange socks. My mind tried to process all the information at once and I felt myself becoming confused. I looked down at the ground and took a few deep breaths. When I looked up again, I stood tall, and I gazed at the man with the number one above his head.

I studied his face, his shoulders, the way he was built, but nothing seemed familiar about him at all. I moved on. I studied each man for an exorbitant amount of time, thoroughly looking at every part of them exposed to me. I didn't think I'd find him, but it wasn't going to be for lack of trying. The fifth man proved to be unfamiliar as well. He was much too short and skinny. I remember the outline of the man who shot me and he was imposing.

When my eyes fell upon the sixth man, I felt a zing of electricity shoot through me, almost like my body had been asleep and was waking up. Pins and needles. It was there and then, just as quickly, it dissipated. I looked over at Dillard and he was stone-like. I turned back to the sixth suspect and my eyes took in everything about him. He was tall, bigger than the other men he was standing next to, and his eyes we trained on a spot on the floor. Again, I looked at Dillard.

"Can you ask Number Six to stand up straight?" I was surprised that my voice came out as calm and strong as it had.

Dillard walked to a button on the wall, pushed it, and spoke into a speaker just above it.

"Number Six, step forward, hands at your side, stand up tall, and look straight ahead." The button made a crackling noise when he released it and I watched as the man bit his lip, took a few steps forward, and stood up straight. It seemed as though he looked straight at me, but his eyes never met with mine. He was looking into a void.

I took another step towards the glass, narrowing my eyes at him. Suddenly, I saw a flash of the man in the dark hoodie. The hooded man was looking at the ground, it was dark, but then he raised his head to look at me, and I watched the shadow move over his face. The first part of his face I saw was his chin. It was prominent with a dimple in the middle.

Just like Man Number Six.

In my mind, the image of the man in the hoodie became clearer and as the shadow moved up, more of his face became visible. His nose – crooked. His eyes – light. His hairline – a widow's peak.

Just like Man Number Six.

"That's him," I said firmly, with conviction. "Number six." I looked over at Dillard and he gave me no indication as to whether or not I was right.

"Have you looked at all the suspects?" He asked as he leaned casually against the wall.

I turned back to the wall of men, the last two men were nothing like the man in my memory. I looked back to Dillard. "That's him. None of the others match the man in my mind. That's him. I know it."

"Ok," he said, taking my elbow and leading me out of the room.

"Wait, *ok*? That's all you're going to say? Was that Jason Ramie? Did I pick the right one?" I *knew* I had; I just wanted to hear it from him. He didn't say anything, just led me back to the room where Porter waited. I walked in and rushed to him, wrapping my arms around his shoulders. His face burrowed into my neck and I heard him take in a deep breath. After a moment he pulled away and framed my face with his hands.

"Are you ok?" He looked panicked.

"Hey," I said, trying to get him to focus on my eyes. "I'm fine, Porter. I'm ok." I felt a smile pull across my face and it was the most brilliant smile. I could feel it spreading throughout my entire body. Happiness. Joy. For once in the last year I wasn't fearful. Something snapped back into place within me, something about being in the room and facing the biggest fear I'd ever had was invigorating. "I did it," I whispered through my enormous smile. "I found him." Porter's eyes grew wide and he frantically looked around for Dillard.

"Was he in there? Did she ID him?"

"Why don't you both take a seat," Dillard said, motioning towards our abandoned chairs.

"Fuck sitting, Dillard. Tell us what happened." The detective looked like he was trying to decide whether he was going to let Porter talk to him that way, but slowly a smile spread across his face.

"She did beautifully. She positively identified Jason Ramie. He's being taken into custody as we speak and will be charged with attempted aggravated murder."

Even though I knew I'd picked him out, I couldn't help the surprised gasp that left me. My hand captured the breathy cry that left my mouth and I turned to Porter. He looked just as shocked as I felt.

"You did?"

I shrugged. "I remembered."

"Of course you did," he said, pulling me into him again, kissing my forehead. "What happens next?" His question was directed at Dillard, but his eyes stayed on me.

"Well, like I said, he'll be formally charged and in a couple of days he'll have a bail hearing and then he'll enter a plea."

"A bail hearing? He could get out on bail?"

"Unlikely. Usually in murder cases like this the bail is set very high and I can't imagine the boy has money like that laying around."

Boy? He didn't look like a boy to me. He was big and burly. He might have been young, but he was no boy.

"But there's a chance?"

"A slim one."

"Still..." Porter continued.

"Hey, it's ok. Everything is going to be ok," I said, trying to soothe him. Porter looked back to me and I saw a little smile pull at his lips.

"Well, this is a pleasant turn of the tides. Ok," he brushed the back of his hand down my cheek. "If you're sure you're ok, I'll let it go for now."

"I'm fine. He's locked up tonight. I remembered."

"You did fantastic," he said gently.

"She really did," Dillard interjected. "I was worried at first that the whole thing would overwhelm her, but she was methodical and thoughtful. She made her way down the line and she grew more confident as she went along. If it weren't a shitty situation, I would say it was a pleasure to work with her."

Porter looked at me with so much pride it made my heart swell in my chest, and I felt some of the walls I had built around it shatter and fall to pieces.

"So, we're free to go?"

"Definitely. I will call you to let you know when the bail hearing is, just in case you want to be there. And you should definitely call your lawyer."

"Thank you, Detective," Porter said, shaking the man's hand.

"No problem. You did great, Mrs. Masters," he said as I shook his hand. I smiled up at him.

"Thanks for being patient with me and thank you for catching him."

Chad waited at the entrance of the police station and when we approached, he looked to Porter for instructions.

"Chad, thank you for waiting. I'm sure you want to get home. I'll contact you in the morning."

"I don't mind. Do you want me to follow you and Ella home?"

Porter looked at me and smiled. "No, they've caught the man who shot Ella. I think we're going to drive home alone tonight."

"That's wonderful news, Sir. Ma'am, I'm happy to hear he's been caught. Have a good evening." With that Chad walked away and Porter and I were alone, in the evening, not in our house, for the first time in weeks. It shouldn't have felt foreign, but it did. To just be the two of us was a novelty. I leaned into him and heard him breathe in a content breath.

"Let's go home," he said into my hair, making me smile.

"That sounds fantastic," I said into his chest. When we pulled up to our house, there was no police cruiser parked down the street and I reveled in the feeling of safeness I felt in that moment. Perhaps we were going to be ok.

Chapter Nine

Ella

My nerves spiked as Porter drove us down the gravel driveway that would lead us to our house. In the past weeks, I knew the house was getting closer to being complete, but Porter had many warnings of insulation and paint fumes and kept me off the property. I trusted him to build us an incredible house, so I wasn't nervous about being kept out of the loop on decisions. Hell, if we could have just transplanted the beach house right here on our twenty acres on the outskirts of Salem, I would have. But if Porter could build a house that beautiful on his own, he didn't need me meddling in the process.

So I let him design, build, and construct our house, only offering opinions when asked. Houses were his forte so I intended to let him shine. I knew I'd love whatever he conjured up and that notion extended to every aspect of our life. However, when his truck pulled around the bend in the road and our house came into view, there was nothing in my imagination that could have prepared me for the beauty of the structure.

"Oh my God, Porter!" I exclaimed, simply stunned by the finished product.

"You like it?"

My head snapped to the side to look at him.

"Like it? Porter, it's incredible!"

"Ok, well, this is just the outside. I hope you like the inside too."

My eyes took in the massive structure. Obviously, I had seen the house in its unfinished form, but not for a month or two. The driveway was circular and led up to the front of the house. There was a side road that led to the back of the house where I knew there was a three-car garage. The house was two stories tall and boasted tall arched accents with exposed beams. The wooden beams stood out against the warm yellow paint and cool-colored stonework that encased the bottom of the house.

The front door was wooden and matched the beams in color, a nearly red chestnut, and small path lights led you from the driveway right to the magnificent door.

Porter parked his truck and came around to open the door for me, lending me his hand, knowing full well that my equilibrium was off-kilter with the big, protruding baby belly I was now sporting. He helped me from the truck, but didn't release my hand, his thumb rubbing gentle circles over my knuckles as we walked towards the house.

"It's *so* beautiful, Porter. I can't believe we get to live here."

"It's ready to go, all finished, we could move in tomorrow if we wanted."

"Really?" My excitement was palpable. This would be our first real home together and I couldn't wait to start the new chapter of our lives.

When we reached the front door he opened it but stopped me before I could go in. I laughed and yelped as he bent down and picked me up, one arm under my knees, the other behind my shoulders, carrying me over the threshold. When he put me down, all I could do was gawk at the gorgeous house. It reminded me a lot of the beach house with its open floor plan, but it was different still, newer and a little more modern. Where the beach house felt much like a beach house, this structure had more of a country feel.

The front door opened into an entryway with a built-in hall tree that I wanted to run my hands over. I could tell from looking at them that Porter had built them. He pulled me by the hand through the hallway and we entered into one great big room that was the living room, family room, and kitchen all combined into one.

Between the kitchen and the family room was a big island that had a tall counter that served as a breakfast bar. All the cabinets were the same wood that the beams outside were made of and the chestnut color was warm and comfortable. The kitchen boasted stainless steel appliances and I itched to cook in this kitchen.

"This is so incredible." I spun around slowly, trying to take it all in. "And so big."

"It'll shrink down a little once we get some furniture in here. Come on," he said, tugging on my hand, leading me up the stairs, "I've got something to show you."

He led me slowly up the stairs, letting me take my time and admire his work. When we got to the master bedroom, he slowly pushed the door open and let me walk in first.

Of course Porter had something planned; he always had something planned. My heart lurched when I saw the picnic he'd prepared for us and my thoughts immediately went rushing back to all the romantic picnics he'd planned: the first one on the beach, the picnic we had while hiking

Multnomah Falls, the picnic on the floor of Dahlia before it had opened when he proposed. Porter gave good picnic.

"Babe, this looks wonderful," I said, my eyes sweeping through the room. Our room boasted a large gas fireplace and a cozy fire was lit, casting a romantic firelight over the room. On the floor there were blankets spread out with an abundance of pillows. A picnic basket sat in the middle of the blanket, along with an ice bucket with a bottle of sparkling cider and two champagne flutes.

"I made sure there were enough pillows because I know sitting on the floor won't be comfortable for long, and that's apple cider in there, not champagne."

I giggled because he sounded nervous. I had never really seen Porter nervous before. Anxious, yes. Angry and protective, yes. But never really nervous. I found it to be terribly endearing.

"It looks incredible, Porter. You're too sweet."

"I just always want you to remember our first meal in our new home."

All I could do was nod in response, my lower lip being worried in between my teeth, trying to keep my eyes from watering. How did I manage to find him? How in the world did I ever manage to live before him? I tried to shake away the feelings as he placed a soft kiss on my forehead. I looked up at him and smiled.

"You're amazing, you know that?"

He shrugged. "Just trying to take care of my baby momma." He led me over to the stack of blankets and helped me sit which, in reality, turned more into a lean because there weren't enough blankets in the world to make my ass comfortable on a hardwood floor. But I found a comfortable spot and relaxed, taking in the view of the fireplace and the sun setting outside of the French doors that led to our room's balcony.

"We'll have to get some nice chairs to put out there so we can enjoy the sunset when it's warm."

"Sounds like a plan," he said as he poured me some cider.

We talked throughout the meal, making plans for the house, decorating ideas, plans for the yard and the property. Somehow I had talked him into getting some animals. Nothing too crazy, maybe just some chickens and a goat. What was the point in having all this property if we weren't going to use it? He laughed at my logic and just made me promise I'd wait for at least a year before obtaining any animals.

The food was delicious and simple. He'd brought strawberries and pretzels with hummus, and I smiled when he brought out the celery sticks with peanut butter because I'd been craving those every night for nearly three weeks. He was a smart man.

"I didn't give my mom enough notice for cheesecake, but I did get these brownies at a bakery in town."

"Shut. Up." I said, nearly drooling over the brownies he hadn't even managed to unwrap yet. What was it about chocolate and pregnancy? For just one split second I had an image in my mind of wrapping a soft, warm brownie around a stalk of celery with peanut butter on it. It sounded like the most delicious thing on earth, but I knew in the back of my mind that anyone not growing a person in their belly would think it weird. So I kept my craving to myself, vowing to try it one day while Porter was at work. When he finally handed me a brownie, it was just as warm and soft as I had imagined it to be and I couldn't help the overtly sexual moan that escaped my lips as I chewed.

I heard Porter startle, choke and cough, having inhaled a piece of his brownie. "Damn, Ella," he said between sips of cider, trying to clear his throat. "You can't make noises like that right now."

"Why not? This brownie is absolutely orgasmic."

"Because it's not fair. No respectable man would have sex with his six month pregnant wife in a house with no furniture, and when you moan like that it makes it impossible for me to think about anything besides, well, that."

"Sex?" I asked with a smile.

"Listen, what I'm imagining doing to you is more than just sex."

I swallowed loudly. "Oh."

"Yeah. So cool it with the moaning."

"Well, why don't we bring some of these brownies home with us later and then we can both get what we want."

His eyes grew dark and he leaned in towards me slowly. "And what is it that you want, Mrs. Masters?"

I closed the distance between us, placing my lips right over his. "I want more brownies, but this time I want them…" I pressed my lips into his, kissing him slowly, but firmly. I pulled away just enough to look in his eyes. "With milk."

It took him just a few seconds to take in my words, but eventually he threw his head back and laughter filled the room. His laughter quieted although he continued to chuckle as he started cleaning up our picnic. "I can provide you with milk," he said, still laughing.

"Are we headed home?" I asked as I finished folding the last of the blankets, piling them up against the wall.

"I've got one more thing I want to show you," he said, plopping some pillows down on the mound of blankets. He took my hand and interlaced our fingers, leading me out of the room and down the hallway. He stopped at a door just a few down from ours which I knew, based on the blueprints and plans we made, was to be the nursery. He gave me a shy smile and then opened the door.

Surprise was the first emotion I felt when I saw the room, but surprise soon morphed into overwhelming love and appreciation for the man standing beside me. I looked at him, again with tears brimming my eyes. I stepped farther in the room, both my hands coming to cover my mouth, trying to hold in the cries I knew were coming.

The walls were painted to look like a sky, only not the sky you'd see from the ground, it was as if you were sitting on clouds. White, cotton ball-looking clouds lined the entire room, ending at about waist height, giving way to a deep dark blue sky, complete with metallic stars painted in all different sizes all over the room. The most impressive part, however, was the ceiling. I looked up to see thousands of tiny lights shining down and twinkling. Some lights were bigger and brighter than others, making it look absolutely realistic.

"Porter how did you do this?"

"Well, I commissioned a local artist to come and paint the clouds and stars, and then the guys and I installed these fiber optic lights in the ceiling. It was pretty fun actually. We got to be a little creative and actually try to make it look like a starry sky. Plus I figured it would make a pretty good nightlight for the baby. There's a dimmer on the wall and you can make the stars as bright as you want."

"It's so beautiful," I said, wiping my eyes.

"You're not mad?"

"Mad?" I asked, turning to him with a shocked expression on my face. "Why in the world would I be mad?"

"Well, I kind of hijacked the nursery. I don't want you to feel left out or like I went over your head. I just wanted to give you something beautiful."

"Porter, this is perfect and so much more beautiful than anything I could have come up with. It's spectacular, really. And I still have so much to do in here like decorate and pick out furniture. You didn't hijack the nursery, you just gave it a jump start. I love it." I turned to him and wrapped my arms around his neck, trying to pull him close but found my belly always to be in the way. I felt him bend his knees slightly and lower himself to me, making it easier to reach around his neck. His hands came to rest on my lower back, gently rubbing circles where I always asked to be massaged.

"You are a remarkable husband, Porter. And you're already a phenomenal dad. Our baby is so lucky to have you."

He was quiet for a moment, still rubbing my back, making my eyes flutter closed with the wonderful feeling of the tension leaving my body.

"Are you hoping for a girl or a boy?" He asked quietly. I thought about his question. It wasn't as if we hadn't had this conversation before, but usually the common answer came out of my mouth – that I would be happy with either sex as long as the baby was healthy. That was still true, I wanted a healthy baby beyond anything else, but I also wanted a baby that had his wonderful traits.

"I really don't care. There are days I think I want a little girl and then the next day I think I want a boy. But in reality, I just want the baby that's already in here," I said, placing my hands on my belly. "This baby was made out of the best love I've ever experienced and is going to be the luckiest baby ever. I don't care, either way, but I won't complain if he or she has your gorgeous brown eyes and dark hair." I tilted my head back up to smile at him and found him looking at me with wonder.

"You're going to be the best mother, Ella." His hands came up to frame my face. "I'm so honored that you wanted to have my children. The best gift I'll ever give our kids is you."

He kissed me and I simply melted. I would never grow accustomed to Porter and his beautifully woven words that instantly and easily liquefied me, leaving me a puddle of emotions. I loved his words and what they did to me.

"I want to take you home and feed you brownies in bed," he said huskily against my neck, running his nose along the curve from my shoulder to my ear, sending goose bumps all down my arms. "And then I want to do other things to you in that bed."

All the parts of me that had melted just moments before were suddenly afire, and growing warmer by the second.

"I think after all your efforts here today, I'm willing to let you do just about anything you'd like to me."

"And I thought the look on your face when you saw the nursery would be my payoff." He nuzzled in further, his tongue darting out to taste the skin behind my ear, making my knees wobble. "Looks like the real payoff is going to be the look on your face when I slide inside of you."

I gasped as his tender licks and kisses turned into bites and nibbles.

"Those are some pretty big promises," I managed to rasp, my fingers threading through his hair.

I shrieked as he slapped my ass and then pulled away to look me in the eyes.

"Let's go, Baby. I plan on delivering."

Chapter Ten

Ella

"If you make me trip and fall at my own baby shower, you'll officially win the prize for worst sister ever." Megan led me through my parent's house, insisting on covering my eyes. She wanted a big reveal moment when I saw the shower decorations, and her enthusiasm convinced me to trust her enough to lead me blind.

"Oh, hush. You're fine." We took a few more slow and hesitant steps and then we stopped. "Ok, just keep your eyes covered for one more minute." I sighed and kept my hands over my eyes. I heard her moving around the room and then she said, with much excitement, "Ok! Open your eyes!"

I blinked away the darkness and my eyes roamed around the room. The first thing I noticed were the hundreds of tiny, sparkling stars hanging from the ceiling throughout the great room. My eyes landed on the banquet table pressed against the far wall and I was taken aback by the three tiered cake sitting in the middle. Each layer was made to look like clouds against a dark sky with more stars adorning it. On top of the cake was a bigger star wrapped in a blanket, laying on a pillow, sleeping on a cloud.

Hanging above the table was a banner that read, "Twinkle Twinkle Little Star, We Can't Wait to Find Out Who You Are". The theme was obviously stars and clouds, and it was so beautiful.

"Megs, this is incredible," I said quietly, still trying to take it all in.

"Your sister worked very hard on this for you," my mom said from behind me. I turned and smiled at her.

"I can tell." I walked to Megan and wrapped her in a hug. "Thanks, Megan."

"Anything for you, Fella, and my future niece or nephew," she said, gently rubbing my belly, which was, honestly, getting a little out of control. She pulled away and ran off to put some finishing touches on something. I pulled out my cell phone to send a picture to Porter. Within half a minute he replied.

Wow. Looks like Megan missed her calling as a party planner.

Right? It's so beautiful. It'll all be torn apart by the time you guys are done golfing, so you won't get to see it in all its glory.

Trust me, I'd rather be there with you than golfing. I hate golfing.

Why did you agree to go? I'm sure Patrick would have found something to do that you enjoyed had you told him.

It's fine. Patrick likes golfing. Maybe he can teach me how to not suck at it.

Well, you have fun walking around in the sun all afternoon. I'm just going to sit here, open presents, and eat cookies and cake and get even more fat.

Ella, love, eat as much as you'd like. I like all the extra Ella I've been able to grab ahold of lately.

I smiled. Even through a text he could still make my blood run quickly. He had been enjoying my new, rounder, lusher body. And I'd been enjoying his enthusiasm for me.

Hmmm. I will, but not for your benefit. Love you. Have fun.

Love you too.

"Is that Porter?" Megan said as she walked past me with a platter of deviled eggs.

"Yeah. He just told me he doesn't even like golfing. He's so funny sometimes." I shook my head, making a mental reminder to tell him how silly the whole thing was.

"Well, they're probably drinking too, so that should help. But honestly, if he would have told Patrick, he would have come up with another idea."

"I know," I waved her worry away. "I think sometimes Porter is so used to just making other people happy, he goes with the flow. It can be really attractive sometimes, to have someone who just wants what you want. But sometimes, it's like, Porter, what do *you* want? Ya know?" Megan nodded and walked back into the kitchen as my mother came to sit next to me on the couch.

"Any new developments on the case?" My mother wore her worried eyes. Everyone in my family was worried, and I understood that, but I hated that they looked at me like I was going to break open at any moment. Granted, I had a history of falling into deep bouts of darkness, but I felt stronger in the last few weeks.

"Not much has changed. He can't make bail, so he is waiting for trial in jail, thank God."

"And he's still pleading not guilty?" I nodded.

Jason Ramie pled not guilty to the charge of attempted aggravated murder and so the process became so much more than I had ever imagined. We were headed for a jury trial. All our lawyers and Detective Dillard told us it was a slam dunk case. With the testimony of the person who gave the police his identity, the surveillance video at Poppy, and the new forensic evidence that matched the bullet found at the scene to a gun Ramie had in his possession at his arrest; all signs pointed to guilty. The most damning piece of evidence they had, of course, was me.

Porter argued for hours with our lawyer, telling him that there was no way in hell I was getting up on the stand and testifying. He was convinced that I had been through enough and that they didn't need my testimony. The lawyer, bless his heart, listened to Porter, but never wavered. The case was *good* on its own, but with me it was golden. I let Porter assert himself, let him rant and rave, and do his best to keep me safe, but eventually I told them both that I would do, gladly, anything that helped put Jason Ramie behind bars.

That evening I was so worried about Porter. I'd never seen him so uptight. He was angry with me and I didn't know how to make him understand.

"Porter, please, talk to me." He banged things around in his workshop in Lincoln City, moving things from one spot to another, tossing things, ripping up papers from his desk.

"I can't talk to you right now." Those words hurt. He never denied me anything, especially not himself. My air was stuck in my throat. Everything in my body seized up.

"Please," I squeaked. His face turned towards me, but he was still all the way on the other side of the shop.

"I won't sit by and watch you torture yourself, Ella. I won't sit in that courtroom and watch you relive all the terror you've experienced in the last year. They don't need you to win this thing. You're volunteering to be torn apart, and I'll be damned if I'll stand by and let it happen." His chest moved up and down, labored by his heaving breaths. I'd never seen him this angry before. We'd had arguments, of course, but he'd never been upset with me.

"That's not how I see it," I whispered. His eyes shot over to me. "I just want to help. I can help end this. I can do it."

"No one is questioning whether or not you're capable, Ella! Not one person cares if you can pull it off. I know you can. I know you'll sit on that stand and you'll tell them everything. You'll give them every tiny detail you can remember, shredding yourself for him, again. You'll let him take another piece of you and no one but me seems to care what effect it will have on you, or on me. I'll be forced to watch you fall apart, again, and just be reminded that I failed you." His voice broke and his head fell forward, hiding his face from me.

"Porter, no," I whispered, my voice breaking, my head shaking back and forth. "Please, don't think that way."

"I can't help it. I've tried for a year now to bury the voice in my head that tells me everything could have been avoided if I'd found a way to protect you, but all I'm left with are the images of you laying in that hospital bed, or you sitting on that porch with blood covering you..." He ran his hands through his hair and huffed out angry breaths. "You've been through enough and if I can keep you from having to relive it, I swear to God, Ella, I will."

I slowly took a step towards him, trying to gauge how he would react to me. He didn't move away, so I took another step towards him.

"I'm not going to try and convince you that I'm fine, because I'm not. I'm changed. Altered. Different. But I'm not broken. I might have been, for a little while, but I've managed to put myself back together. You helped me with that, Porter. You helped me find the pieces of myself I thought I'd lost and helped me put them together again. But the same way you won't sit by and watch me fall apart, I won't sit by and let you blame yourself for this."

I took another step towards him. We were just feet from each other now.

"Two very terrible men are responsible for this, not you. Not in any way is this your fault. To hear you tell me that you feel that way almost hurts worse than anything either of them did to me." I swallowed, closing the distance between us, only inches now. "I can do this, Porter. I can walk into that courtroom and tell everyone who can hear me what that man did to me. I can do that. I *need* to do that." I reached up and cupped his face, rubbing my thumb across his cheek. "But I need you more. I need you to be there, being strong for me, supporting me. I can't tell you how much I need you."

"I'll always be here for you," he whispered, leaning into my hand. "But sometimes, it seems like that's not enough."

"What do you mean?"

His hands found his hair again and I watched as his face gave away all the emotions he was feeling: angry and sad. "You've suffered so much, Ella, and I haven't been able to take any of your suffering away. These men, Jason and Kyle, they've hurt you in ways that I can't fix."

"They've hurt us both, Porter. I hate that our relationship centers around you trying to keep the baby and me safe, or that you have to worry if I've got a guard with me, or if I can handle a testimony. I want us both to be happy, to be free of this dark cloud that's been shrouding us for so long. The best and easiest way to end this, for good, is for me to testify. I want to sit in that chair and look Jason Ramie in the eye and tell him what he's done to me. I want a jury to hear about my anxiety, the amnesia, everything that has happened because of his actions. He deserves to hear it and I deserve the opportunity to tell my side of the story."

Porter's hands fell to his sides and he let out a long and exasperated breath. Then he reached for me, and I felt my body relax into his chest and his lips kiss the top of my head. "I hadn't thought about it that way." I felt him breathe me in and his arms fell around me, cinching around my waist. "You do deserve that. I'll support you one hundred percent."

Porter would always support me, but his concerns about me testifying were the same concerns my whole family had, which is why my mom had the worried look across her face as she sat across the couch from me.

"You're still going to testify?" She asked me with hopeful eyes, obviously wanting my answer to have changed since the last time we spoke about it.

"I am. If I didn't testify and he was found innocent, there's no way I could live with myself. He needs to pay for what he did and I will do whatever I can to make sure that happens."

My mother nodded her head and placed a hand on my knee. "I understand, Ella. I just want you to be healthy."

"I've never felt healthier," I said with a smile, rubbing my belly. "I think I'm going to walk around for a bit until I'm forced to sit in a chair for too long." I got up and offered to help Megan with any last minute preparations. In no time at all, guests arrived, cake was cut, and gifts were opened. Women near and dear to me spent a good hour oohing and awing over tiny little baby outfits, all of which made my heart swell just a little more with excitement about someday soon having a tiny little baby to put in all of them. I heard many complaints about the difficulty of buying gender-neutral gifts, but brushed them off knowing that everyone was just excited to meet the little baby.

When the men returned from their golfing trip, I was caught off guard by Porter's grim expression.

"What's the matter? Couldn't Patrick teach you how to not suck?" I asked, running a hand through the hair at the nape of his neck.

"The lawyer called while I was out."

"On a Saturday?"

"Yes, on a Saturday. We pay him a lot of money so I'm ok with him working on the weekends."

"Ok," I muttered, completely caught off guard by his grumpiness. "What did he want?"

Porter exhaled loudly, running his hand through his hair. "The defense attorney wants you to come in for a deposition." His eyes drifted towards the floor, not willing to make contact with mine.

"Hey," I said gently as I hooked my finger under his chin, urging him to look at me. When his eyes found mine I smiled, hoping to bring him out of his funk just a little. "We knew this was coming. Everything is going to be ok. I promise, I can handle this."

"It goes against every instinct I have to let you walk into a room where people are waiting to hurt you." His eyes never left mine, but I watched them go from desperate to angry.

"They don't have the power to hurt me, Porter. I am the one in control of the situation." I ran my hand up and down his bicep, again, trying any trick I could think of to get his mind off of the trial. "Do you want to look at all the adorable baby things we get to take home?"

His eyes wandered to the pile of gifts that still sat next to the chair I'd occupied while opening gifts. A look of shock and surprise floated over the features of his face and I smiled because it was very seldom I got to see a surprised Porter; he was usually the one surprising me. "Where in the heck are we supposed to put all of that?"

"Looks like we might need some more storage in the nursery. It's all gender neutral stuff, so it can easily be saved and used for the next baby. It will actually make having baby number two way easier." My voice trailed off, as did my thoughts. I contemplated armoires and chests of drawers, weighing my options for how to best utilize the space in the nursery. I looked to Porter, about to ask him if it was too late to have built-ins installed and his face morphed again into something that resembled euphoria. A smile came over me, impossible to look at him happy and not smile, and I was curious about what brought on this sudden and turbulent mood change. "Babe, you ok? You are all over the emotional map today."

His attention turned to me and his arm wrapped around my waist, not getting as far around me as it used to, but still doing a good job of pulling me closer to him.

"I just had the best vision of you, holding our child, a toddler, with your belly round with baby number two." He lowered his head and shook it gently. "Just when you think you can't fall in love with someone any deeper, you realize there's so much more you have yet to experience with them, and every single day just makes me love you that much more."

I was stunned by his words, by his thoughts. Sure, we've always planned on having "kids" or "babies". Our future planning had always had plural children, so it wasn't a far fetch to jump from Baby One to Baby Two. And then I had my own little day dream; Porter with one child riding on his shoulders, little chubby hands gripping his head, while he walks hand-in-hand with another littler person. The image could be a painting, it was that precious. And I feel exactly as he does, filled to the brim with love, yet still longing to add more love to our life. I took one small moment and placed his hands on my belly, mine resting over his, and then I felt his forehead against mine and I leaned into him.

"How'd we get so lucky?" I whispered to him, hoping that the entire party isn't witnessing our intimate moment.

"I don't question it, Ella. I'm just thankful for it."

Monday morning, bright and early, Porter and I walked into our lawyer's office and were brought back to a conference room. There was a cart with coffee and muffins, which normally I'd be all over – hello, eight-month pregnant lady here – but this morning I was too nervous to put anything in my stomach. Porter could tell I was anxious, which sent him into a protective frenzy, nearly forbidding me to leave the house. I tried explaining to him that I wasn't worried about the questions; I was more apprehensive about the process. I'd never been deposed before. It was all new to me and a little nerve wracking.

After a few minutes, more men entered the room and took out folders, laptops, and an audio recorder which they placed in the middle of the table. Our lawyer introduced us to Jason Ramie's legal team. I shook their hands, trying to keep myself from thinking terrible things about a man who would shoot a woman, trying to kill her, and tried to remind myself that more than likely they were appointed by the state to defend him. Deep breaths in and out. The legal system in our nation gave him the right to a fair trial. Even though it would have been easier had he just admitted to the crime, I was almost looking forward to testifying. I wanted everyone in that courtroom to hear what he'd done to me. That was a kind of justice I couldn't get anywhere else. So a trial was fine by me.

Everything was very formal and I didn't get asked any questions I hadn't answered before when being questioned by the police or my own lawyer. Porter's hackles raised a few times when the lawyers asked about my relationship with Kyle, and I did my best to calm him with a soothing hand on his thigh, or linking my fingers with his. He was there as a support to me, but I didn't mind offering him my support. In fact, I reveled in it.

At one point, the defense attorneys asked me about the off-shore accounts Kyle had set up and whether or not I had any knowledge of them. I blinked at the question, but answered honestly with a no.

"So, you really didn't notice tens of thousands of dollars being syphoned out of your own business?" The man's voice was accusatory and snide. I fumbled for words, not really sure how to answer him. Luckily my lawyer came to my rescue.

"Mrs. Masters is not on trial here today, gentlemen. I suggest you change your line of questioning or we will end this deposition early." The defense hardly looked phased by the threat from my lawyer, but moved on to what seemed to be safer questions about the shooting itself.

When everything was finished and we headed home, I could feel the tension radiating off of Porter in the car. He held something back, kept something inside of him, most likely for my benefit, or so he thought.

"Hey," I said as I rubbed his thigh. "Are you all right?"

"Not really," he said, his eyes glued to the freeway ahead of him as we made our way back to Salem.

"Wanna tell me what's going on in your head?"

He didn't answer me right away, but I let him think his thoughts through, not in any hurry. "I almost jumped over the table at that defense lawyer. I wanted to punch him right in his assuming face."

"Whoa. Wait, what?" My head snapped to the side to look at him. His face was scrunched up in anger now. I obviously was not doing a great job of calming him down.

"He was insinuating that you were involved in the embezzlement, Ella."

I thought back to his question and the more I thought about it, the angrier I got. In the moment I had been so surprised by the question I didn't really process it fully, then they started asking a million other questions and I never gave it much more thought. Sure, Kyle had taken advantage of me and my trust and stolen money from me, but I hadn't found out until he died. And even then, I really didn't dig for information about it. It didn't matter to me anymore. He was dead and the threat was gone. Was it the smartest decision not to investigate how he was able to steal so much money from me? Probably not, but at that moment in my life, I was in self-preservation mode. I was more concerned with not drowning in a pool of darkness having taken a human life, than trying to figure out the logistics of embezzlement. Not once had it occurred to me that someone might think I had been involved.

"Why would I embezzle money out of my own business?" I was shocked by the accusation.

"Tax evasion," he answered quickly. He was obviously three steps ahead of my in the thought process.

"Tax evasion?"

"Yeah, the less revenue you bring in, the less you have to claim on your taxes and you could fall into a lower tax bracket."

"Wait, you don't think…"

"No, Ella. Don't even ask that question." He interrupted, not even letting me finish.

"You have to know I couldn't ever pull something like that off."

"Ella, there are many reasons why I *know* you weren't involved in illegal affairs involving your business, but your capability isn't one of them. You're a very smart woman and just because you haven't used your intelligence to commit crimes doesn't mean you couldn't." He gave me a grin. I couldn't quite figure out if he was giving me a compliment or not, but regardless I was glad his scowl had taken a break.

"Well, capable or not, I still don't know *how* he managed to steal the money."

"Do you want to know how?"

I shrugged. "I didn't, not in the past, but after today I think maybe I should find out. I don't want anyone else to think these terrible things about me." My mind raced, suddenly consumed with questions. How did he get the money from Poppy without me knowing? What did he do with the money? Where is all the money now? I felt a warm, strong hand on my thigh, this time he was trying to comfort me.

"Don't go slipping away from me again."

I gave him a little smile. "I'm not. I'm just thinking about it now, wondering how it all happened."

"We can hire an investigator. We can get those answers."

I nodded at him. "Ok. I think that would be best, don't you?"

"If it brings you more peace of mind than stress, then yes, I think it would be a good idea."

"Ok, let's do it." It seemed like even though Kyle was gone and buried, recently, he was being resurrected a little more every day. I took a few deep breaths in, trying to manage the panic before it had a chance to get out of hand. Panic, for me, was funny because half the anxiety came from the fear of the events, but the other half came from the fear of living my life this way for the rest of eternity. The panic was triggered by thinking about what had happened, but then it continued because I didn't want to live my life this way.

I knew high blood pressure was not good for the baby, and I could tell the stress was affecting the little person in my belly because I felt a foot poke out right by my ribcage.

I took a few more calming breaths and rubbed my belly, trying my best to comfort the baby I couldn't hold yet.

"You ok? Baby ok?" He split his focus between the freeway and my face, giving me worried looks.

"I'm fine, Babe. We're fine, just a big kick. I've been sitting for too long." I squirmed in my seat, trying to relieve some of the pressure off my tailbone.

"Want me to drop you off at Dahlia? I could pick you up for dinner later."

"That would be great. Can I opt out of cooking tonight? Maybe we can go out?"

"Of course," he said, smiling at me, twining his fingers with mine. "I'd love to take my beautiful wife out for dinner." His thumb traced small circles on the back of my hand and it caused goose bumps to rise up and down my arms.

"Perfect. Any chance you want to give your beautiful wife a full-body massage after you take her to dinner?" Massages had become a frequent occurrence in our household at about six months. Sometimes they were very necessary. It was possible that sometimes I also played the pregnancy card to get frequent massages when they weren't completely necessary. Then there were the times when I just wanted to feel my husband's hands running over my skin and this was my passive way of asking him to get me naked and touch me. I never fooled him though. He always knew when I was making a ploy for sex.

"I'm sure that could be arranged," he said, the words falling from his mouth in a slow and sexy timbre. He knew exactly what I was asking for and by the sound of it, was planning on delivering. My core clenched with just his words and the way he said them. I felt my face start to heat, sure I was turning red. "You getting hot, Babe? Need the AC turned up?" His sexy voice was now also playful.

"Shut up," I said, smiling as well. Then I reached forward and adjusted a vent to blow directly on me. I heard him snicker and looked over at him. He was trying so hard to keep in a big laugh and just seeing him happy made the events of the day seem insignificant. One moment of happy with Porter could make a terrible day fade into darkness. How lucky was I?

Chapter Eleven

Ella

Having a baby, even though you are constantly surrounded by women who've done it and heard about it for your entire life, is something you can never fully be prepared for. The birth of my precious baby will always be the shining moment of my life. Until I have another, the moment I held my baby for the first time will forever be the moment I cherish most. I love Porter more than I ever thought I could love anyone, but my love for my child couldn't compare to my love for any other person. It was different. More. Completely encompassing. There was absolutely nothing like it. I couldn't explain it – it was something one had to experience to fully understand. But even after what could be described as a 'less than simple' birth, the only thought I had was, *I would do that a million times over again for this little baby in my arms. Gladly. I would do anything for my child.*

I woke up in the middle of the night, not unusual at all for me anymore. I groaned, a little perturbed to be disrupted as I slept, but then after waking up a little more fully, realized that it had finally happened. I peed the bed.

"Shit," I whisper-yelled, completely mortified. Over the duration of my pregnancy I gained a new appreciation for my pre-pregnant bladder, but this was ridiculous. "Gross, gross, gross," I said as I hobbled out of bed, heading for the bathroom. I made it to the bathroom and started stripping my clothes off and heard Porter rustling around.

"You ok, Babe?" His sleepy voice called out. I groaned inwardly, not wanting to admit to what had happened, completely mortified.

"Yeah," I whined. "Ew. Ew. Ew. Yuck…" I cried as I peeled my yoga pants down. "I'm so done with this whole pregnant thing," I yelled out, frustrated. I looked up to see him standing in the doorway, legs crossed at the ankle, hands gripping the top of the door frame, shirtless. I glared at him. How dare he look like a GQ model while I stood there huge and gross.

"You're nearly done," he said sweetly.

"Ok, well, I just peed the bed, so unless you can ensure that won't happen again, being *nearly done* isn't good enough. Oh, and yesterday I couldn't make it down the stairs at the beach house. I couldn't see the stairs, Porter. My big-ass belly was in the way and I *couldn't see the stairs*. I had to go down them sideways. SIDEWAYS. I can't get up from the couch on my own, I can't sleep on my stomach, I can't eat a turkey sandwich, and I *really* want a turkey sandwich." I was seething at this point and could feel my heart beating rapidly. I stopped and took a few deep breaths in and out. "I love this baby, Porter," I said, looking him in the eyes. "I do. But I want it out, like, now." He walked to me and wrapped his arms around me.

"I can't imagine what it feels like to be pregnant, but I can tell you that you're doing a wonderful job. The baby will come when it's time." I groaned into his naked chest. After a moment, I pulled away and waddled into the shower. When I emerged, feeling clean again, I smiled at the fresh pajamas folded neatly on the counter. The gross ones were gone and I decided my husband needed some sort of award. I dried off, dressed, and then made my way back into the bedroom only to find Porter putting clean sheets on the bed.

"You're the best. I'm sorry you have to clean up after me."

"If I could take all the pain and uncomfortableness from you, I totally would. But if all I can do is change some sheets, you best believe I'm gonna be the best sheet changer there is." I walked to him and wrapped my arms around his waist as he placed a kiss on the top of my head.

"We're going to laugh about this someday, right? Like, one day this will be funny and not mortifying?"

"Honestly, Ella, I'm already laughing." I smacked him on the stomach and then looked down at my legs.

"Mother Fucker." This shit was not funny. "I think I just peed again." I shook my head, still looking down, confusion taking over. "This is weird. I didn't even feel like I had to go."

Porter gave me a look that probably mirrored mine, confusion furrowing his brow. "This might be the weirdest question I'll ever ask you, but, are you sure it was pee?"

"What do you mean?" I asked him, but I knew what he meant. "I'm not due for two more weeks."

He shrugged his shoulders. "Due date or not, the baby comes when the baby wants to." Even as he said the words I could feel more liquid oozing out of me. Not a lot, but enough that I could feel it and it made me squirm.

"Let's call the hospital." I said the words and then I felt the nerves take over. I called the number for the labor and delivery wing and spoke with a very nice nurse. I explained the situation to her, much to my embarrassment.

"Well," she said sweetly, "if you're feeling fluid coming from your vagina, and you don't have to urinate, there is a good probability that your membrane has ruptured. What did the fluid smell like?"

"Uh," I stammered. "I didn't smell it." I tried to hide the disgust from my voice. Who goes around smelling the sheets they just soiled?

"Well, amniotic fluid smells different than urine, so that's one way you could rule out urination."

"I'll go smell it," Porter said, standing up from the bed.

"You will not!" I yelled. There is no way that I would ever recover from my husband smelling my sheets. I just couldn't. All the mystery would be gone. I could never, *ever*, feel sexy around him again if he smelled my sheets. "I'll smell it."

"Amniotic fluid smells sweeter than you'd imagine and, funny enough, a little like semen."

Gross. "Ok, so what if it is amniotic fluid?"

"You should start to experience contractions and we would want to see you in the hospital when your contractions were three to five minutes apart."

"I haven't had any contractions." I said, immediately worried I'm doing this whole labor thing wrong. I couldn't even contract when I was supposed to.

"It might take a few hours, but you should start contracting soon. It was more than likely contractions that ruptured your membranes. You just couldn't feel them because they aren't strong enough yet. You could be contracting right now. It's just a matter of waiting until they're strong enough to do some damage." I cringed at her nurse jargon; I didn't need any damage done to me. "However, it's important that we deliver the baby within twenty-four hours of the membranes rupturing, so if you aren't contracting within the next, oh say, ten hours, you should come in anyway."

"Then what happens?" I asked, horrified.

"Don't get ahead of yourself, Mrs. Masters. First, determine whether or not it was urine on your sheets and go from there. I'm looking at your chart and there's no reason why you shouldn't expect a totally normal delivery. Is this your first?"

"Yes." I said sadly, suddenly wishing I knew what I was doing.

"It'll be ok. I would bet money that you didn't wet the bed. It sounds like you ruptured." Again, I cringed. She needed some different verbiage. I hung up with the helpful nurse and went to smell the sheets. I lifted the offending linens to my nose and gave then a hesitant sniff. I immediately and unconsciously felt my lips turn into a surprised pout.

"Huh," I said out loud to Porter who stood just outside the door. "She was right. It does smell like semen." I smelled the sheets again to confirm my opinion and then stopped, realizing what I was doing.

"Wait," he said, a huge smile coming across his face. "It doesn't smell like pee?"

I shook my head and then, damn it, smelled the sheets again. I stopped mid-sniff and threw the sheets to the floor to discourage my nose from trying to smell them again. "No, it's definitely not pee." I saw the smile on his face and it took me a few more seconds to put all the puzzle pieces together. "Oh, shit," I whispered as soon as I caught the wave he was already riding.

"Babe, your water broke."

"Holy shit."

"Stop swearing. The baby can hear you," he said with a warm smile, joking with me.

"Oh my God."

He shrugged. "That's a little better."

"Porter! Stop it! This is serious!" I squealed. I pointed down to the sheet. "That's not pee!" Now he laughed, beautiful joy shimmering all over his face. I heard big belly laughs and saw his gorgeous smile. It was contagious. I started laughing too. At first, just small spattering laughter. Then it grew into the kind of laughter that made your eyes water, laughter that bent you in half and made you grab your stomach. My stomach was huge, but it still shook heavily with laughter. Then I laughed even harder as more fluid trailed down my legs. The whole situation was hilarious.

But then all the hilarity ended when my stomach was ignited in hot fire as I experienced my first honest-to-goodness contraction.

"Oh holy shit," I said as I grabbed my belly, wincing in pain. Porter had no jokes about language as he flew to my side, instantly alarmed by my discomfort.

"What's wrong?" He asked, panicked.

"Contraction," I managed to utter, still clutching my belly. The pain started very low, but shot out and felt like my entire belly was in a vice grip. It lasted forever, or about thirty seconds, which in labor time *is* forever. When it was over I took a few deep breaths to stop myself from vomiting and then stood up. "That was terrible. I thought they were supposed to get worse as labor progressed, not start off so painful you wish you were unconscious." I looked at Porter for answers, but his face looked pale and confused. He would obviously not be offering me any labor advice at the moment.

"Maybe…" he managed to speak. "Maybe you are really good at labor and skipped the easy part."

I laughed, forgetting the pain I had been in just minutes before. "That's the stupidest thing I've ever heard," I said through giggles.

Three hours later I was no longer laughing at Porter. It seemed as though he'd been partly correct is his assessment of my situation. I was really good at labor. Within an hour of my contractions starting they were four minutes apart and I was in some serious pain. Pants were pointless because with every contraction I leaked even more fluid and couldn't stop chanting "Ew, that's gross," through each one. We did the stereotypical speeding car race to the hospital as I was sure the baby was going to fall right out of me. This was pain like I had never experienced.

You could imagine my surprise when, after arriving at the hospital and making quite a fuss about how I was going to give birth right there in the emergency room, I found out I was actually only dilated three centimeters. That's right, seven to go.

"Are you sure?" I asked the nurse with her hand shoved uncomfortably up inside me. "Can you check again?"

"I am checking, Honey, and you're only at a three, maybe three and a half."

Well, for goodness' sake, don't rob a woman of that half a centimeter.

They hooked me up to monitors and that was, by far, the best part – getting to listen to the heart beat all the time. It was a soothing sound, however, it did nothing to make the pain go away.

Porter tried his hardest to make me feel as comfortable as possible, and in return I tried my hardest not to physically harm him. The contractions came and I turned into a woman I had never met before. I swore. I yelled. I was just plain rude. But when the contractions went away I apologized and promised to be better during the next one.

It was a vicious cycle of pain and lies. It hurt more every time and I never got any nicer. Eventually on a down swing, I told Porter that I wouldn't hold it against him if he left me.

"I'm sorry," I cried. "I don't know why I'm being like this. I wouldn't want to stay with someone like me. You can go, in fact, I insist. I don't deserve you." I blubbered. I had come unhinged.

"Baby," he said sweetly as he brushed the sweat-soaked hair from my forehead, "I'm not going anywhere. You're doing great. I love you and you're not doing this without me. You swear at me and call me names all you want. I promise I won't hold it against you when all of this is over." His words just made me cry harder. He was a saint. "Now, Ella, don't get upset, but what do you think about getting some pain meds?" He looked as if he was waiting for me to smack him upside the head.

"We said we were going to try to do it naturally…" I whined. We had a plan. I wanted a peaceful, calm, productive labor. Ha.

"Baby, you're doing so well, but I think maybe it would be good if you got just a little help with the pain." He ran the back of his fingers down my cheek and I leaned into him. Pain relief sounded wonderful, but admitting that was breaking my heart. I had wanted so badly to do this right.

"There is no right way to have a baby, Ella," he said, reading my mind. "You've put in a lot of work, but maybe your body is trying to tell you that it needs a little help." He kissed my brow.

"You won't think less of me if I get an epidural?"

He laughed a little. "No, Baby, I won't. I think it might save our marriage."

"I just wanted everything to be perfect," I whispered as he leaned down to embrace me.

"It's up to you, Ella. I'll stand here until the end of time listening to you yell, taking your insults, but it's killing me not being able to help you at all. Watching you in this much pain tears me apart. Plus," he said with a gentle smile, "I think you're scaring some of the other moms in the maternity wing." My lips turned up into a smile, but then turned right back around as another contraction came upon me. This time I buried my face in my pillow and stifled my screams until it was over, trying not to break Porter's fingers as he held my hand. When it finally subsided, years later, I looked up at him with fresh tears in my eyes.

"Ok, I think it's time for an epidural." He let out a huge sigh of relief. I pushed the little button on my bed and heard a voice come over a speaker system telling me she'd be there soon. When the nurse appeared, I was just finishing another torturous contraction.

"How are you doing?" The nurse asked with sincere concern.

"I think I want an epidural." I said, trying to hide the shame in my voice.

"Ok, well, there are a few things to consider. First, let's do an exam to see how far along you are now. If you're too far along you won't be able to get one. Do you feel any pressure when you have a contraction? Urges to push?"

"No," I answered. "Just the distinct feeling like someone is ripping my stomach to pieces." My comment came out more snarky than I had anticipated.

"Ok, you're going to feel a little pressure now," she said, breezing past my rude comment. She lied when she said 'a little' and I cried out from the seriously uncomfortable feeling of someone trying to shove their fist inside my cervix. "Alright, you're at four centimeters so you can still get an epidural if you want one."

"FOUR?" Porter and I both cried at the same time. The nurse tried to hide the fact that she rolled her eyes at us and then patiently continued.

"Yes, four. Would you like me to call the anesthesiologist?"

"I've been sitting here in agony for hours and you're telling me I'm only at FOUR centimeters?" This woman was a pro because she did not even bat an eyelash at me.

"This is very typical, I can assure you, Mrs. Masters. This is your first delivery. You could be here for hours and not make any progress. Now, would you like for me to call the anesthesiologist?"

Oh, she was good. "Yes, I would very much like the epidural."

Epidurals are scary. In theory, you go into it knowing what is supposed to happen, but when someone actually tells you to sit still, through your contractions, while they put a needle into your spine, it very quickly becomes terrifying. There's no way I would have been able to get through it had I not been leaning up against Porter's chest. I think the doctors planned it that way. They know you're going to freak out, so they tell you to lean against the one person who is supposed to make you feel better. Leaning up against him, smelling him, almost took away the fear, but not totally. Wood and soap, those scents are what got me through it.

Slowly and gradually, over the next thirty minutes I started to feel the pain lessen until, eventually, I felt nothing. Well, I felt nothing except exhaustion. It was four in the morning and I could barely keep my eyes open.

"Babe," I heard Porter's raspy voice but couldn't bring myself to turn my head to look at him. "Get some sleep. I'm going to be here the whole time." I felt him take my hand and it was the last thing I thought about before I fell asleep.

Chapter Twelve

Porter

Even though I was exhausted, I knew there was no way I was going to be able to sleep. It felt like there was sand in my eyes, they were so dry and red. I wanted to close them so badly and just fall asleep like this, with Ella's hand in mine, but I made sure to keep my eyes open. The two most important people in my life were lying in a hospital bed and if something was going to go wrong, I was going to be the first person to know – and to get help.

I tried to keep the dark thoughts away. I tried to focus on the fact that this was a happy occasion. Hospitals didn't always have to be a place where you almost lost the one person you love the most. It could also be the place where you found a brand new person to love. I tried to focus on that. We weren't here to lose; we were here to gain.

Ella slept for about three hours, never stirring, sleeping peacefully. I watched the screen just to the side of her bed that monitored her contractions. The screen showed her contractions as hills and as far as I could tell the hills were getting taller and wider. I'd watched the screen enough to understand that meant her contractions were getting stronger and lasting longer, and for that reason I was glad she was still asleep.

Ella was, by far and away, the strongest woman I had ever met, but it was agonizing to watch her suffer through labor. For nine months she'd spoken about trying to have a natural birth. I have no doubt she very well could have made it – she's stubborn enough – but I wanted her to give herself a break, to not push herself so hard that in the end she was worse off than when she started.

The hills were getting bigger and wider still and with every contraction my eyes darted back and forth between the screen and Ella, watching to see if she was uncomfortable at all. She slept through every single one, not looking like she was affected at all. Modern medicine really was astounding. To my left, through the wall, I heard the distinct sound of a baby crying. The cry was gurgled and frantic. It sounded new. I felt a little uncomfortable hearing someone else's baby's first cry – like I'd stolen something from them. But then I smiled to myself thinking that if I could hear that baby's cry then the parents were also hearing their baby's first cry. Excitement washed over me, looking forward to sharing that moment with Ella, hoping someone in the rooms next to us might use our special moment as motivation.

I finally allowed my eyes to close, trying to have faith in the fact that Ella was asleep and not in any pain. My hand was clasped around hers and I pulled her it close to me as I laid my head on the bed next to her. I tried to keep my mind from wandering to the last time I was in this exact same position and instead, focused on trying to imagine what our baby would look like. I fell asleep to the image of a beautiful baby with pink skin and blue eyes, just like her mother.

I awoke to the sound of the door to the hospital room opening. My head shot up and I saw a nurse walking through the darkened room, making her way towards Ella. She gave me a silent smile and proceeded to the print-out of all the hills that made up Ella's labor. I looked at the clock and noticed that two more hours had passed. I look back to the nurse who is making marks on the paper with a pen.

"Is everything all right?" I whispered to her. She looked over at me and smiled again.

"Everything looks very normal and healthy. I'm going to ask the doctor to come check her progress in a few minutes."

"Is it ok that she's been asleep this whole time? I mean, she's not in any danger, is she?" Even though I was glad she wasn't feeling any pain, it was a little unnerving that she could sleep through all her contractions.

The nurse gave me a sweet smile. "The epidural blocks the nerves that send pain signals to the brain. She can't feel anything below her chest. So, she's sleeping as if she's in no pain, because she isn't. It's perfectly normal and actually beneficial that she's asleep right now. She'll need all the energy in the world when she's pushing and after the baby is born." Her whispered response goes a long way to ease my worries and I thanked her softly before she left the room.

I laid my head back down, but just as I felt myself drifting off the door opened and the lights came on. I saw Dr. Bronson enter the room and she gave me a comforting smile.

"Hello, Porter. How's Ella doing?" I stood and looked to Ella, who still slept, and back to the doctor.

"She's doing well, I suppose. The woman could sleep through an earthquake at this point," I laughed.

"Well, I hate to wake her, but her chart indicates she might be close to pushing, so I want to check her."

I nodded and then leaned down to her ear. "Ella, Baby, wake up." I brushed the back of my hand down her cheek, trying to rouse her. "Sweetheart, wake up." I pushed her hair off her forehead. I saw her eyes start to move beneath her lids and she took a deeper breath. I smiled, watching her come back from sleep, like a princess in a fairy tale. I couldn't help myself so I leaned down and placed a chaste kiss against her lips and I felt her smile against me. I pulled away and saw the bluest eyes in the world staring back at me.

"Hi," she whispered.

"Hi, back. How are you feeling?"

"Good."

"Good." She smiled at my response.

"Good morning, Ella," The doctor said from across the room as she washed her hands. Ella's head whipped around to look at her and then she smiled again.

"Hi. I didn't even see you there."

"Well," the doctor said with a playful lilt to her voice, "I'd be distracted if I woke up to that too."

I blushed.

"He can be very distracting," Ella said as she patted my hand.

"Good. You're going to need some distraction because I need to check your progress." Dr. Bronson moved to the side of her bed and lifted up her blanket, exposing her legs.

"I'm going to help you move your legs because I know you probably can't right now." I watched as Ella's face strained a little and then she laughed.

"I can't move them at all."

"That's good," the doctor said. "That means the medicine is doing its job." She pushed both of Ella's feet up towards the rest of her body and then gently placed her knees to the side. I winced because it looked a little uncomfortable. "I have to warn you though, Ella," she said as she started to examine her. "In order for you to push, we'll have to lower the dosage. We don't want you to be in too much pain, but you have to be able to feel at least a little in order to push effectively." The doctor's eyebrows furrowed a little and she sat back on the bed, finished with her examination. "And it looks like the time is now. You're fully dilated. Are you ready to push?"

My heart skipped at the doctors words and excitement rushed through my body. I looked to Ella to see the excitement on her face but was confused when I saw she started crying.

"What's wrong?" I asked her, confused in her sudden change in emotion.

She looked up at me with tears welled in her eyes. "I don't know," she cried, the tears falling from her eyes. "I'm a little scared, I guess."

I kissed her brow. "Everything's going to be ok. I'll be right here with you the whole time."

"What if I can't do it? What if something bad happens?" She sniffled and wiped away the tears from her cheeks.

"The baby has been safe in there for nine months, what if something goes wrong?"

"Ella," Dr. Bronson's voice rang out and we both looked to her. "It is normal to be apprehensive about giving birth, especially if you've never done it before." She gave Ella a supportive smile. "Your baby is ready to be born. They want to meet you and you'll do great. Next to your husband, I too, will be here the whole time." She patted Ella's leg and tilted her head, waiting for her response. I never asked her before if she has her own children, but I'm sure she does. Or she had the best bedside manner I've ever encountered. Either way, I just gained a new appreciation for her.

Ella wiped her tears again and then sat up a little straighter. "Ok, I can do this." She took in a deep breath as if she was readying herself for battle.

"Good girl," I said, wiping away the last of her tears.

"Ok," Dr. Bronson said, clapping her hands together. "Showtime!"

The next few minutes were a flurry of activity. People entered the room with a lot of equipment and something that resembled a little crib on wheels. The bed folded down and transformed to allow the doctor to get even closer to Ella and I laughed because all I could think about was how I wanted to call the bed Optimus Prime now that I knew about its transforming capabilities. Ella looked at me funny when I laughed, wanting in on the joke.

"Later," I told her. Now was not the time to tell her I'm thinking about cartoons from the eighties as she's about to start giving birth to our first child. "I'm going to give an update to our parents." She nodded.

"Hurry back," she said, and then she winked at me. Even in this moment, when I knew she was scared and nervous, she could still make my blood run hot. I shook my head at her and made my way to the waiting room. Sometime last night, I couldn't really remember when, I called our parents and let them know Ella went into labor and they all insisted on coming to the hospital. Ella and I both appreciated their support, and also appreciated that they all understood that Ella and I wanted privacy during the birth. Both our moms were very understanding, even though I knew either one of them would give anything to be in there when the baby was born.

When I made it back into the room, even more people were there. All of them seemed focused on the jobs they were performing. I went back to my side of her bed and gripped her hand, kissing her forehead.

"Both our moms give their love. And your dad said, and I quote, "Go get 'em"." Ella laughed, which was the best sound I'd heard all morning.

"Ok, Ella, we're going to do a few practice pushes." Dr. Bronson was literally right up in Ella's business. I imagined Ella would be a little uncomfortable with the doctor's proximity, but she seemed unfazed. "Your epidural should be wearing off a little making it easier for you to feel the contractions, but until then you can look at that screen. When the line starts to move up, you're having a contraction. You need to pull your knees to the side and up towards your head. Then you need to push. Porter will count to ten and then you can rest, ok?" Ella nodded and looked at me with worried eyes. I smiled at her.

"Everything will be ok," I said, softly, trying to make her feel more at ease.

"All right, Ella, you see how the line is going up? That means it's time to push. That's it, pull your knees back and bear down." Ella followed the instructions perfectly, as if she'd done this a million times. "Alright, Porter, now you count to ten. Not too fast, but not too slow."

When I reached ten, Ella collapsed back down on to the bed and looked up at me. "Count faster next time," she said with her eyes closed. Dr. Bronson slowly shook her head at me and mouthed 'No'.

"You did great, Babe."

"Next time, Ella, we're going to push until the contraction is over, taking a small break between each one – just a few seconds." Ella nodded and I just watched her. When the next contraction came, she did just as she was supposed to and so did I. She gave three good pushes and then the doctor told her to relax. She leaned back into the bed, but then suddenly gripped her stomach in pain.

"Oh, ouch!" She cried, drawing in a sharp breath through her teeth making a hissing sound. "That really hurts," she said, rubbing a spot low on the right side of her belly. "Like, really hurts," she said, looking at the doctor with a question in her eyes.

The doctor placed her hands on Ella's knees and said calmly, "The epidural is likely wearing off. It's normal to feel some discomfort."

"But this is just one spot, right on the side, and I'm not having a contraction."

"Your body is just adjusting. The baby's heart rate is normal. Everything is going well."

Ella just nodded while still rubbing the spot bothering her, breathing in through her nose and out through her mouth.

This went on for hours.

Ella pushed through every contraction, and then when she wasn't pushing, she complained about the pain in her side. The doctor was patient with Ella. It was obvious that she was trying, but even the nurses seemed to be getting restless after a while.

With every push she made a little progress, but then when the contraction was over the baby would sneak back up, away from us. I tried to help her. I held her legs, I kissed her forehead, and I wiped her brow. I must have counted to ten at least a hundred times by now. I'd count to ten a million times if it helped her. I'd do anything at this point to just help her.

"Is it supposed to take this long? What if something is wrong?" I asked the doctor between the contractions. I didn't want to say it, but she'd started to bleed and it seemed like a lot of blood to me. I passed worried an hour ago and was now moving into terrified. It was easy to get caught up in the happiness of pregnancy, easy to take an simple delivery and healthy baby for granted. I hadn't stopped to think about the fact that something might not go right, but I was thinking about it now.

"Porter, Ella, the baby's heart rate is good, Ella is holding up through this. I just need you to dig deep and do your best to get this baby out." The doctor sounded confident, but a little worried as well.

Another hour went by, Ella pushed and pushed, but the baby made little progress. She started to fade, reaching new depths of exhaustion, I imagined. It was hard to believe she held up this long. Thoughts kept racing through my head, things I was unable and unwilling to say out loud. Why was this taking so damn long? How long did she have to do this until they decided it was long enough? Wasn't there anything they could do to help her? Between contractions her eyes fluttered closed, but she still quietly moaned in pain, clutching the same spot on the right side of her belly. Something wasn't right. I panicked on the inside, but tried to remain calm on the outside, not wanting to cause Ella to panic as well.

"Ella, look at me," Dr. Bronson said, a new edge to her voice. "I need you to focus, look at me." Ella opened her eyes and groggily gazed at her. "This is it, Ella. You've got three more tries to get this baby out, but then I'm going to have to *take* the baby out. I know you can do this. I know you can."

"I don't want a C-section," Ella said, barely able to keep her eyes open.

"And I don't want to give you one. But you've got to rally, Ella. You need to get the baby out on the next contraction or I will have to take the baby."

"I need something to hold on to," she said raggedly, obviously at the edge of exhaustion.

I didn't understand what she meant, but the nurses did. One of them reached into a cabinet and pulled out a sheet, tying a knot in one end and handing it to Ella. The nurse held on to the other end and stood behind the doctor. I bent down so that my mouth was against the shell of her ear.

"I'm so proud of you, Baby. You can do this. I know you can." She smiled and leaned her head against me.

"Ok, Ella, here comes a contraction. It's time. Push your baby out."

I watched as Ella gripped the sheet, pulling herself up, using it as leverage to push. A nurse held up her left leg and I held her right. I watched and waited, hoping that this worked.

"Porter, count!" Dr. Bronson yelled, focusing on Ella. I quickly began to count, a little embarrassed I'd forgotten my one job. When I made it to ten, the doctor yelled again. "Don't stop, Porter, count again. Ella, it's working, keep pushing!"

Ella took another deep breath and bore down, pulling on the sheet, giving the nurse on the other end of it quite a jolt and she had to readjust her footing to keep from falling over. I smiled on the inside, knowing Ella dug deep. I made it to seven this time before the doctor yelled again.

"One more push, Ella. The baby is right here!" She turned to the nurse beside her and said much quieter, "I'm not letting this baby get stuck."

Ella took another deep breath and started all over again, pushing and groaning, working harder than I'd ever seen anyone work at anything. I watched her face as I counted, not sure I was even counting correctly. For all I knew, I could have been saying all kinds of random numbers for all it was worth. I just held her leg close to me and said words that I thought were helping and watched her do the most miraculous thing anyone had ever done.

Suddenly she collapsed back onto the bed and a whole new flurry of activity happened. People moved all over the room. I watched as Ella's eyes slowly opened and then grew wide. I dropped her leg and saw a beautiful and spectacular look of love spread over her face. Her hands reached forward and grabbed something as tears started spilling from her eyes.

"Oh my God," she said through her tears. "She's beautiful."

She's beautiful.

She.

A girl.

My eyes moved from Ella's face to her hands and something new and wonderful clicked inside of me. Ella held my baby. Our baby. She was small and pink and loud. She cried as if she was trying to tell us all how much the last few hours had been so horrible. I couldn't move for watching her. Watching them. Ella. And my daughter.

My daughter.

Our daughter.

Ella looked up at me, the happiest tears I'd ever seen from anyone coming from her beautiful eyes, and softly she said to me, "Thank you." Stunned, not having moved much or been able to say anything yet, I crashed my lips against her mouth, trying to convey every emotion I was feeling at that moment through our kiss – an impossible task. I broke away and although the kiss was short and chaste, it was the first time I'd kissed Ella as a mother and it was beautiful. She was beautiful.

"Porter," I heard a fuzzy voice in the back of my head. "Porter, would you like to cut the cord?" I looked up to see Dr. Bronson smiling at me. After a moment to piece together what she'd said, I nodded and took the scissors she held out to me. She showed me where to snip and I did, eliminating the last physical tie the baby had to Ella. She was really, truly, here. I handed the scissors back to the doctor, still looking at the cord I'd just cut.

My gaze swept back down to my daughter as Ella positioned her against her chest, moving her hospital gown out of the way so that the baby lay against her, skin to skin. Ella's left hand rested on the baby's back while her right hand glided softly over the baby's head. She closed her eyes and her head fell back to rest against the hospital bed, completely exhausted but with a look of pure, exalted joy across her face.

I watched my wife hold our daughter and felt as if I was floating above everything. This had to be a dream. Love like this didn't exist in real life. You can't meet a person, a baby, and love them this deeply, irrevocably, in an instant. If all parents loved like this, if every single person who had a child felt this way, how did life go on? How could there be anything after this?

We stayed like that for a few moments, then the buzz of what was happening around us brought us back to reality.

"We're going to have to weigh and measure her now," a nurse said with an apologetic smile towards Ella, obviously knowing giving up her baby in that moment would be painful.

"You're not taking her away, are you?" She asked, a little panicked.

"No. I'm just going to take her over there," she pointed to the cradle on wheels I'd noticed earlier. "She won't leave the room, I promise. We just want to check her out. It'll be five minutes, tops."

Ella kissed our baby on the head and then pulled back quickly, a look of terror on her face.

"What is this?" Ella cried, looking at the baby's head, her fingers feathering over it. I looked down and saw what had Ella worried and my heart began to pump rapidly.

On top of the baby's head was a bump – a big bump – and what looked like a scrape. And there was blood. The nurse reached for the baby, taking her from Ella gently, bringing her over to where the rest of the medical staff stood ready to examine her. Dr. Bronson was still at the edge of Ella's bed doing Lord knows what.

"Ella, Porter, it looks like the baby has what is called a subdural hematoma. There seems to have been some head trauma during the birth. They are fairly common and not necessarily dangerous."

"What do you mean 'not necessarily'?" I asked, angry at the game of verbal dodgeball we seemed to be playing. I wanted to know what was wrong with our baby, and I didn't want it sugar coated or danced around.

"Well, what I mean is, it might not be a cause for concern. We'll have to watch her. It literally is just a collection of blood underneath the surface of the skin. It will eventually just dissipate and be absorbed back into her body. The main concern is with jaundice. So, over the next couple days we'll just need to watch her bilirubin levels."

"Her what?" Ella said, sounding scared.

"Bilirubin. It's just a fancy word for how clean the blood is. Too much bilirubin is bad, and when the blood dissipates from the hematoma it can cause a traffic jam, of sorts, for the liver, causing the baby's skin to turn a yellow color." The doctor said all of this while focusing between Ella's legs. I found myself wondering what she could possibly be looking at with such concentration.

"That sounds serious." Ella's voice was faint and frightened.

"It can be, if you don't watch it. Don't worry, she's in good hands." The doctor stood and removed her gloves, throwing them in the trash can by her feet. She came up to Ella's side and pressed her hands against Ella's stomach, feeling around for something. "Ok." She placed a hand on Ella's shoulder and gave her a smile. "Your uterus is still contracting and making very good progress on shrinking back down. You lost a lot of blood so I am going to prescribe you some iron. You needed four stitches so you'll need to be extra careful for a few days while those start to heal." She paused and gave Ella's shoulder a small squeeze. "You did really well, Ella. I was worried for a while, but you did a great job."

"She's going to be ok?" Ella asked, hopeful.

"Everything looks excellent," a nurse said as she brought the baby back to her. She handed her over, wrapped in a pink blanket, a hat on her head, covering the large bump, hiding it from view. "Eight pounds, four ounces, twenty-one inches long. Scored a nine on the Apgar test." The nurse noticed the confused look on Ella's face. "She's perfect." She laughed. "Don't let the bump bother you. She's perfectly healthy, just needs a little extra care. She had a rough exit, seems like the side of her head might have gotten caught on your pelvis."

"Is that why my side hurt so much?"

The doctor and nurse both just smiled at her. That bothered me. How many times did Ella tell them she was in pain while she was pushing? They hadn't paid much attention to her complaints and it seems like there might have been something legitimately wrong. I liked Dr. Bronson, and I wanted to believe she did what she thought was best for Ella and the baby during the delivery, but a small part of me was angry they had let her push so long when it turned out the baby had been in distress the whole time.

I tried to let my feelings of anger go, now was not the time to harbor negativity. Now was the time to cherish the little girl that was currently snuggled against my wife.

"So," the nurse said, upbeat. "Do we have a name for this little, darling girl?"

Ella turned her head and looked up at me, smiling, eyes shining, looking like the most beautiful woman I'd ever seen.

"Yeah," I said, not breaking eye contact with her. "We do."

Chapter Thirteen

Ella

When my parents and Tilly walked into the hospital room, I couldn't contain the smile that spread across my face. Watching their faces light up, witnessing their eyes go wide as they found the little bundle of bliss currently resting against my chest; it was a moment of pride for me. I wanted to show off the perfect little baby I'd made. I wanted to watch them fall in love with her, just like I had, and take all the credit for their happiness. She was my most impressive accomplishment, and also the most precious one. In an instant, just one moment in time, she'd become the singular and most crucially vital person in my life. All she had to do was *be*. She existed and therefore, so did I. It was amazing.

Mom and Tilly instantly cried. I expected nothing less. She was perfect and worth crying over. My dad walked to Porter and shook his hand, saying something congratulatory to him. Porter smiled as he shook his hand but then turned back to me and the baby, just as enraptured as I was.

"Oh my word, Ella, she's just perfect," my mother said, looking adoringly down at her sleeping face.

"I know," I said, my eyes gliding back to her soft cheeks, one of which was mushed against the swell of my breast.

"Well," Porter's mom said through happy tears. "What's her name?"

My eyes darted to Porter, nodding, letting him know he could reveal our secret.

"We've decided to name her Matilda Rose," he said softly, watching his mother closely. It was like watching an artist create a painting. First you saw both of our moms hear the name, then you could see the understanding cross their faces, and then the best part: The surprise, the joy.

"You named her after me?" Tilly asked, tears now coming quickly, flowing over cheeks big from smiling.

"Well, actually, we named her after both of you," I said looking between Tilly and my mother. My mom's eyes were just as wet as Tilly's.

"Matilda for you, Mom," Porter said, holding back tears I could hear in his voice.

"And Rose, for your middle name, Mom," I said. "We really hope that Mattie here," I said looking down at my daughter, "takes after all the strong and important women in her life."

I watched for a few minutes as the two moms passed their granddaughter back and forth, cooing at her, touching her, loving on her. I was still baffled and completely in awe of everything happening right in front of me. Was this how my mom felt about me when I was born? I can't imagine it's possible that my mom loves me as much as I love Mattie. But when my mom's eyes fluttered from my daughter up to me, I saw it; I saw her love for me. It's always been there, but now it was different. I saw my mother differently, Tilly too. How lucky was Porter to have such an incredible mother? It was easy to take a mother's love for granted, until you were one.

A nurse came in and smiled at the obvious and copious amounts of love in the room.

"Hi, I'm Fran. How are you feeling?" She asked me.

"Pretty good, just a little sore from sitting in this bed." I squirmed, trying to alleviate some of the discomfort.

"You'll be moved to the Mommy and Baby wing in about an hour and the beds there are much better. Would you like to try and nurse?"

"That's my cue to leave," Dad joked. He stopped by my bed and kissed my forehead. "Good job, Princess. She's perfect." He shook Porter's hand again and then made his exit, going to sit in the waiting room until my mom was ready to leave. I looked up at Tilly and my mom.

"Will you guys stay?" Honestly, I was a little nervous to try and feed Mattie for the first time and could have used all the help I could get. Both of them agreed with smiles; I don't think wild horses could have dragged them from the room. Tilly handed Mattie back to me and the nurse helped me adjust her and myself to try to get her to latch on. At first, it was awkward and a little embarrassing. Mattie seemed more interested in sleeping than eating so I was just rubbing my nipple on her face, trying to tempt her, and it seemed a little strange.

The nurse was very helpful and kept talking so that even though I felt awkward, She made it seem like the most natural thing and I guess, of course, it was.

"Let's unwrap her and see if some cold air won't wake her up." She laid Mattie out on the bed and unwrapped the blanket from her. I felt my heart flutter as I watched her curl up, trying to escape the cold air, her little legs bending up towards her chest, her tiny butt perfectly round and cute. I fell in love with her a little more just then. Her eyes didn't open, but she moved around, so the nurse brought her back and did all the dirty work, manipulating my breast for me, getting Mattie to open up her mouth.

Again, I felt uncomfortable as this strange woman's hands gripped my breast, but I tried to go with the flow, tried to pretend like this isn't the most unusual position I've ever been in. But suddenly, all my concerns about modesty and shyness floated away and dissipated when I felt Mattie's mouth latch on to me. I looked down and saw her perfect mouth wrapped around me and I couldn't help the tears that formed in my eyes. She suckled and made the tiniest whimpering noises I've ever heard.

"Oh my God," I whispered. I felt Porter press a kiss against my temple, but I didn't dare look up at him. I couldn't. I stared at Mattie for as long as I could. I don't think I could ever tear my eyes away from her, from this. I'm connected to her like I've never been connected to anyone.

Eventually Mattie fell asleep and no longer fed, but just slept with me in her mouth.

"She's asleep," I said quietly to the nurse who was making polite conversation with our moms while I nursed Mattie, all of them laughing and smiling as if the most miraculous thing in the world wasn't happening in my arms.

"Newborns are so lazy," she said with a smile. "You might find her to be more lethargic in the next couple of days due to the hematoma, so you'll need to try extra hard to get her to latch on. If I'm not here to help, there's always a lactation specialist on the floor, so don't hesitate to ask for help."

"What hematoma?" Tilly asked. We spent the next five minutes explaining Mattie's condition, taking her hat off and showing our moms her injury.

"You should try to feed her at least every two to three hours, and if she'd too tired to eat, make sure you're pumping. Ring the bell if you have any questions." Fran said goodbye to everyone and just as she left, another nurse entered and informed us it was time to change rooms. There was a flurry of activity, but I kept my eyes on Mattie and my arms wrapped around her. They didn't allow me to hold her as we moved rooms, but they did allow Porter to wheel her in a bassinette.

Our parents decided to leave us, all needing sleep just as much as we did. We said our goodbyes and the nurse got us situated in our new room – and, yes, the bed was much more comfortable. I was given a ton of instructions from the nurse, all of which were overwhelming, and she could tell I was exhausted. She left us, claiming she'd return soon to check on us.

Suddenly, it's just Porter, Mattie, and me. The three of us. Alone. I looked at him and it occurred to me that he had yet to hold his baby. I was instantly ashamed that I hogged her, that I let everyone else hold her first.

"Porter, you haven't held her yet," I said, urging him to come to us. "I'm so sorry. Why didn't you say something?" He shrugged.

"Watching you with her has been the most wonderful experience I've ever had. I didn't want to take her from you," he said, simply. My heart liquefied at his words. It was typical Porter to put me and my needs before his own.

"Come over here," I whispered, scooting over on the bed so there was enough room for him to sit next to me. Once he was so close to me I could feel the heat radiating from him, I passed Mattie over, gently laying her in the crook of his elbow. He didn't falter, didn't seem nervous at all. He took her and he held her firmly, without hesitation. He was a natural. Her tiny, perfect head fit snuggly against the strong muscle of his bicep, and her pristine, creamy and pink face looked flawless against his tanned skin.

"She's so beautiful," he whispered, his eyes not blinking, using every moment to just look at her. I leaned my head up against his arm, listening to him breathe, watching him caress the feather-soft tuft of hair at the nape of her neck. "She's perfect, you know," he said quietly, looking into my eyes. "You made a perfect little girl."

"*We* made a perfect little girl."

He kissed my forehead. "You did most of the work."

"Well, that I won't argue with you about." I sighed and leaned my head against him again, exhaustion taking me over.

"I was really scared there for a little while." His voice was still quiet, but now it was hesitant and almost weak. I looked up at him, wondering what in the world could ever possibly make my husband sound so broken.

"What do you mean?"

"For a while there I was afraid you and the baby weren't going to make it through that delivery. You were so brave and so determined, but she just wasn't coming out. You were bleeding so much and trying so hard..." His voice trailed off and I watched him take a few shuddering breaths, his fingers never leaving the baby's fine hair peeking out of her hat. "I refused to let myself think what would happen to me if I lost you, but I'd be lying if I said I wasn't scared today." He turned his face to look at me, eyes wet but not spilling over with tears. "I don't ever want to find out what life is like without you. I need you, Ella. We need you."

I thought about his words and tried to imagine what the birth must have looked like from his point of view. I imagine I would have been nervous and scared had I witnessed that too.

"What's funny," I began, hoping my insight might make him feel a little better, "is that I wasn't ever once concerned about myself or the baby." I leaned back against his arm and looked down at Mattie, still comfortably sleeping in her father's arms. "I just kept thinking that I only had one job and that was to get her out. I was going to push and push and push until she was here. But when the doctor said it was now or never, I just knew it was up to me." I shrugged a little, my eyes drifting closed. "I just did what I had to do to protect her," I said, sleepily.

We sat there in silence for a few moments and I could feel myself drifting away. I was nearly asleep when I had a thought of panic and I sat up, looking around for the baby. I breathed a quick sigh of relief to see Porter still awake and looking down on her.

"I don't feel comfortable sleeping with her in the bed. Maybe you could take her to the rocking chair? Or put her in the bassinette?"

"Sure. No problem," he said, slowly standing up and moving to the chair.

"But, uh, Porter?"

"Yeah?" He said as his beautiful brown eyes found mine.

"Don't fall asleep while you're holding her. If you get tired just put her down, ok?"

He laughed at me and smiled. "Don't worry, Ella. I'm not going to break her. But I promise I'll put her down if I get tired."

"Thank you." I laid back down and pulled the thin hospital blanket up around my shoulders.

"Ella?"

"Yes?" My head sunk into the pillow and I felt myself starting to relax.

"Thank you for giving me a family."

I opened my eyes and saw him staring down at Mattie and I saw so much love beaming down on her. "Yeah, well, thanks for being a good son and driving a total stranger home in a rain storm."

He looked over at me and we both smiled, knowing that so much more was in store for us.

Chapter Fourteen

Ella

The first two weeks of having a new baby was nothing like I had expected it to be. I can't really remember what I was expecting, mainly because remembering anything, including my own name, at some points was a stretch.

Mattie was the perfect baby – during the day. She slept beautifully – during the day. She cooed and cried and opened her beautiful eyes every once in a while to take in her surroundings. But at night, well, things could have gone better. The baby cried, I cried, and sometimes Porter looked as though he was a deer in headlights. The poor man didn't know up from down some days and there were times I was no help at all. I had my fair share of breakdowns in the darkness of night, having absolutely no idea why my baby cried for hours.

One thing I did learn, though, throughout all the madness of that transitional time, was that sometimes you had to throw out all the advice and parenting books you'd read and just listen to your baby. Mattie wouldn't sleep or stop crying until she laid directly on me. So guess where she slept? That's right: on me. This particular arrangement made it difficult for me to sleep, but I was happy to lay in the dark, half dozing, if it was quiet and Mattie wasn't crying. Porter did everything he could to help; if she was awake, he was awake. But if she was sleeping it made no sense for him to lie awake with me. I used those quiet moments in the dark to reflect on how much my life had changed, to imagine where we'd be in another year's time.

Thankfully, I never found myself drifting into the darkness in my mind. The events surrounding my shooting and Kyle would seep into my thoughts at times, but I never wallowed. I allowed myself to process the thoughts, I even wrote some of them down if I thought it would be helpful in court, but then I moved on. I let my mind wander elsewhere. I never panicked and I never worried. It was a new feeling of being content I'd never experienced.

I also expected that after having a baby, for a little while at least, my sex drive would be gone and, in some ways, it was. I definitely didn't want to have sex; sitting was a hardship sometimes. But seeing Porter shirtless holding our baby, talking to her about her day, was the biggest turn on ever. He was so gentle with her, so careful. If I had thought he'd used soft hands with me before, I was wrong. He was soft with Mattie, soft for her. The sun rose and set with her. She had the secrets to the universe and he tried to coax them out of her every evening, rocking with her, telling her stories, running his fingers over the soft hair on her head.

For two weeks now we focused on Mattie and I wouldn't have it any other way. We loved her and would do anything for her. But when I realized that, for the first time since we'd been home from the hospital with her, she was asleep in the middle of the day and I wasn't completely exhausted, my mind immediately started thinking about how much I missed my husband.

I found him in the laundry room, moving clothes from the washer to the dryer – bless him. He was focused on his task and didn't hear me approach. I felt him startle a little when I slid my hands around his waist from behind, pressing my front to his back, snuggling in. His hand slid over top of mine, caressing me, causing my breaths to come faster. It had been so long since we'd been together and I was now a little angry at the fact that we still had four more weeks to wait.

I breathed him in, cherishing the familiarity of his scent. He always smelled the same and I came to rely on it, expect it, love it.

"Hey, Babe," he said softly, aware of the fact that Mattie was asleep, not wanting to wake her. "What's up? Gonna go lie down?"

"Nope," I said, popping the P, with my face still resting against his back.

"Can I get you anything?" He asked, making me smile against him.

"Nope." This time I popped the P loudly, making him chuckle.

"Ok."

I loosened my grip and walked around him, placing myself between him and the washing machine, and looked up at him, my hands now on his chest.

"Hi," I whispered.

"Hey." He looked at me with pure confusion, a smile playing on his face as he tried to figure out what it was I wanted from him, his eyebrows raised in question.

"I miss you." My whisper was even softer, my insecurity coming over me, a little embarrassed to be putting myself out there so blatantly. His brow relaxed at my words, but a new look of concern had worry lines forming around his eyes. There was a very large part of me that I just now realized was hanging by a thread, scared to death that he would reject me. My hands slid around his neck, fingers running through the hair there, gently urging him down to me. He came willingly, but stopped short, his forehead resting against mine.

"I'm right here," he said breathily, his hands coming to rest against my back, right at the swell of my backside.

"Are you? Because you feel pretty far away right now." I couldn't keep the hurt from my voice. He knew what I was asking for, yet he held it just out of arms reach.

"Ella, we can't. Not yet. I don't want to hurt you."

"Not sex, Porter, just… I don't know… us." I dropped my hands from his neck and pulled back, putting some distance between us. "You use to hold me every night. You would hold my hand at the dinner table, touch me as you passed by, find any reason you could just to touch me." He tried to open his mouth to interject but I put my hand up. "Let me finish." I took a deep breath, finding the courage to continue. "I know things are different now. I know that there's a baby in our bed and I don't look the same." My words became a little strangled as I felt a lump forming in my throat. "I just don't want to lose that part of *us* that I love so much, the part where we're never close enough to each other."

I continued to look down, not wanting to witness his rejection or his dismissal. But goose bumps raised up all over my skin when I felt a single fingertip bring my chin up. When our eyes met, I couldn't ignore the concern still written across his face.

"Don't ever question my need for you, Ella. Don't insult our relationship that way. Don't insult yourself either. I'm sorry if I've done a poor job of making you feel secure." He said and his hands ran up my shoulders, coming to rest on either side of my neck, his thumbs smoothing over my jaw. "I've been so focused on making sure Mattie is taken care of and then making sure you're taken care of, I just feel like I can't do enough for either of you. But don't doubt, ever, that I want you." His face moved down and his lips rested just barely on my ear. "I crave you," he sighed into me, the air from his mouth moved against my ear and I melted even further against him. "I refuse to be the husband," he said, splaying kisses gently across my neck, "who pressures his wife," more kisses, "who's just given him the greatest gift," wetter kisses now, "to have sex with him before she's ready." His hands roamed, one still on the back of my neck, the other moving down my side, grazing my ribcage.

"I don't need sex, Porter. I just need you." He stepped into me, pressing my back against the washing machine, his hands grabbing ahold of me firmly where they lay. His eyes suddenly peered into mine, both of us breathing hard, my heart beating rapidly. Then slowly his mouth lowered to mine.

His kiss started slow and gentle, as if her were afraid he would break me if he pushed me too far. We'd done little more than peck on the mouth since Mattie was born. She was our focus, but right now, I wanted to feel something besides his concern, besides his need to care for us. I wanted him to remember the passion we shared between us, needed him to bring me that point where he was my everything and I was his.

When his tongue teased the seam of my lips I opened for him, moaning into his mouth as his tongue sought out mine, pressing against it firmly, guiding our kiss. His hands came to my cheeks, angling my face just right so that he could devour me. What started out gentle was now heated, and he kissed me like I was the last little bit of air left in the world and he was drowning. He breathed me in, using me, taking me, and I loved it.

His hands were suddenly on my waist, hoisting me onto the washing machine and he stepped in between my knees, his stomach pressing firmly in between my legs.

"You tell me what you want, tell me when to stop if I go too far." His mouth returned to mine, one hand brushing the hair back from my face as he kissed me, the other making its way below the hem of my shirt, gliding up the skin of my back. I pulled back and yanked his shirt over his head, throwing it to the floor, then pulling him back to me, my hands finding his hard muscles.

"I love your body, Porter," I said against his mouth and I meant it. He'd always had a nice body, but I hadn't found a lot of time lately to admire it. But now, with my hands running smoothly and bravely over the contours of his perfectly sculpted torso, I was free to admire how wonderfully built he was. "You're perfect."

He groaned, wrapping one strong arm around my middle and sweeping me off the washing machine, his other arm holding me behind my knees, he carried me from the laundry room. My arms wrapped themselves around the back of his neck and I continued kissing him, remembering that last time he carried me like this when we had come home from our honeymoon. Him always the traditionalist, carrying me over the threshold. I smiled against him, the memory having a serene effect on me.

He sat on the couch and we both landed with a thud, but it mattered not because his mouth was back on mine and he pulled me closer to him still. I sat on his lap but couldn't get as close as I wanted, so I moved to straddle him, one knee on either side of his hips. It was only when I had pressed my center against him that I thought it might not have been a good idea. He must have sense my unease because he pulled back and his eyes found mine.

"Are you ok?" His voice was gravelly and raspy in a way that made every hair on my body stand at attention. "Ella?"

"Mmm hmm," I mumbled, moving my lips to his neck. Hearing him gasp as my lips met the skin there, tasting him, thrilled me. Perhaps, even though I wasn't as skinny as I used to be or as put together, maybe I could still get to him, still turn him on and affect him the way he affected me.

I tentatively and very slowly used my hips to grind into him. I could feel him beneath me, feel his arousal, and I desperately needed to feel him against me.

"Ella, no, stop." My heart stopped, not accustomed to hearing him put things to a halt between us. He brought his lips back to mine and continued to kiss me, but my confusion was keeping me from enjoying his mouth at the moment. "I don't want you to get hurt," he said by way of explanation. He was worried about me.

I was acutely aware of my body, obsessively so, in fact. I had been ever since I'd given birth. At first, everything had hurt, with good reason; a baby will seriously mess everything up. It hurt to sit, it hurt to stand, it hurt – period. But as the days went by and things began to heal, I took note of what was still painful and what seemed to be comfortable again. It had been two weeks since the birth of Mattie and I felt almost normal again. I didn't feel like running a marathon and I didn't want anything coming even remotely close to the inside of my vagina, but being with him, like this, felt wonderful. Well, it had until he'd told me to stop.

"Porter, please, I need this. I miss you."

"If I hurt you, Ella, I wouldn't be able to forgive myself."

"It doesn't hurt," I whispered as I slowly rocked myself against him, watching his eyes roll to the back of his head, groaning. "It feels incredible." I took his lower lip in between my teeth and pulled gently, trying to convince him to let me play, to trust me enough to give me this. "This is all I want. Nothing more." My lips went back to blazing a trail along his throat, over his neck, behind his ear, and I felt the moment he gave in. He wrapped his hands around my hips, not stopping me but aiding me.

I moved my mouth to his, thanking him, cherishing him, and we kissed like teenagers under the bleachers. We kissed like we were afraid of getting caught. We kissed like two people desperately in love who hadn't kissed in ages. We kissed like it was the only thing keeping us alive anymore.

His hands pulled my shirt up over my head and I had one tiny moment of fear that his seeing my bare stomach might end this, but then his mouth moved down my neck, his hands pulling down gently on my hips, and I forgot I was supposed to feel self-conscious. I forgot everything except the way he was making me feel – which was incredible. Loved. Wanted.

I was only wearing a pair of thin yoga pants – my new mommy wardrobe – and the elasticity of the fabric made it possible for me to feel every ridge of the bulge in Porter's jeans. His hand slid around my waist then under the material of my pants as he grazed my ass. I felt a gentle yet firm grasp against my backside as he pulled me on to him further still. I gasped against his mouth, suddenly a little afraid of what might happen between us. I had not had an orgasm since before giving birth and I wasn't sure what it would feel like now. Should I be expecting pain? Should I stop this before it went too far?

Porter pulled against me again and I felt nothing but unadulterated pleasure, which I showed with a guttural moan. His hands moved from my backside and roamed over my stomach, gliding up my torso and cupped my breasts. I nearly melted at the care and gentleness with which he treated me. He didn't grab or squeeze; I felt the slightest feather of touches as his thumbs floated over my nipples, causing a whole new wave of arousal to flood through me.

"Porter," I gasped, so close to the edge.

"Just let go, Baby. I'm here."

I felt his hands grasp my cheeks, my forehead being pulled down to meet with his, and his ragged breath upon my face. I whimpered loudly as he braced his arms against my back, putting more pressure against me, and my orgasm burst through me. Mouth gaping open, foreheads still touching, fingers curling against his biceps, I found my release and floated like a feather back to reality.

My eyes were still closed and his hands were trailing down my back, waiting for me to return to him. When I finally blinked and pulled back to look at him, he wore a concerned look on his ruggedly beautiful face.

"Are you ok? Did I hurt you?"

My hands came up to cradle his face. "That was anything but painful." I tried to reassure him by kissing him gently, but when I pulled back he was still wearing the same face. "I promise. It was wonderful. Thank you." I moved just a little, trying to climb off of him, and felt his hardness still beneath me. "Do you, um, need me to…"

"No." He said curtly.

"No?" My insecurities came racing back. He'd never denied me before. What man turns down a blow job? Was it because he wasn't attracted to me anymore?

"Hey," he said, a little softer this time with less edge to his voice. "This was for you. I'm not expecting anything in return." He leaned forward and kissed my forehead, then pulled back to stare at me some more. I tried to take his words for their value, tried not to read into them too much, but my insecure mind was racing around with thoughts of stretch marks and pregnant bellies. Obviously, my mind concluded, he wasn't attracted to me sexually anymore.

"Hey," he said again, only this time he sounded angry. My eyes darted back to his at the new emotion I heard in his voice. "Don't do that, Ella. Don't let your mind wander off with your thoughts. I can see it all over your face and you're wrong." His thumb came up and traced a line down the edge of my jaw, starting at my chin and working back towards my ear.

"Watching your body change to carry my baby was the sexiest thing I have ever seen, and the way you look now," his hand that was just gentle at my jaw had moved back into my hair and gripped me firmly. "I could never stop loving this body, Ella. This body gave me the most beautiful creature in the world, and I want to worship you, I do." He pulled my face towards him, so close that his mouth was right next to my ear. He breathed his words against my skin, making me shiver against him as new waves of pleasure rolled over me. "But the next time I come, I want to be buried deep inside of you. I want to enjoy your new body to its fullest." His teeth nipped at my earlobe and my breath caught in my throat.

"Ok, then," I managed to mumble, even with his mouth on my neck.

"And Ella?" He said, again, his mouth still sending goose bumps along my neck.

"Yes?"

"I can't wait to be buried inside you again."

"Ok."

Chapter Fifteen

Ella

Porter took a leave from work for two weeks after Mattie was born, and those were two glorious weeks filled with both of us learning how to tread these new and rough waters of parenthood. Of course, all our families came to visit, but mostly it was just Porter, Mattie, and me trying to make it through another day. We had many tumultuous moments that involved crying, and many more beautiful moments, like coming across your gorgeous husband sleeping on the couch with your even more gorgeous baby girl asleep on his chest. The sight of Porter with Mattie nearly did me in every time.

But when Porter went back to work, it was a whole new ballgame for us girls. We had to adjust all over again to doing things on our own and sometimes Mattie wasn't fully cooperative. The first time I ventured out to the grocery store, just Mattie and me, I only came home with one third of what I needed because right in the middle of the store Mattie decided to get hungry and I didn't have the patience or experience to nurse her while I shopped. So we went home without our groceries, Mattie screaming the entire way.

Even though Porter worked more than a full day, he would always come home and help me. This was both incredibly helpful but also not surprising in the least. He had always been one to go the extra mile; he never did anything half way. So, when he would come home and simply take Mattie from me and tell me to go to bed, I always would, and I always told him 'thank you'.

I rolled over in bed one morning, hoping to see Porter's sleeping face, but was a little disappointed when I realized he wasn't there. I'd missed him again. He left for work so early and refused to wake me if I was sleeping, claiming that I needed sleep more than he needed a goodbye kiss. Some days I wouldn't argue with him – I'd take sleep over anything. But today, I missed him and wanted him in our bed.

I was appeased, however, by the sight of Mattie, softly snoring on his side of the bed. Laying in a fort of sorts Porter must have built around her, trying to keep her from rolling off the bed and prevent me from rolling onto her.

I watched her sleep for a moment, captivated by how much I loved her. After a few moments my hand reached out to gently brush her cheek and I was immediately caught by the heat radiating off of her. I sat up quickly and then placed the back of my hand on her forehead and again, gasped at how warm she was. But she wasn't just warm. She was hot.

"Mattie, sweetheart, what's the matter?" I asked softly as I lifted her and brought her forehead to my mouth, pressing my lips against her skin only to affirm that, yes, indeed, she was hot. Too hot. She stirred a little, as if I was bothering her, but she didn't wake up fully. I put her back down on the bed and as I undressed her, the idea being to cool her off, I tried to figure out what one was supposed to do with a three-week-old baby who had a fever.

She was just in her diaper now and I placed her back in her bed fort. I reached for my cell phone and immediately dialed the number for her pediatrician. When the receptionist answered, I explained the situation and she put me on with a nurse who I then explained the situation to again. All the while my hand kept going back to Mattie's forehead or arm or belly, wishing the fever away. Hoping that I'd feel her again and it would be gone, that I had been wrong all along.

The nurse listened to me and then asked some questions about when she'd eaten last and other baby things. I answered her and then my nerves took over when she finally gave me some instructions.

"The doctor is full this morning with appointments, but your baby needs to be seen soon. Can you take her to an urgent care facility?"

"You think it's urgent?"

"Yes, sweetie. When babies that young get fevers, it's urgent."

"Ok, yes, I can do that." I said the words, which for all intents and purposes were confident, but I sounded anything but. I sounded scared and worried, because I was. "Where should I take her?"

The nurse gave me directions to the nearest urgent care clinic and once I'd hung up the phone I did my best to dress without having a panic attack. I packed a bag for Mattie, although I could never have told you what was inside that bag. I pulled on some clothes, most of which I believe were clean, but I couldn't have told you which top I was wearing. My objective was to get my baby to the clinic.

Once we were in the car and headed to our destination, I pushed the button on the console that allowed me to make a call to Porter as I drove. He answered and I immediately heard the familiar sounds of construction: lots of banging and buzzing, sounds of men talking and shouting over equipment.

"Hey, Babe. How's it going?" He answered, sounding completely worry-free, which he was, but I called to end that.

"Mattie's sick," I blurted out, nearly crying as I said the words.

"What?" He asked, as if he hadn't heard me.

"The baby," I said louder. "She's sick."

"What do you mean sick?" He asked, sounding a little more worried than he had before.

"Sick enough that the nurse at her pediatrician's office told me to take her to urgent care."

"What's wrong with her?" He asked impatiently.

"I don't know, Porter!" I yelled and then began to cry. I tried not to lose control of my emotions, but I didn't have any more answers than he did, and I hated not knowing what was wrong with her.

"Ok, Baby, calm down. It's ok. Everything's going to be fine. Where are you taking her? I'll meet you."

I gave him the information and directions to the clinic and apologized for snapping at him. He told me I didn't need to apologize to him for anything and that just made me cry even harder.

When I arrived at the clinic, I parked hastily, grabbed her car seat out of the backseat and quickly walked inside. A woman with long brown hair saw me enter and met me halfway into the building.

"Is this Mattie Masters?" The woman asked me.

"Yes," I answered, trying not to cry in front of a stranger.

"Come back with me. The nurse called and told us to expect her, so we've got a room all ready."

"Thank you," I managed. I followed her and she led me to an examination room.

"Why don't you take her out and get her undressed."

I started taking her out of the car seat and undressing her, a little concerned when she hardly stirred.

"How'd she get that bump on her head?"

"It was a sub-dermal hematoma. It happened during birth. The doctors all said it would go away." She listened to me, but just nodded. I placed Mattie on the white paper which covered the examination table, the crinkling and crackling sound it made seemed loud and intrusive in the quiet room.

"Ok, let's see what's going on with this little girl." The nurse gently rolled Mattie to her side and pressed a stethoscope against her back, listening intently. I was afraid to breathe, afraid to move, afraid to blink even. She moved away after listening to a few different spots and put the stethoscope away, pulling out a different device I didn't recognize. She went to place it on Mattie's head and my hand shot out.

"Wait," I said loudly, halting the nurse. "What does that do?"

The nurse laid a hand over mine and gave me a few reassuring pats.

"I'm sorry to have frightened you. This is just a thermometer. I'm going to take her temperature." I watched as she rolled the thermometer over her forehead and ended up behind her ear. It was the strangest thermometer I'd ever seen.

"I'm sorry. I have never seen a thermometer like that. It just scared me a little. I'm sorry."

"You don't have to apologize, Sweetie. You're the momma. She's your baby. I'd be concerned if you *weren't* worried about her." She sighed when she looked at the tiny digital screen on the device. "Her temperature is higher than we'd like it though." She turned to the computer in the room and typed in some information then turned back to me.

"The doctor will be here in just a few minutes."

I nodded and picked Mattie back up, cradling her against my chest, slowly rocking her back and forth. She wasn't upset, wasn't crying, wasn't fussing at all. But I needed the comfort. I needed to hold her and press her against me, wanted her to feel me, know that I was there with her. A few tears fell down my cheeks, but I tried to keep it together.

When the door opened again, a woman wearing a white doctor's coat walked in and gave me a sympathetic smile.

"Hi, I'm Dr. Bailey. How is little miss Mattie doing today? Let's take a look." She reached for Mattie and took her from me, unwrapping the blanket from around her tiny body. I saw her press her fingers onto her skin and then pull them away. She did this a few times and then listened to her breathe just as the nurse had. After what seemed like a lifetime, she handed Mattie back to me.

"So, Mrs. Masters, here's what I'd like to see happen: We're going to have an ambulance take Mattie to the children's hospital at OHSU up in Portland. She has some sort of infection and it's important that we get her to the hospital as soon as possible."

My world stopped spinning.

"An ambulance?"

"Yes." She gestured towards the baby again and unwrapped the blanket from her. "You see how when I press on her skin, it turns white, but then when I pull away it takes a long time for the color to come back? That's not good. And with a baby her size and age, any fever is cause for concern."

"Will she be ok?"

"We need to get her to the hospital." Her refusal to answer my question only made me worry more. "There is a special pediatric ambulance service and I am going to give them a call. While we wait, I think we should try to draw some blood from Mattie to start investigating where the infection is."

"Take her blood?" My mind raced and even though I tried to keep up with everything happening around me, I couldn't catch my breath. I couldn't register what was happening. All I heard was infection and ambulance and Mattie. I squeezed her closer to me, afraid to let her go, afraid that once I handed her to someone else I might not get the chance to hold her again.

"We'll take good care of her. I promise you that." Dr. Bailey held her hands out, waiting for me to hand Mattie over, but I was frozen. "The ambulance will be here shortly. We don't have much time. I'm so sorry, but this is important." I looked up at her again, then back down to Mattie. I brought her tiny little body close to me again, pressed a kiss against her head, and then gave her to the doctor.

Dr. Bailey quickly took her and left the room, leaving the door open. I watched her leave and felt all the air leave my body. My hand came to my mouth and I felt a cry trying to escape, but nothing came – mouth open, tears welling in my eyes, lungs burning, but no sound.

How was any of this happening? She was perfectly healthy; we'd had no issues. My head started shaking and finally air seeped into my lungs. I gasped, panicking. I reached for my phone in my purse and called Porter.

"Hey," he answered on the first ring. "I'm almost there. The traffic from the beach was ridiculous."

I tried to answer him, to respond in some way, but nothing came from me aside from gasps of air.

"Ella, are you there?"

I let out a strangled sob.

"Oh, God, Ella what's wrong?"

"Porter," I whispered.

"Damn it, Ella! What's going on? Is Mattie all right?" He sounded just as afraid and broken as I felt.

"They took her from me."

"What do you mean?"

"They said they're taking her by ambulance to OHSU and that they needed to take some blood from her. They took her from me." Just then, I heard my baby cry from down the hall. It wasn't a hungry cry or a sleepy cry – both of which I was familiar with. This cry was something else entirely. It was painful. Something inside of me snapped and I ran out of the room towards the sound of her screams. When I reached the room she was in, I stopped outside of it, looking through the window, allowing me to see something I would never wish on another mother.

My baby was lying on a table, surrounded by nurses and doctors, some of which were holding down her arms and her legs. One woman was holding what looked like a warm compress on her hands, while another woman was trying to find a vein in Mattie's foot.

My mouth gaped open again, but this time the sobs came from me uninhibited, as I watched Mattie struggle against them. "Porter," I cried. "Our baby."

"I'm coming to you, just hang on."

"No," I said shaking my head. They're taking her to OHSU. Meet us there."

"Ella," he said angrily, but I knew he wasn't angry with me, he was angry because he wasn't with me, wasn't with Mattie.

"Porter, by the time you get here we'll be gone. I need you to be at the hospital. Please." I heard him sigh and then I heard what I thought was him hitting his hand against his steering wheel.

"I hate that hospital," he said quietly. My heart broke a little for him then too.

"I know, Babe. I know. Please though, meet us there?"

"I'm on my way."

"I love you."

"I love you both. Keep me updated if anything happens."

"I will. Drive safely."

I hung up the phone and returned my attention to Mattie, still crying, still struggling against the nurses. She was a tiny little fighter at nearly three weeks old. One of the nurses looked up and saw me through the window. She said something to another nurse and then came out into the hallway.

"Are you the mother?"

"Yes," I replied, not taking my eyes off of Mattie.

"Do you want to come with me to get a glass of water?"

My head snapped in her direction, immediately put on guard by her request.

"No. I'm fine right here."

"I know it's hard to watch, Sweetie. Let's just take a walk." She put her hand on my arm, gently trying to lead me away from the window, but I wouldn't budge.

"Your baby is fine," she said, trying to placate me.

"Her name is Mattie."

"Mattie is a strong little baby. Most babies that we see come here in her condition don't fight us at all. It's a good sign that she's crying. I know it hurts your heart, but it's a good sign."

I felt more tears welling up in my eyes at her words. Again, she placed her hand on my shoulder gently and turned me so my back was to the window. I allowed her to turn me, but wasn't going to move away from the window. The nurse then put her arms around me and started whispering in my ear.

"You have to be strong for her, Momma. If you're upset, it upsets her. I know it's scary right now, but trust that the doctor knows best how to take care of her and be strong for your baby." She pulled away and gave me a small smile. "I'm going to go get you some water."

I stood there as she walked away from me, watching her disappear down the hallway. I wondered if she had any children. I wondered how she would be reacting if it were her baby being poked and prodded in that examination room. I knew she was just trying to get me to calm down, but there was a smug part of me that gloried in the idea that very few people could truly understand what I was going through in that moment, and I'd be damned if someone was going to tell me how to react.

I turned back to the window, and saw that the nurses were trying now to get a needle into her hands where there'd been warmers on them. I made an instant decision and pushed the door open, walking past all the nurses and doctors and made my way to stand closest to Mattie's head.

I started by gently smoothing the baby-fine hair on her head and whispering to her.

"Mommy's here, Baby. I'm here, Sweetie." Mattie calmed almost immediately at my words, only letting out slight whimpers. I kept my voice soft and soothing, trying not to cry as I told her how much her daddy and I loved her. I just wanted her to know I was there. She hadn't been out of my sight since the moment she was born and I didn't feel like now, of all times, was when we should be separated. I watched the nurses give me strange looks, as if I'd crashed their party, but I didn't care. She was my baby and I was going to be with her, wherever she was.

For nearly ten more excruciating minutes I watched as the nurses failed miserably at trying to find one of her veins. She'd been poked in every available part of her body.

"Should we try the frontal vein?" One of the nurses asked the doctor. Before she could answer I interjected.

"What is that?"

"The vein that runs down the middle of the forehead," the nurse responded almost robotically.

"Absolutely not," I stated. "She's been poked enough for now."

"It really would benefit everyone if we got a line in," Dr. Bailey said, trying to convince me.

"Is it necessary?"

"She will need bloodwork, yes."

"No, I mean, is it necessary that you take her blood right here, right now? Is it vital?"

Dr. Bailey watched me closely, her lips pressed firmly together. Then I saw her shoulder relax. "No, it isn't vital."

"I want this whole procedure halted. Let her rest. They can try again at the hospital." I heard my voice and I sounded firm. I sounded like I was in control. It was exactly the opposite of what I was feeling. Dr. Bailey nodded and moved back, as did all the nurses in the room. I picked Mattie up and pressed her to me again, swaying back and forth. She started rooting around and I breathed a sigh of relief to see that she was hungry. "Would it be ok if everyone left so I could nurse her?"

"Sure," Dr. Bailey said softly. "I'll alert you when the pediatric ambulance gets here." After her words, she left along with everyone else, and I was left in a room with just Mattie and me.

"Sweet baby," I said as I situated her at my breast. I spent ten glorious minutes alone with her, cherishing what I considered might be our last quiet moments alone for quite a while. "I'm going to take care of you, Sweet Girl. I promise."

When I heard a soft knock on the door, I knew it was time to go. Mattie had fallen asleep as she ate and it hurt my heart to remove her from me. I tried to hold the tears back, but it was impossible. When the door opened, a softer Dr. Bailey stepped in and spoke quietly.

"The ambulance is here. You can either ride with them or you can follow behind."

"I'll ride with her."

She nodded and led me back to the original examination room and helped me pack and get everything together. When the EMTs showed up with a gurney, I tried again, unsuccessfully, to hold it together, but still a few tears managed to make trails down my face. I watched as they strapped her car seat to the gurney and then one of them nodded at me.

"Follow us," he said. And so I did.

We walked through the clinic and I felt like I was in a dream. I saw everyone's eyes follow the gurney, see the car seat on top, see my baby, and I felt their pitiful stares. I knew, if I'd just been a person in that waiting room and had seen a tiny baby being wheeled out on a gurney, it would have broken my heart. I would have looked at the mother and felt so sorry for her. I felt that. I felt people looking at me like the worst thing in the world was happening to me.

And it was.

I couldn't argue with their looks, couldn't even put on a brave smile. There was no bravery left in me. All I had to hold onto was hope. And even that was slipping away.

Chapter Sixteen

Porter

For the second time, I found myself racing toward the hospital on the hill. Much like the first trip, when Ella had been taken there after Jason Ramie shot her, I was panicked. The feelings of not being in control, not being informed, took over and I found it difficult to stay calm. My heart pounded, my chest ached, and my hands shook.

The difference this time was, even though I felt uninformed and lost, a new feeling came over me: terror. I was frantic when Ella was in the hospital, afraid I'd lost her before I'd ever even really had her. But I *had* Mattie. She was mine. The very thought of losing her, of her light being taken away from me, caused me to lose the air in my lungs.

My whole body shook with sobs. I cried harder than I ever had before. One hand on the steering wheel, one hand covering my mouth or wiping tears from my face – I was a mess. I didn't know what was wrong with Mattie, but if she was being taken by ambulance, I could only imagine that it was serious, and the unknown was the scariest and darkest place to be. My mind was full of images that were shredding me from the inside out. I imagined myself getting there too late, that she'd already be gone by the time I got there. Another sob racked my body as I imagined Ella having to deal with this all on her own. I prayed she wasn't alone, but I also harbored really hateful feelings towards anyone who was with Mattie and Ella right now as I was stuck in this godforsaken truck, alone, on the freeway.

My mind continued to torture me until I suddenly found myself parked at the hospital. I blinked, surprised that I hardly remembered the drive. I climbed out of the truck and walked into the emergency room. I stopped at the first desk I saw.

"My daughter was brought here by ambulance. Where can I find her? Mattie Masters."

"How old is your daughter?"

"Three weeks."

"Ok, she would have been taken to the pediatric ER." The woman gave me directions and I was off. I found the entrance and picked up the phone to get admittance. I told the person on the phone who I was, and who I was looking for. She told me the room number Mattie was in and the door next to me made a buzzing noise. I hung up and pushed through the door.

The hallway I entered was lit brightly with florescent lights and smelled exactly like a hospital should: stale, clean, and like chemicals. My eyes darted to the numbers next to the doors on each side of the hallway. I kept walking, forever it seemed, until I finally found the room I was looking for. I pushed the door open and what I saw nearly broke me.

My eyes first found Mattie, so small and so pale, cradled in Susan's lap. She had two sensors on her chest, wires coming from them connecting them to a machine that beeped rapidly. Her tiny, fragile hand was wrapped with something blue, and through it I could see another tube coming from her, and an I.V. that was attached to a bag of fluids. She was sleeping, but she looked different. She looked sick.

The next thing my eyes took in was Ella, standing in the corner of the room, facing the window, looking out over the river and the Portland skyline.

"Baby," I tried to say, but it came out a strangled whisper. She heard me and her head whipped around to find me and then we both lost our composure. She ran across the room to me, crying the instant her head met my chest. I cradled her against me, gripping her so tightly to my body, thankful to be together in this moment. "I got here as soon as I could," I said against the top of her head, my lips moving against her hair, my tears dropping into the blonde locks.

"Trust me," she said, still crying against me. "You didn't want to be around for what happened earlier." My body steeled at her words, fury raged through me, worried that she'd had to endure something terrible while I wasn't with them to help or to comfort. I held her, my hands rubbing up and down her back, trying to offer her anything I could, even though I knew in this moment there wasn't anything that could take away the fear I felt, which I was sure she felt deeper than even I did.

I loved Mattie, with everything that I was, but I could also concede that Ella loved Mattie in a way I could never understand. Ella's love for our baby wasn't better or worse than mine, it didn't take anything away from how I felt about my child, but the connection I witnessed between Ella and our daughter was inarguably the deepest tie I'd ever seen two people have to each other. It made me love Ella that much more.

After a few minutes of crying with each other, I pulled away and used my thumbs to wipe the tears away from Ella's face.

"What do we know? What's wrong with her?"

Ella shook her head. "They don't know yet. They think it's some sort of infection. They said babies her age don't get fevers unless it's an infection. They tried to take her blood at the clinic…" Her words cut off and new tears sprung from her eyes. "They couldn't get a vein, and Mattie was just crying, and I wasn't in the room." She leaned into me again. "I could hear her crying from down the hall. They took her from me and I wasn't with her." Hearing her words, feeling her body shaking against mine, broke my heart all over again. I knew it didn't compare, but if someone had tried to keep me away from Ella in the same position, I wouldn't have stood for it and I would have been just as broken as she sounded.

"Babe, it's ok." I tried to soothe her, but I knew what she'd experienced today was something she'd likely never forget. "You got her to the doctor and now the hospital, where they'll take care of her." I pressed a kiss against her temple. "You did everything right." She pulled away again, wiping her newly shed tears away and I turned to see Susan still holding my girl.

"May I?" I asked, motioning towards Mattie.

"Of course," Susan said automatically, smiling down at her granddaughter. She stood up slowly and let me take the chair, then gently laid my girl in my arms. When we got her all situated, being careful that none of the wires or tubes coming from her were tangled, Susan walked to Ella and wrapped her arms around her.

I tried to keep my eyes off of the pair of them, watching Ella cry was hard enough, but watching her cry into her mother's shoulder was another level of gut-wrenching. Instead, I focused on my angel, trying to make sure she was as comfortable as possible.

We waited an eternity, switching between me holding Mattie or Ella nursing and snuggling with her. I was relieved that Mattie would eat; surely that had to be a good sign. Nurses kept coming in and out of our room, checking her stats, making sure the tubes and wires were working properly, but then they would leave and offer us no news of what was actually wrong with her.

As the day went on, we all grew more and more anxious. All our family members were anxious to hear of Mattie's status, and due to hospital rules, no more visitors were allowed. The entire family came to a halt, waiting to find out what exactly was ailing Mattie.

Around five pm, a new person came into the room and gave us all sympathetic smiles.

"Hi, I'm Dr. Edwards." She reached her hand out to Susan and Ella, but smiled and gave me a polite nod as I held Mattie.

"We've gotten back the preliminary lab results for Mattie here and I'm afraid we are going to have to admit her." I watched Ella take in her words, process them as she nodded her head, and continue to look to the doctor for more information. "Mattie seems to have an infection in her kidney, her bladder, but most importantly, in her blood."

"How does a three week old get this sick?" Susan asked.

"It's pretty impossible to tell where the infections stems from. We just have to treat it fully and hope for the best." Dr. Edwards flipped open Mattie's chart and kept talking as she looked at the clipboard. "It also seems that one of our pediatric nurses might have heard a murmur in her heart, so we're going to check that out as well."

"What is the treatment for this infection?" I asked, still trying to process everything being told to us.

"We will need to administer aggressive antibiotics intravenously starting immediately."

"How long do you think she'll need to be here?" Ella's voice was sturdy and strong.

The doctor stood up straight and looked Ella right in the eyes.

"Unfortunately, Mattie is very sick. You're lucky you caught the infection when you did. Had you waited another day or two, this might be a very different conversation. However, she will still need treatment for a few weeks. She could be admitted to the children's hospital for anywhere from two to five weeks, depending on how she responds to treatment."

"Five weeks?" Susan stammered.

"I don't want to downplay the severity of the infection. A blood infection in a three-week-old baby is serious. If we don't treat it fully and entirely it could be devastating. The timeframe is just an estimate. We need to get Mattie on antibiotics as soon as possible. Then we need to see how she reacts to them and we'll go from there."

"When can we get the antibiotics started?" Ella's voice came from across the room and she sounded almost stoic.

"Just as soon as you sign these consent forms. We'll get the meds to her and transport her upstairs to the children's hospital."

Ella looked over at me, her eyes silently asking me what my thoughts were. I knew what she was thinking and I was on the same page. If they thought Mattie needed it, we would do it. I nodded at her and then looked down at Mattie still sleeping in my arms.

"What do I need to sign?" Ella walked towards the doctor and I knew she had it handled. I didn't move from my seat or look in their direction. I focused on Mattie and trusted Ella to get everything sorted out.

What came next was a flurry of activity as nurses came in and hooked Mattie's I.V. up with a second bag which contained the medicine the doctors were hoping would heal her. Dr. Edwards came back and listened to her heart again, speaking to the medical student that was now accompanying her.

"Ok," the doctor said with a sigh. "I did hear an abnormality, but I can't be sure it was a murmur. It could be nothing at all, and most likely is, but I want to take every precaution. I will schedule an echocardiogram. For now though, hang tight and when they are ready to take Mattie upstairs, someone will come and transport you all."

I walked over to the doctor and shook her hand, having missed the opportunity when we first met.

"Thank you, Doctor. I appreciate it."

"She's in good hands," she said before she nodded at Ella and Susan, then left the room.

Ella walked back to the hospital bed and gazed down at Mattie. "She's so small," she said quietly. The baby laid in the middle of the hospital bed, looking quite tiny against the big bed. I came up behind Ella and made sure her back was pressed up against my chest, offering her someone to lean on. Sure enough I felt her relax into me and I placed my hands on her shoulders.

"She may be tiny, but she's strong like her mother." Ella's hands came to cover my own and we stood there, watching Mattie sleep.

"It's funny because this is what babies do, right? They sleep. That's pretty much all she's done since she's been born. So why, now that I know she's sick, the more she sleeps the more nervous I am? What if the whole time she's been alive, she's been ill?" Ella's hands left mine and wrapped around her middle. "What kind of mother doesn't notice when her baby is sick?"

"Hey." I wrapped my arms around her chest, hugging her from behind, bringing her closer into me. "You *did* notice she was sick. That's how she got here. You've done everything right, Ella. Kids get sick, right?"

"No, kids get colds and the flu. Babies don't get blood infections, Porter."

"You can't beat yourself up over this, Babe. This could have happened to anyone. You heard the doctor, you brought her in at the right time. She's going to be fine."

"I know she is," she said softly, surprising me.

"You do?"

"She has to be."

I pressed a kiss against her temple because I couldn't argue with her.

Ella

Our new hospital room reminded me a lot of the room we'd spent two days in after Mattie was born. Same uncomfortable half-bed that was disguised as a bench seat. The same box TV hanging from the ceiling, same hospital smell. The only difference was that there wasn't a bed. There was a crib, but it actually resembled more of a cage. It was taller than me and really did become a cage if you raised up the only movable side all the way. It was everything we'd worked so hard to avoid at home. It was cold and hard and uncomfortable. It was stale and flat. It wasn't soothing and warm, or soft, or loving. It was clinical and it served a purpose.

My mother had been with us nearly all day, but when visiting hours were up, she had to go. She promised she'd be back in the morning and she promised she'd bring me coffee; her small way of trying to make this awful situation not as unbearable and I loved her for it. Porter went to grab us some dinner from the cafeteria and I was left alone with Mattie in another hospital room, but this time the happy baby haze was missing. I wasn't busy falling in love with a little person I'd just met. No, instead I was trying to think of any way I could help heal the little person I'd already fallen madly in love with.

I stood next to her crib, watching her breathe, obsessively making sure she took her next breath. I'm not sure exactly what I'd do if she stopped breathing, but I knew I'd be the first person to notice and find someone to help her. I had a contingency plan for almost any scenario I could think of. I would fix her if it was the last thing I did. I had to.

Slowly I watched as she started stretching, a normal baby thing to do. Only, she couldn't lift her right arm because it was wrapped so heavily with the gauzy fabric that kept her I.V. from coming out. It didn't seem to bother her that she was restrained – she'd spent nine months in a cramped belly, so I assumed she was used to it by now. Her little mouth opened in a toothless yawn and she was all gums. I gave a small laugh and a smile to see her be so babyish while experiencing something no baby should have to endure.

"Hi, Sweetie," I cooed at her, brushing the hair on her head with my hand, relishing in the feeling of her silky baby locks on my skin. "This is a pretty silly way to get my attention." I sniffled when I realized I had started to cry softly. I reached into her crib and started to unwrap her from her blanket, finding the diapers and wipes the nurse had supplied us with. "If you wanted some alone time, I could have sent Daddy to work on his boat." I continued to talk to her as I mindlessly changed her diaper, something that had become second nature to me now. When she was all changed and wrapped back up, I carefully picked her up, minding all her wires, and sat down in the one chair in the room to feed her.

"The problem with Daddy, though, is that he never takes no for an answer. You can try to send him away but he never really leaves. Once he's made up his mind, once he's decided to hang around and help you get your car started even though you tried to tell him time and again that you had it under control, well, Sweetie, he just never seems to give up." Her little fist was wrapped around my finger and I brought her sweet little hand to my mouth and pressed a kiss against her fingers. "If there's one thing I learned from your daddy, Mattie, it's that he always fights. Always. He sets his mind on something and he is persistent. He winds his way into your life and makes himself so vitally important to you that you forget that you ever were happy without him. That's exactly what you've done to me, Mattie. You've wiggled your cute little, tiny, baby butt right into my heart, and I'll be damned if I'm going to give you up without a fight."

I used her soft, pink blanket to wipe an errant tear that escaped. "So, you promise you're going to put up a fight and I promise I'm going to fight for you too. Okay?"

"Can I get in on this?" I turned to see Porter standing in the doorway, a tray full of cafeteria food in his hands. He put the tray down on the counter and walked over to us, kneeling next to our chair, and I watched in wonder as he bent down and kissed Mattie's head gently while I nursed her. The image took my breath away and had we not been in a hospital room, surrounded by beeping monitors and crib-cages, I might have thought it a wonderful moment. It was still memorable, but more so because it was sad, not the beautifully moving moment it would have been had it been experienced in our warm bed or in the rocking chair I purchased with exactly this moment in mind.

Suddenly, I was overwhelmed with everything, pushed over the edge by the polarity of the moments I was getting versus the moments I was promised.

"I can't lose her, Porter. I just can't."

"Shhh." He said, pulling my head down to rest on his shoulder. "We're not going to lose her, Baby. Like you said, we're going to fight with her and for her. She's going to get through this."

"How can you be so sure?"

He didn't answer me; he just kissed my forehead and kept us close to him. It didn't matter that he didn't answer my question, because I knew what he was thinking – It was the same answer I had running through my head all day.

She would get through this simply because she had to, because without her we both would simply fall to pieces.

Chapter Seventeen

Ella

The next twenty-four hours were filled with tension and aggravation. We woke up to find that Mattie's I.V. had come out, something that apparently happened with children a lot. I was, again, faced with watching people in white lab coats poke and prod her tiny hands and arms trying to find a vein. During the ordeal, our nurse came into the room and saw me crying into Porter's chest while Mattie lay crying in her crib.

"Hello, Ladies," our nurse, whose name tag read Melody, said to the lab assistants torturing my baby. "I think Wendy is on shift right now. Why don't I have her try?" Melody efficiently shooed the white-coated women out of the room and then wrapped Mattie back up in her blanket, picking her up. "Would you like to come with me?" She asked, looking at me.

"Where are you taking her?"

"We've got a nurse on the floor who use to work in the NICU. She's really good at finding tiny veins. She would be much better at this than the vascular access people. They don't often get to work on such small patients."

I nodded and wiped my tears, following her down the hallway. She found the nurse she was looking for and I followed them into a room that looked like it was used for storage more than anything else, but it had a bed in it and a very bright light. They chatted amongst themselves and I stood near Mattie's head, trying to just *be there*. I steeled myself, getting ready for more heartbreak as Wendy went near my baby. She spent what felt like forever inspecting

Mattie's arms, something the other white-coated women had never done.

"I think the left arm is the best bet," Wendy said, getting out the needle. I cringed as she went for Mattie, waiting for the crying to start, but I watched as she got it in with one poke and Mattie never made a peep. My eyes shot up to Wendy and Melody, shock filling them.

"I told you she was good," Melody said with a smile.

"I never want the people in the white coats to come near her again," I said, sounding more forceful than I had intended. It wasn't a request; it was a demand. Melody just smiled brightly at me.

"Not a problem," she said as she wrapped Mattie back up, placing her in my arms. "Let's get back to her room so we can get some more meds in her." As we walked back, I learned that Melody was a nursing student in her final year of nursing school.

For the rest of the day Melody was around, checking up on us and taking care of Mattie. Every time she came into the room, she was smiling and something about her made me feel better about our situation. She was so sweet to Mattie and that went a long way with me.

As the day wore on, Mattie napped and Porter and I wound up sharing the God-awful bench in the room, both trying unsuccessfully to get comfortable.

"I hate to say this," I sighed as I sat up, "but maybe you should go home and get some sleep." As much as I wanted him here with me, we needed to be realistic about this room. "We can't both sleep here tonight."

"How about we take shifts? I'll stay here tonight and tomorrow we can trade."

I looked over at him and I'm sure I had a wicked look on my face. "I'm not going anywhere, Porter."

"Babe, you have to go home at some point."

I couldn't help the immediate rage that came over me. "Porter, I'm not leaving this hospital unless Mattie is leaving with me. What makes you think I'd leave her here all alone?"

"She wouldn't be alone. I'd be here with her. If you stay here, you'll go crazy, locked in this room," he paused, carefully choosing his next words. "It's ok to leave her, Ella. It doesn't make you a bad mom if you need a break."

I stood up and walked across the room, needing some distance from him in that moment.

"She's three weeks old, Porter. Three weeks old. That's it. If I were at home with her, you wouldn't be asking me to leave her with you while I went to the grocery store. Where she goes, I go. I'm not leaving her."

I saw the moment understanding came over him, and I watched as regret washed over his face, softening his features. He sat up, his elbows resting on his knees, face in hands, with his brow furrowed as his thoughts, clearly written across his face, worked their way through his mind. As soon as I knew he understood where I was coming from, the anger seeped from me and I let it go. He wasn't trying to hurt me or force me to leave. He was just worried about me.

"I can handle this." I said softly, moving closer into him, letting my hand come to the back of his neck. I felt his hands cup the sides of my thighs as I stood in front of him. "This is supposed to be the time in our lives when we're connected all the time. I'm supposed to be with her twenty-four-seven. Just because it's inconvenient, and we happen to be in a hospital, it doesn't make me less of a mom. I'll be with her, here, until they release her."

"You know I'm just concerned about you," he said, pleading with me to understand his point of view, looking up at me with so much love in his eyes I felt a tug at my heart. "These aren't normal circumstances, Babe. This isn't you leaving her for thirty minutes to go run an errand. This is you and her, locked in a room, for who knows how long."

"I know. But this is what I signed up for. This is what being a mommy is all about. If she's here, so am I." Porter was silent for a moment, but I still took the opportunity to run my fingers through the hair at the nape of his neck. "There is, however, no reason for you to be here every night. This room was not made for two parents."

"So, let me get this straight," he said seriously, but with a small grin. "You get to stay here and play the Mommy of the Year role, and I get to go home and sleep in our comfortable bed all alone?"

I leaned down and pressed a long, gentle kiss to his forehead.

"You get to be Daddy of the Year for the rest of her life. Just trust that it would be impossible for me to leave her here."

"As you wish," he said, wrapping his arms around my waist, his head resting against my belly, silently asking for me to run my hand through his hair again; I knew how much he loved it. "So, I'm gonna go home then, and take some time to catch up on sleep and shower. I'll come back later this evening with an overnight bag for you. Anything in particular I can bring you?"

I tapped a finger against my chin, pretending to think really hard about his question.

"If you brought me a chocolate milkshake, I would love you forever," I said with a smile. My smile grew wider as I felt his hands travel around my waist and fall on my bottom. He pulled me against him with a playful gleam in his eyes.

"You were already going to love me forever, but I'll still bring you a milkshake," he said as he firmly yet gently tapped my ass.

"Of course you will," I teased.

We both heard the door open and I turned as Melody walked in, carrying a plastic tub and some more diapers. "Hi," she said sweetly. "Don't mind me, just checking some vitals." I left Porter and walked to the crib to watch Melody examine her. She took her temperature and listened to her heart.

I felt Porter come up behind me and kiss the back of my head. "I'm going to head out then." I leaned back into him and let him take my weight for a moment. He tapped my bottom again and then moved in to kiss Mattie on her head, minding Melody and her work.

"Bye, Princess. I'll be back later with a milkshake for your momma. You want one too? You're gonna have to talk to her about that." He stood up and winked and me. "I'll see you in a bit," he said, leaning in to press a small kiss against my mouth.

"Ok. I'll see you later." I watched him leave and then turned my attention back to Mattie. "Can't you just look at the screen to get her heart rate?" I asked curiously after she removed the stethoscope from her chest.

"Oh, I'm listening for the abnormality. Her heart rate has been stable since she was admitted."

"Can you hear it? The murmur?"

She looked around like she was afraid someone would hear her. "You know," she said as she whispered and leaned in closer to me. "I really can't." She smiled at me. "Not that I think they are making it up, but sometimes when babies this small come in, the doctors just really try to be thorough. I'm sure if Dr. Edwards said she heard something, she's just being thorough." Everything was quiet for a moment while Melody finished her examination.

"So," she said, drawing out the word. "Your husband is very sweet." I could see her trying to hide her smile and it made me smile in return. I was used to women fawning all over Porter. It was inevitable and it usually didn't bother me. I knew exactly what other women saw when they looked at him and I could appreciate it just as much as they could. Seeing Melody turn a pretty shade of pink as she blushed made me laugh out loud.

"He is very sweet. I'm a lucky lady."

"How did you two meet?" She asked, moving around the room trying to avoid eye contact.

"Oh," I said with a sigh. "It's a long story. I guess you could say his mother introduced us."

"Ah ha, well, if he has any younger brothers who don't mind overworked nursing students, I'd be happy to meet them."

I laughed out loud at her.

"Unfortunately, Porter is an only child. But my brother-in-law is closer to your age and he has brothers." I paused and smiled at her. "He's not as good looking as Porter, but he's easy enough on the eyes."

She laughed and our conversation moved on effortlessly as we stood in Mattie's hospital room, prepping to give her a bath. It occurred to me, five minutes later, that this was the first time in over twenty four hours that I didn't feel like my world could collapse around me at any moment. Something about Melody's sweet nature and ability to take my mind off of the very real trauma happening around me, lifted my spirits in a way that I would be forever grateful for.

We had just finished drying Mattie off and dressing her again when the door opened and another white-coated person walked in. My heart stopped and my eyes darted to Melody.

"Can I help you?" Melody asked, her voice firm, but polite.

"I'm here on orders from Dr. Edwards to get another blood draw."

My blood started pumping faster and I could feel the panic starting to come over me at the thought of another incompetent person poking Mattie.

"I very explicitly stated in the patient's chart that there were to be no more phlebotomists sent here to draw her blood. Tell me what you need and I'll make sure the lab gets it."

"Listen," the woman said to Melody. "I just go where the doctors tell me to go. You want to take care of this, be my guest. All the info is in her chart." She swiftly left the room, not looking our way again. I was still a little stunned that Melody had so easily and effortlessly put her in her place, that I hardly noticed when she picked up the phone.

"Hi, who's the nurse in charge up on your floor tonight?" She listened to the person on the phone and I saw her nod. "Great, can I speak with her?" A few moments later and someone else came onto the other side of the line. "Hi, Barb? Hey, it's me Melody down on the pediatric floor. Do you think you could come down here and help me with a special patient? We're trying to draw blood but she's a tiny little thing and we need some extra help." A few moments later Melody hung up the phone and turned back to me. "Barb is the charge nurse up in the NICU and she's going to come down and help. She'll be better at finding a vein and Mattie won't feel a thing."

I stared at Melody and even though my heart still pounded, coming down from the fear that I was going to have to watch my child be tortured again, I felt a warmth swarm it at the same time. This woman, who I didn't know more than a day, had just taken a situation that could have been terrible and eased all my fears. I wanted to hug her.

Words couldn't express how much I appreciated what she had just done for me and for my baby.

"You're incredible," I managed to whisper. "Thank you."

She waved a hand at me as she made some notes on the computer, as if she hadn't just done something for me that I'd remember forever. I knew, years from now when I told Mattie about the time she was rushed to the hospital when she was a tiny baby, I would tell her about Melody and how she fought the white-coated monsters for her. She was my hero in that moment.

I knew I didn't have the words to explain it, so I let her wave it away. I was still silently dumbfounded by the whole situation when Barb made it down to the room, cooing and fawning over my baby. Without one single cry from Mattie, they were able to get what they needed from her.

The following days were difficult. Every morning Mattie's I.V. came out and had to be put back in. Everyone on the floor was very understanding and always called the NICU for help. They took blood from Mattie every day, testing the blood for infection levels, measuring whether the antibiotics were doing their job. The good news, as Dr. Edwards let me know during her rounds on our fifth day there, was that since her first blood draw in the ER, the infection hadn't gotten any worse.

"You brought her in at just the right time, Mrs. Masters. This could have been a very different outcome if you hadn't noticed her fever. You did a good job," she said, smiling at me. "I'm going to order that she be taken off the heart monitor. She doesn't need it anymore."

"She doesn't?"

"No. The first few nights we wanted to monitor her heart because she was a very sick little girl and I wasn't sure how she would do on the antibiotics. But I'm confident she's on the road to recovery. I think she's out of the woods now."

Hearing the doctor tell me that she was essentially afraid Mattie's heart would stop in the middle of the night really scared me. I knew she was ill, but I'd never really stopped to think about the severity of everything going on. My mind had just been focused so fully on getting her better. I never let myself stop to think about the fact that I could have lost her.

"She was *very* sick, Mrs. Masters. I don't want to mislead you," Dr. Edwards said, placing a hand on my shoulder, obviously picking up on my sudden turn in mood. "But you've done a great job taking care of her. She's making remarkable progress. In fact, I think we can release her sooner than I originally anticipated."

"Really?" I was instantly uplifted. After days of feeling the heavy darkness looming over us, the uncertainty of what would happen, this was the first moment in which I felt like, just maybe, everything would be ok after all.

"Yes, but it's going to take a bit of work on your part."

"Anything. If Mattie needs it, I'll do anything."

"I thought so," Dr. Edwards said, smiling. "If we were to release Mattie later this week, she would still need up to two weeks of antibiotic treatment administered intravenously. So, in order to make that happen outside of the hospital, we would need to put in a PICC line."

"What is that?"

"It's essentially a flexible catheter we insert up the vein in the arm and thread it through to the opening of the ventricle of her heart. It's like a semi-permanent I.V. You can both administer drugs through the port and also draw blood from it, so she wouldn't need to be poked every time we needed blood from her and she can get her antibiotics. There also is virtually no chance of the PICC line coming out, like her I.V.'s have been."

"It goes into her heart?"

"No, not directly into it, we just thread it through until it is just above it."

"Can it get into her heart? That sounds dangerous."

"There's a very small probability of that happening, especially since she's a small and basically immobile child. Usually with older children we see problems with the line getting pulled out, by siblings or during play, but since she's just a baby, the risk is really low."

"Why has the duration of her stay changed so drastically? I thought we'd be here for weeks."

"We take the care of our patients very seriously, and our staff is trained to recognize parents who are capable and parents who need help. The nursing staff here has been really impressed with your attentiveness to Mattie, and if we didn't think you were capable of handling her care at home, I wouldn't even be having this conversation with you. That being said," she paused and gave me a small smile, "if you feel overwhelmed and would like for her to stay here while she completes the next two weeks of antibiotics, that's fine too. I don't want to send you home to fail at this, I want everyone to be happy and healthy. But think about it."

"When would this all happen?"

"Well, I'd like to get a PICC line in her regardless of whether you stay or go. So, if you agree, that could happen in the next few days. And as soon as the PICC line is in, I would feel comfortable releasing her."

My heart stuttered a little at her words. We could go home? I could take her home with me and we could just go back to being the little family I had spent nine months imagining?

"This is just one option, Mrs. Masters. Do not feel like you have to go this route."

"I need to talk to my husband about it."

"Of course. Talk about it with him, think about everything I've told you, and feel free to ask questions if they should arise." She paused for just a moment and smiled at me, her cheeks becoming pink and round under her eyes. "Regardless, Mattie is going to be just fine and if nothing else, that's something to celebrate."

Mattie is going to be just fine.

I'd never felt the physical release of tension in my body like I did in that moment. I sighed in relief and felt my shoulders sag with the weight being lifted off of them. My hand came to the base of my throat, resting on the part of my chest where my heart was beating rapidly beneath my skin, tears prickling in my eyes. My baby was going to be ok.

"Thank you, Dr. Edwards. I appreciate everything you've done for us so much. You have no idea."

"Well, you're welcome and I'm just glad to see this sweet girl leave here happy and healthy. Think about what we discussed and let me know. And still, just as a precaution, I am going to order her an echocardiogram today. I haven't heard the murmur in a day or two, so it might have just been something related to the infection, but I want to be sure."

"Of course. That's pretty straight forward right? Just like a sonogram?"

"Yes. They'll come down to you and she'll probably sleep through it," she said with another smile. "I'll let you know as soon as we get the results."

"Thank you."

Dr. Edwards left and I slumped down onto the stiff chair next to Mattie's crib, still trying to take all the information I'd been given.

Mattie.

Home.

Healthy.

It was a reality we'd been losing a grasp on for the last week and now it was back. Our girl could go home. I grabbed my phone and sent Porter a text.

When are you planning on coming to the hospital?

I'm on my way in just a few minutes. Need me to bring you anything in particular?

No. I just want you.

Good, cause I'm on my way.

I smiled to myself, thinking about the look on Porter's face when I got the chance to tell him the good news. My smile only lasted a few minutes until my mother showed up with Megan. I excitedly explained to both of them what Dr. Edwards had told me, that there was a way for me to take care of Mattie in the comfort of our own home.

Immediately I saw my mother's face contort into a look of fright.

"What is it, Mom?"

"Don't you think it would be safer for Mattie to stay here? Where the doctors are?"

I didn't answer her right away, because I couldn't quite nail down my reaction. Not only was I angry that my mother was questioning my ability to take care of my own child, I was also hurt that she didn't think I was capable. Megan, smartly, remained quiet in the corner, not interjecting with her opinion at all. I walked over to Mattie, picking her up, seeking the calming effect holding her usually had over me. I knew she could feel my tensions, so I forced myself to relax.

"I don't think they would let me take her home if it were dangerous." I tried not to let my words bite, but they came out sounding harsh and jagged.

"Well," my mother said with a huff. "I don't think I would trust myself to take a sick baby home. What if something went wrong? A catheter? Right next to her heart? Ella, that sounds dangerous."

Although the anger flared, suddenly I was overcome with insecurities. Was I putting my comfort above my baby's health? Did I want out of this hospital so desperately that I would risk my child's health to escape? Could taking her home harm her, and if so, how would I handle that? The high I felt from the doctor's words was hastily and hurriedly ripped out from under me, only to be replaced with a brand new low of self-doubt.

"Well, Mother, this is a decision for Porter and I to make together. Thank you for your unwavering confidence though." I felt the tears welling in my eyes and I knew I didn't want to cry in front of her, didn't want her to see that her blatant lack of belief in my capabilities as a mother. I turned away and quickly wiped a tear from my eye, hoping that neither her nor Megan noticed. A long and uncomfortable silence filled the room, stifling and filled with tension, broken finally by my mother's voice.

"I think I'm going to go to the cafeteria and grab a cup of coffee. Can I bring you anything, Ella?" Her voice was softer now and I thought I heard a small sliver of remorse in it, but I just shook my head, refusing to face her. "Megan?"

"I'm good, Mom."

I heard the door open and then close again, my breath rushing out of me as I let out a sigh filled with tension.

"She's only worried about Mattie," Megan said softly, obviously trying to smooth over the rift that was just put between my mother and me. I didn't want to say anything.

I didn't trust myself not to break into tears if I opened my mouth to speak. I felt like I was being held together by one single thread and at that moment the thread was being pulled in two different directions, promising to snap at any moment.

"So," she said loudly, trying to change the subject. "Something really strange happened at Poppy yesterday."

My head snapped around to look at her. I welcomed the distraction of discussing work. "Like what?"

"A man came in and said he was a private investigator, hired by Porter to look into the embezzlement."

"Oh." I knew Porter had mentioned hiring a P.I., but I hadn't really given it much thought. Life had gotten in the way of everything else. "What happened?"

"Well, since no one had told me about a private investigator, I called Porter just to confirm that the strange man was legit, but once he got the all-clear, he was really only interested in talking with the girls. I think he looked through some of the files on the computer, but I just kind of let him do his thing."

"He didn't ask you any questions?"

"Not really. He told me that Porter had told him I wasn't involved in any way and that unless I was helping him with information he needed, I wasn't to be bothered."

Of course Porter would protect my sister. "What did he ask the girls?"

"Only Brittany was there, Sarah had the day off, but she didn't have much to say about it." Megan shrugged her shoulders and gave me a helpless look.

I let out another sigh, trying not to let the stress of the situation rile me back up.

"I'm sorry if it was inconvenient for him to be there. We had talked about hiring someone, but with Mattie... we should have warned you."

"Oh please, don't worry about me. I want to know how He-Who-Shall-Not-Be-Named managed to take so much money from you too."

I gave her a smile, finding her snarky humor brought up my spirits when I needed it most. And then, as if the universe knew how much cheering up I really needed, the door opened and Porter stalked in. My face lit up at the sight of him, wanting him to wrap his arms around Mattie and me, taking away all the stress of the last hour.

"Hey, Babe," he said in greeting, but his voice sounded strained and worried. No, no, no. We didn't need any more bad news and I had a feeling that was exactly what he was bringing me. "Hey, Megan," he said, giving her a small and unconvincing smile.

"Hello, Porter. I met your friend the P.I. yesterday."

"Oh yeah? Did he come by Poppy?"

"Yup. Had a look around the office and chatted with Brittany for a few minutes."

"He didn't bother you, did he?"

She smiled at him, almost laughing. "No, I just showed him where the computer was."

"Good." He said with a nod, then turned back to me. "How are my two favorite ladies?" He walked towards us and pressed a kiss against my forehead and then leaned down doing the same to Mattie, effectively melting my heart. When would watching my husband interact with our baby cease to be a huge turn on?

"Well, we were doing really well until my mom got here and ruined everything." Porter's head turned as he looked back and forth between Megan and me.

"Don't look at me!" Megan said, holding her hands up in surrender. "I'm the only one here who isn't a parent so I refuse to have an opinion."

"What's going on?" Porter said, his face softer and concerned.

I took a deep breath and then launched into all the details that Dr. Edwards had given me and also my mother's less than positive response. I tried to keep to the facts and not let my emotions run away with me again, but I felt my face heating up and my eyes start to sting with tears again when I thought about how inadequate my mother had made me feel. I tried to wrap the story up quickly though, because I knew she would be coming back soon. Porter listened and watched me, taking Mattie from me halfway through, cradling her in the nook of his elbow.

When I had finished explaining the situation, Porter said nothing but reached into his back pocket pulling out his wallet. He held his hand out to Megan, urging her to take his wallet.

"Can you go get me something to drink from the cafeteria?" He asked her without taking his eyes off mine.

"Sure. But I don't need your wallet," she responded, standing up and stopping to press a kiss against Mattie's head before she left the room. Porter shook his head and put his wallet away.

"Now, Ella," Porter said, placing the baby down in the crib. "Tell me what's really bothering you." He came to stand right in front of me, his hands rested on my arms, sliding up and down, trying to soothe me.

I took a moment to compile my thoughts; I didn't want to just spew emotions all over him.

"I was really excited to take Mattie home and my mom just made me feel like I would be endangering her by taking her out of the hospital. As if I couldn't take care of her well enough on my own." So much for not spewing emotions. Tears made their way from my eyes and I found my voice shrill and shaky. I felt his hand come to the back of my neck, gripping me just slightly, pulling my head into his chest. His other hand found its way to the small of my back, his hand splayed over me, bringing me even closer in to him.

"Your mom is most likely just worried about Mattie." He took his hand from my neck and I immediately missed the warmth. He began to trail his fingers through my hair and I knew he was trying to calm me down. "You can't fault her for wanting the best for her grandbaby."

"I'm what's best for Mattie," I said with more conviction than I intended, but it was how I truly felt. I could take care of her. I knew I could.

"I agree," he said, his lips pressed against the top of my head. I exhaled against him, letting him take all the tension away. He was kind of magical that way. I wrapped my arms around his waist and moved my head back to look him in the eye.

"So you think we should take her home?" His opinion was vitally important to me and I knew that whatever he had to say would impact our decision on what to do from here. I wanted to know how he felt.

"I think that if the doctor thinks she would be fine with us in our home, then yes, I think we should do it. Will there be obstacles? Probably. But there has to be some setbacks to keeping a newborn in the hospital unnecessarily. Think of all the germs that she could be exposed to being in the hospital with other sick children."

I hadn't even thought about that part. He was right and I loved him even more for believing that together we could handle whatever was thrown our way.

"So, we take her home then?"

"I think so," he said, leaning down and pressing a small kiss to my lips. "Your mom has her opinion, but in the end we're Mattie's parents and we make the call. That's the beauty of having your own children, I suppose. It's our chance to mess up."

I laughed, realizing that he'd managed to make everything better just by holding and listening to me. The fact that he'd agreed with me was just icing on our proverbial cake. Also, there was the fact that not once since Mattie was born had he called me hormonal. I knew I was, any woman who had a baby and then stood by while they were taken by ambulance to the hospital was bound to be. But not once did he ever indicate that I wasn't entitled to any and every feeling I had. My hands wound their way up to link behind his neck and I pulled him down to me for a real kiss.

His lips pressed against mine and I sighed as his hands gripped my waist, pulling me against him again. His tongue skimmed the seam of my lips and I opened for him, eager to taste him, to feel connected to him in that way. Our tongues met and shivers ran through me as his slowly caressed mine. Fast and frenzied was incredible, but no one did slow and sensual like Porter. His hands slid up my sides, gliding over me, leaving a trail of goose bumps. When they finally made their way to my face, each hand cradled one side, his thumbs rubbing gently under my eyes. Suddenly, he tilted my face, angling my mouth just so. I heard him growl, felt the sound reverberate through his chest, as he took my mouth. My heart leapt, overpowered by the sudden need I felt coming from him. Slow and sensual turned into heated and heady.

My fingers threaded themselves through his silky hair, gently tugging him closer to me, only to be rewarded with another moan from him. I was on fire. The flames were building causing heat to pool between my legs. The kissing continued, never losing steam, never lacking intensity.

Eventually, when he finally pulled away, breathing heavy and very hard against my belly. He sighed and pressed small kisses along my neck.

"Two more weeks," he said against the sensitive skin below my ear.

"Until?" I asked, too caught up in the feeling of his lips against me to fully comprehend his words.

"Until I can bury myself in you again." His teeth nipped at my earlobe and I moaned, quite involuntarily.

"Mmm. You're a tease," I sighed. I frowned when I felt him pull away, but was turned on all over again when I saw how dark and full of lust his eyes were.

"Trust me, Ella. If we weren't in a hospital room right now, I'd be finding all kinds of alternative ways to use my mouth."

"Oh God. Please, don't say things like that," I said, pressing my forehead against his chest. I breathed his scent in, trying to come down from the high he'd given me. "How do you always smell so good? And always smell the same?"

"How's that?"

"Like wood, soap, and sexy as hell."

He laughed, his chest rumbling beneath me. I loved the sound of his laughter, especially when I was the one who caused it. His laughter died down and we stood there in each other's arms for a few minutes, both of us just watching Mattie sleep.

"So," I heard him say hesitantly. I leaned back and looked up at him.

"So, what?"

"I got a call from our lawyer this morning."

"And?"

His hand came up and he ran the back of his fingers over my cheek, obviously trying to lessen the blow of whatever he was going to tell me.

"They moved the trial up."

"Ok…"

"It starts tomorrow." My stomach dropped and my eyes widened. "If you still plan on testifying, you have to be there."

"But, Mattie…"

"I know…"

"I can't leave her…" My head shook back and forth feverishly.

"Shh…" he said, pulling me against him again.

"Porter, I can't leave her."

"You don't have to."

I did though. If I wanted to make sure Jason Ramie was put in jail, if I wanted my chance to tell him and a jury exactly what he'd done to me, I would have to leave her.

"What am I going to do?"

"You're going to do whatever you're comfortable with and I'll support you either way."

The door to the hospital room opened and Megan and my mother walked back in. Both of them stopped in their tracks when they saw us, clearly noticing something was wrong.

"Oh, Ella. I didn't mean to upset you," my mother said walking to me, obviously thinking I was still upset over our argument. She placed her hand on my back and I turned to her, wrapping my arms around her, suddenly needing the comfort of my mother, regardless of how angry I had been with her just ten minutes ago. I cried into her shoulder as Porter explained the situation. All the while I felt my mother's hands rubbing up and down my back, continually calming me, letting me know she was there for me.

"Fella, whatever you need, just let us know." Megan's voice was soft from across the room and I gave her a weak smile over my mother's shoulder.

"Truly, Ella. If you want us to stay with her while you go to the trial, we'll be here, no matter what. Or if you just want us to help you while you're here, we'll do that. And if you decide to take her home, like the doctors said, I'll help you with that too. Anything, Ella." My mother's voice was filled with emotion and I knew she was apologizing for what had happened earlier.

"Thank you, Mom." I pulled away and wiped my eyes, feeling like the breakdown had passed for the moment. I looked to Porter and saw his eyes trying to gauge what I was thinking. My eyes drifted to Mattie next and I took in a deep breath and let it out loudly.

I spent the next few hours just holding Mattie, rocking back and forth in the uncomfortable chair the hospital provided, nursing her, kissing her, feeling her satiny hair beneath my fingers. I listened to Porter interact with my family and I tried to add a word in every once in a while, but I was busy loving on my daughter. No one seemed to notice or mind. Eventually my mother and sister left, kissing us both and giving Porter hugs, telling him to let them know what I decided to do.

Chapter Eighteen

Ella

Sometime that evening, as I held Mattie in my arms and spoke to her about little lambs and curds and whey, the door slowly creaked open and I was surprised to see Brittany poke her head into the room. Her face was painted with hesitation and worry, instantly setting off my internal alarm – something was wrong.

"Hi, Brittany, come in," I said quietly, not wanting to wake Mattie. Porter stood and opened the door all the way for her and she shyly made her way into the room. When she made it fully in I saw that she carried a bouquet of colorful wildflowers. She set them down on the counter and twisted the vase so that the most beautiful and colorful flowers faced us.

"I wanted to come and see how Mattie was doing," she said timidly. My eyes flitted downward and I noticed her hands were trembling. Something wasn't right. Brittany took the few steps that brought her right next to me and she looked down upon Mattie and a smile grew wide across her face. "She's so beautiful. Is she going to be ok?"

I nodded and looked down at her as well. "The doctors say she's through the worst of it and can go home soon."

"That's fantastic," Brittany said, but her voice didn't match the sentiment. Tears welled and she trembled.

"Why don't you sit down," I said, standing up and offering her my chair which she took quickly. "Porter can you go and get her some water?" He was up and heading towards the door instantly.

"No, wait, he should be here for this too," Brittany said, halting him.

"You're scaring me, Brittany. What's going on?" She took a few deep breaths in and out, seemingly trying to calm herself down enough to speak. My eyes met Porter's and I knew he was just as confused as I was.

"I remember when I first started at Poppy," she started, with a trembling voice. She looked down at her hands, wrung them together, still giving me no reason to calm down. "I remember thinking that I was so lucky. I got this amazing job working for this incredible woman who was everything I wanted to be." She looked up at me then, tears falling down her cheeks. "A few weeks after I started this awesome job I met this awesome guy. He was so sweet and attentive, always calling and texting, I thought I'd hit some sort of jackpot. First the perfect job, then the perfect boyfriend." She sniffled and wiped her nose on the sleeve of her jacket, emotions leaving no room for politeness or manners. Her eyes locked on mine and she looked at me with so much hurt and found myself close to tears just to see her that way.

"When our relationship became physical, I spent many nights wondering what the catch was. The other shoe had to drop at some point, right? Things were too perfect."

Porter shuffled on his feet, obviously uncomfortable listening to Brittany talk about her sex life. "I'm going to take a walk," he said gently.

"No, I'm really sorry Porter, but it's important that you stay."

He looked at me with wide eyes, silently begging for me to rescue him. I shook my head slightly and motioned for him to stay.

"His name was Bobby and he was wonderful. We dated for over six months before we slept together. He travelled frequently for his job so when we could see each other it wasn't usually for a long period of time and he was always coming and going. In all that time he never once pressured me. He was so patient and kind. And when we finally did sleep together, it was wonderful. I felt like he really loved me."

She began to fully cry and I handed her the small box of Kleenex from the end table.

"I'm sorry. I've never told anyone this before."

"Brittany, it's ok. Take your time. We're not going anywhere."

She took a few steadying breaths and then trudged forward.

"When he asked me to let him take pictures of me naked, it caught me off guard, but I didn't say no right away." She shrugged and then shook her head, obviously having an argument with herself in her mind. It seemed as though she's had this discussion with herself a few times. "Lots of people let their boyfriends take pictures of them, right? My first instinct was to say no, because, well, it's a naked picture. But I didn't want him to be angry with me and I wanted to make him happy. I wanted him to want me."

At that point I stood and brought the baby to Porter and then returned to Brittany, placing my hand on her, trying to convey that I wasn't judging her. She was neither the first or last young woman to let her boyfriend take naked pictures of them.

"I eventually let him take the photos and I won't lie, part of me liked how much he seemed to enjoy them. After a few weeks I had grown accustomed to him taking the pictures of me, but when he then asked to take pictures of us *during* sex, I was surprised."

Porter was visibly uncomfortable with what he was hearing and he turned his back to us, trying to give her as much privacy as possible. I could feel the tension coming from him.

"He was really persistent and had strong arguments. He kept asking what the difference was between naked pictures and sex pictures? If I trusted him with one I shouldn't be bothered by the other." She cried still, her words chopped up by sobs and sniffles. "I couldn't answer him," she said with a twinge of panic. "I'd already let him violate me, what was the difference?" She shook her head and I squeezed her hand, hurting for her, wanting to tell her that it was wrong of him to put her in that position.

"When I finally relented, he seemed so pleased with me. The pictures, to me, were disgusting. I didn't like looking at them, but he seemed to like taking them. I always asked him to erase them and sometimes he would, but I knew sometimes he kept them."

She was quiet for a few moments. Then she seemed to gain some strength and continued.

"He became more demanding and even though I wasn't happy anymore, I thought perhaps if I did everything he asked he would become the man I had originally fallen for.

If I could just make him happy…" She trailed off and my heart broke for her. I started thinking back to the first year when she worked at Poppy with me and I couldn't think of any time when I noticed she had been unhappy. Could she have been going through something this traumatizing without me having even noticed that something was wrong?

"The first time he ever took a video of us having sex, he said it was an accident."

Her words were cold and removed and my heart broke in half for her.

"He said he had been trying to take a picture, but it had been on video by mistake. Immediately, I panicked. I grabbed for his phone and tried to make him erase it and he backhanded me. In that moment I knew the first Bobby I met, the man who cared for me and was sweet and kind was never coming back. He said that the video wasn't a big deal and that he already had pictures, so what was I so upset about?" She looked at me like I might have an answer for her, but I was in shock and couldn't help but feel disgusted for her, terrified for her. "This went on for a few more weeks. He would make me have sex with him, lording the video over me, threatening to post it on the internet, email it to my parents, basically anything he could think of to hurt me, he used it against me."

Brittany raised her eyes to mine and a new sadness had taken over, remorse and regret filled her to the brim and I ached for her. "I'll never forget the first time Bobby walked into Poppy. I panicked because he'd never come into my work before and I was afraid he was there to out me, to show my employer these disgusting videos and photos I'd *let* him take of me. And you can imagine my horror when you walked right up to him, kissed him on the cheek, and called him Kyle."

My brain started piecing things together, started connecting all the dots she'd so bravely laid out for me.

"What?" I whispered.

"Yeah," she said, so nonchalantly, wiping tears from her eyes. "I had been sleeping with your boyfriend. Not just sleeping with him though, making sex videos with him. I was shattered. I was completely disgusted with myself."

I looked to Porter whose jaw was tense and clenching and I knew that if Kyle wasn't already dead, he'd be on a rampage right now looking for him.

"Why didn't you tell me?"

"I couldn't! That day he came in to Poppy, he was taking you to lunch and when you went in the back to get your coat, he told me that if I said anything to anyone he would release everything." She paused and took in a shuddering breath. "That's also how he forced me to steal all that money from you."

My heart stopped and my breath was stuck in my throat. In the corner of my eye I saw Porter place Mattie in her crib and start pacing the room, back and forth.

"I'm so sorry, Ella. I never meant to do any of this and if I could go back and change everything I would. I just didn't know what to do. For so long, years, he had a thumb over me, taunting me with the videos, telling me he'd post them all over the internet and my future would be ruined. A few times I almost refused, almost let him follow through with his threats. There were other times I also thought about ending it all. I just wanted to be that carefree, fun, happy girl I use to be, ya know?"

"Oh my God, Brittany, I can't believe he did that to you," I whispered. Even after everything I'd been through with Kyle, learning the depths and lengths his evilness spanned was always still surprising. I wouldn't put any of this past him, but still found it hard to believe that someone I'd wasted so much of my time on could even think of pulling something like this off.

"When I heard that you'd killed him, that you had shot him dead, that was the most wonderful moment of my life, and that alone made me so sad. The idea that the death of someone gave me some sort of freedom, well, that really messed with my mind. But I couldn't get over the happiness. Finally, I thought, finally it's over." She sniffed again, wiping her nose on a kleenex.

"But then the private investigator came into the store and I knew I either had to tell someone, or I was going to be found out." A new wave of panic moved over her and I watched as she simply fell apart.

"I'm so sorry, Ella. Oh my God, I'm so sorry. I would never have stolen from you – not in a million years. I know what you must think of me and…"

"Brittany, don't say another word." Porter's voice was loud and firm from across the room. He walked over and knelt in front of her. "If this is the true story, if he really did this to you, and I don't have one tiny sliver of doubt that he did, you need to talk to the police. Ella and I, of all people, understand that Kyle was by far the worst person that ever walked this earth, and I am so sorry that he did that to you. It wasn't your fault and we could never place blame with you. But you have to tell this to a detective."

She nodded, sniffling at the same time. "I know. I just wanted Ella to hear my side of the story before I turned myself in."

"What do you mean turn yourself in?" I asked, finding my voice suddenly concerned with what she was planning to do.

"I'm going to the police station to tell them what I've done."

"You mean what you were coerced and blackmailed into doing?" All of a sudden I was filled with rage that Kyle had tried to ruin someone else's life. However mad I was, I was even sadder knowing he had probably succeeded a little with Brittany. Even from the grave he was still causing pain. "Brittany, there is no active investigation right now about the missing money. We hired a P.I. because we were curious as to how he did it. But no one is looking to press charges against you. You did nothing wrong." Brittany looked at the ground and nodded her head, but she still looked defeated. I couldn't imagine what she was thinking, or the bravery it took for her to come here and tell her story. "You'll go to the police station, Brittany, but not to turn yourself in, to give a statement, to aid them, perhaps, but that is all."

Porter reinstated his purposeful march across the room, angry steps leaving angry thumps in their wake. Mattie slept peacefully as years of drama unfolded around her. I watched Brittany and she looked down to her lap and cried, softly mumbling how she never meant to hurt anyone.

We were all better off now that he was dead.

It was a harsh statement. It was also a true statement. He hurt more people than he helped. If I hadn't defended myself last year, if I hadn't killed him, not only would I be dead, but he'd still be hurting other people. Brittany might still be under his thumb. For the first time in maybe ever, the guilt over killing another person wasn't weighing so heavily down on me.

Once she'd quieted down and pulled herself together a little bit more, Brittany stood and made to leave. I hugged her and tried to remind her that none of this was her fault, that what he had done was wrong. She nodded at my words, but I knew she wasn't agreeing with me. It would probably take her a very long time to accept that fact, but I hoped that someday she would. She told me she would go to the police station straight from the hospital and I gave her Dillard's name, telling her to only talk to him. I hugged her again and then watched her walk out of the room.

My eyes found Porter and they were wide, my mouth hanging open a little, completely and totally shocked at what the last hour of our lives had left us with.

"Can you believe any of that?" I asked him, hoping he was just as shocked as I was.

"I know I've said this before, but he's lucky he's dead already, because otherwise I'd find him and finish him off myself. What a worthless waste of a human being."

"He seemed so normal…"

"Yeah, well, if all the crazy douchebags of the world would wear neon flashing signs around their necks warning us all, the world would be a better place."

I had to laugh at the image of Kyle with a sign hanging from his neck flashing the words "Deranged Psychopath". I let out a sigh, finding that all the day's events were finally catching up and finding me exhausted.

"Have you thought about what you're going to do tomorrow?" His voice was light and concerned all at the same time. I could feel his need to protect me as a physical force, his need to keep me safe wafting over me. I nodded and met his eyes.

"I'm going to go to the trial."

He nodded, silently, then ventured another question.

"And you trust your mom enough to leave Mattie here with her?"

I shrugged. "I don't know if I trust my mom, or sister, or Kalli, or anyone enough to be here with Mattie without me. But it doesn't matter, because the only other person on the planet I'd leave her with is going to be here with her – you."

His eyes grew wide in surprise and he took a few steps towards me. I kept my face still, not letting my feelings show as he moved closer to me. I'd seen Porter get worked up quite a few times since we'd been together, and I knew he would never hurt me, but this was fury I'd never seen Porter direct at me before.

"You're crazy if you think I'm going to let you testify tomorrow, even be in the same room as that poor excuse for a man, without me." His finger was pointed angrily at me, his voice was firm and furious, and his eyes were wild. He was really scared. And I knew he would be. This was exactly the reaction I was expecting from him. Even though I knew he was furious, it made me smile.

"Porter, the only place I *need* you tomorrow, is here, with our baby." I stood up and walked to him, taking his hand in mine and wrapping his arms around my waist. "I have no doubt that I can testify tomorrow, on my own, just fine. And I would love it if you could be there with me, holding my hand, and offering me sweet words of comfort, just like I know you would. But I *need* to know that Mattie isn't alone, isn't sensing that we're both gone and wondering where we've went. That would hurt me more than anything. So you need to stay here. Can you do that for me?"

He grunted.

"The idea that he'll have his eyes on you, that he'll even be breathing in the same room as you makes my skin crawl, Ella. I don't think I'll be able to handle knowing you're there without me."

"We've been dealt some pretty shitty cards, Babe. Trust me, I'd be the first to tell anyone that when it comes to us, our relationship, and our lives, we've fought more battles than I think necessary. But I'd fight them all over again for our little girl. That's what tomorrow will be for me: a battle. But I can win this one, Porter. I can walk in that courtroom and I can put him away. I will. And on top of all of that, the part that makes me almost excited to fight that battle, is that I feel like I can do it on my own."

I leaned into him, resting my forehead against his chest, soaking up every ounce of calm that being near him offered. "I'm finally strong enough to fight this on my own. I need you for so many things, Porter. I need you to love me, and make me laugh, and be a father to our child, and comfort me, and to build me beautiful houses, and to take me on picnics." I looked up at him, using my eyes to beg him to trust me in this. "But tomorrow, I can fight that battle by myself. In fact, I need to. I want to. And I'm going to win." He used one of his big, strong, callused hands to sweep my hair behind my ear, and then his gentle hand cupped the side of my face.

"I'm so proud of you," he whispered, his words caressing my face, opening up my soul, and hiding inside my heart. He pulled me into him again and I smiled against his chest. I felt his hand drop to the small of my back while the other cradled my head against him. I breathed him in again, loving what his embrace could do to me. "I am *so* proud of you," he repeated, even quieter and closer to my ear. Only I could hear him. I felt as if it were a gift he was giving me. His pride. There were a few things I knew in life to be true – undoubtedly, one-hundred-percent, absolute truths. I knew that Porter loved me. I knew that we were supposed to be together. I knew that Mattie was destined, fated, to be ours, just waiting in the wings for her cue to arrive. I knew he supported me, wanted me, cherished me, and appreciated me. But to hear him say he was *proud* of me was fulfilling in a soul-lifting kind of way.

I took his praise and I felt it inside of me, lighting me up. But his sentiment only mirrored what I already felt inside.

I was proud of myself.

We both knew that a year ago I would have been reduced to a puddle of panicked goo on the floor with even the idea of being in a room with my shooter, testifying against him. I would have needed Porter and possibly medication to get myself through that event. But today I was confident that I would handle everything capably. Would it be difficult? Yes. Might I be uncomfortable? Probably. But I knew that, even if I panicked a little, I could work through it. Testifying against him was important enough to me.

I sighed against him and again felt the exhaustion of the day. All the ups and downs and revelations dragging the energy right from me. I brought my hand up to cover a yawn and felt Porter still running his hands through my hair.

"So will you do me a favor and show up here really early tomorrow so I have time to go home and get ready before I have to be in court?"

"I'll do you one better. How about we share this God-awful excuse for a bed they've given us and you spend the night cramped up against me?"

I smiled up at him, unable to imagine anything better.

Chapter Nineteen

Ella

Leaving the hospital the next morning couldn't have been more difficult. I got up early then broke every parenting book's rule and woke up my sleeping baby simply to nurse her. I desperately needed that connection to her before I walked out that door. It did occur to me that I was being overly dramatic and emotional, but I was only four weeks post-partum and leaving my new baby in a hospital to testify against the man who tried to kill me. So, the emotions were warranted I supposed.

Porter laid on his uncomfortable bench/bed, elbow bent, hand propping up his head of sexily rumpled hair, and watched me cuddle Mattie as I fed her, telling her how much I loved her and that I would be back before she knew I was even missing. I wiped a few tears away, trying not to cry, wanting to be strong.

Porter confided that he was secretly looking forward to feeding her a bottle for the first time and then I broke down at the thought of missing it. Eventually, I knew I was delaying the inevitable and needed to leave. I kissed Mattie and let Porter kiss me senseless and tell me he loved me more than anything.

I left my little family behind and walked down the hall, through the hospital, and out the doors, crying the entire way. As soon as I found where Porter had left my car, I got inside and forced myself to calm down. I told myself repeatedly that Mattie would be fine, that she probably wouldn't even notice I was gone. I dried my eyes and took a few deep breaths.

The day from here on out would be taxing and I had to prepare myself for a different kind of emotional drainage.

One thing I did find some unexpected joy in was dressing for court. It had been months since I'd worn anything besides maternity clothes and yoga pants. I found myself smiling when I realized I could take more than a two and a half minute shower because Mattie wasn't in her bouncy chair right outside the door. I took advantage of my aloneness in that moment and took the shower I'd been dreaming about for a month: long, hot, soapy, and quiet.

I found a gray pencil skirt made of a fabric that had a little stretch, accommodating the part of my belly that hadn't gotten the message that I wasn't still pregnant, and paired it with a soft lavender button up shirt. I marveled at the fact that my feet fit back into my high heels, and even remembered how to put my hair in a French twist. Putting makeup on was like riding a bike, like I hadn't missed a beat.

When I was all ready I looked in the mirror and couldn't help but smile. I looked pretty damn good. It wasn't the same body I'd had a year ago, a had a few curves that were slightly bigger, but I still liked what I saw. I liked it enough to snap a picture on my phone and send it to my husband.

Not too shabby, huh?

I smiled, knowing he'd like it.

I headed back into Portland, grabbing a coffee which I desperately needed as it had already been a full day, but it was really only seven am at that point.

When I made it to the courthouse, I was focused on maintaining the outer appearance of being calm, when on the inside I was positively frightened. I thought that if I could at least convince the people walking on the street next to me that I was calm, cool, and collected, it would somehow become true. I turned to start the haul up the tall stairs that led to the entrance of the courthouse and heard the unmistakable sound of my sister's voice.

"Hot damn, Fella! There's no way you had a baby a month ago!"

I looked up, surprised and truly amazed to see Megan and Kalli waiting at the top of the stairs, both smiling down at me.

"What are you guys doing here?" I asked as I made my way to them. At the top of the stairs, I hugged them both, instantly grateful for their surprise appearance.

"You don't think we'd let you do this alone, do you?" Kalli said, smiling and running her hand down my arm in support. Blame it on having a new baby, blame it on her schedule, blame it on a million things, but I hadn't seen Kalli since the day we brought Mattie home from the hospital. I didn't realize it until that moment, but I had missed her terribly. When Mattie had been taken back to the hospital last week, Kalli had been out of state working, but called and texted us daily, checking in, being as present as she could be.

"I guess that was a stupid assumption on my part," I laughed. "Where's Mom and Dad?" I asked, looking to Megs.

"They're at the hospital with Porter. We wanted to split our support. Dad might show up here after lunch," she shrugged. "Depends on Mom."

I gave Megan a strange look. "What's up with Mom?"

"She's torn. She wants to be here for you, but she's not sure she could sit and listen to you tell the story of how you almost died. Plus she's worried about Mattie. She's just being a mom, I guess," she said almost flippantly, trying to downplay Mom's emotions. Megan didn't realize now that I was a mom, I could understand Mom's dilemma.

"Well, I'll be fine, so Mom should stay with Mattie."

Megan smiled. "I'll let her know."

We walked into the building and continued through metal detectors and had our bags searched. My lawyer was waiting for me and approached me as soon as I made my way to the courtroom.

"Good morning, Mrs. Masters. I'm glad you decided to be here. I know it was a sacrifice for you and short notice. These things happen." He reached out to shake my hand, giving me a rough smile.

"Let's just hope it's not all in vain, Mr. Donaldson."

"Surely not. Here is how the day will look. Trial starts at nine, we have opening statements, and then we will begin presenting evidence. We have a few witnesses, you included, and the defense has the opportunity to cross examine every one. When we're all through with the prosecution, it will be the defense's turn to present. They, too, will more than likely call you as a witness and then I will have the opportunity to cross examine."

"Do you think Jason Ramie will testify?" I asked, suddenly curious if I was going to be gifted with his side of the story.

"If his attorney is smart, no."

I felt a little deflated at his answer. I wanted to hear what he had to say, how he planned on explaining away his guilt. "How long do you expect the trial to last?"

"Depends on a number of factors. If the evidence is presented concisely and the defense is prepared, we could wrap up the first part of the trial today. What could take the longest is the jury's deliberation. It's really anyone's guess when it comes to jurors."

I must have looked worried because he placed a hand on my shoulder and gave it a short squeeze before dropping it. "Once both sides have rested, you won't be needed any more. After you've been questioned by the defense you will be free to go. But you're welcome to stay if you'd like."

"I suppose I'll wait and see how I feel." I leaned closer in to him, dropping my voice to a whisper, not wanting everyone in the hallway of the busy courtroom hallway to hear my next question. "How do you suggest I deal with pumping?" I tapped the black bag hanging from my shoulder containing my breast pump. I would give up nursing my daughter for the day to be here, but I wouldn't risk losing the ability to nurse all together.

Mr. Donaldson didn't miss a beat and answered my question with the same professionalism, which I couldn't have been more thankful for.

"I've made the judge aware of your needs and she's agreed to recess the court every two hours to allow you the time you need."

I raised my eyebrows in surprise. I looked to Megan and Kalli and they were smiling back at me. So far, this was all sounding doable. Mr. Donaldson excused himself from us, promising to return closer to nine. I turned to the girls and we stood in the hallway chatting, waiting for the trial to begin. I pulled my phone from my purse, hoping to check in with Porter before I was unavailable for who knew how long. I saw I had a few messages from him and I immediately panicked, furiously clicking on the screen to get to the messages that I was sure were going to inform me that something terrible had happened in my absence.

Hey Hot Momma ;)

His response to my picture made me smile and blush a little, finding myself a little more than glad that he found me attractive. The other messages were simply pictures and if I were being honest with myself, they were the most adorable pictures that would not have ever been taken had I not left Mattie alone with her daddy. The first was Mattie wearing the University of Oregon baseball cap that Porter sometimes wore to work when it was hot outside. It was huge on her, obviously, but ridiculously cute. The next photo was of her, still wearing the baseball cap, with the television remote rigged to look like she was holding it. It came with the text,

Taking after Daddy already.

I laughed at the picture and the caption, mostly because it was funny, but also because the implication that Porter ever really just sat around and watched TV was laughable.

Adorable. Enjoy your daddy and daughter bonding time. Mr. Donaldson thinks I could be done with the trial today if everything goes well. I'll keep you updated.*

Kalli and Megan did their best to keep me occupied until it was time to go into the courtroom, but I was too anxious to appreciate their efforts or laugh at their jokes. I gave them a few smiles when I thought it was appropriate, but my mind was meandering between my testimony and my family back at the hospital.

When it was finally time to head into the courtroom, Mr. Donaldson indicated for me to take a seat behind his table to the left of the aisle. I was flanked by support, Megan on my right and Kalli on my left. The courtroom was surprisingly empty. I don't know who I expected to be there, but it definitely wasn't the media filled circus that my overactive imagination had whipped up. A few minutes later, Dr. Andrews from OHSU and Dr. Evans, my psychiatrist, both came in, and a moment after that Detective Dillard entered, talking with the head investigator from Lincoln City. All four took seats on the same side of the room as me. It was weird seeing them all together like this, as if my life for the last two years was sitting here, getting ready for a replay. Although, the most important people, Porter and Mattie, were noticeably absent.

On the other side of the aisle sat a woman and a man, both who looked to be in their forties. There was one other person there, seated behind the couple, a man who appeared to be in his twenties and seemed like being there was in inconvenience to him. He kept checking his phone and bouncing his leg up and down.

Suddenly the doors opened again in the back of the room and the men who had deposed me walked in. I recognized them as Jason Ramie's defense team. My pulse spiked and my breath caught in my throat. This experience was quickly becoming all too real. I had wanted my chance to do my part, my chance to defend myself, my opportunity to prove to myself and Jason Ramie that he couldn't take everything from me. But now I felt as if maybe I had been too careless in my evaluation of my abilities.

Simultaneously, both Megan and Kalli grabbed one of my hands with theirs.

"Breathe, Fella," Megan whispered in my ear. "We're right here. We've got you."

I nodded, my eyes glued to the floor beneath my primly crossed ankles.

After that, everything happened quickly. The doors were closed, the bailiff entered, the judge came in, and then Jason Ramie entered the courtroom. He had been kept in a separate room, still in custody of the Portland Police, and was hand cuffed when he entered. I forced myself to look at him and was pleased when the sight of him didn't send me into a tailspin of emotion. It made me nervous when they took his handcuffs off, but I was calmed slightly by the fact that the police officer was never more than three steps from him.

I noticed the couple sitting behind him, who earlier seemed out of place, now looked desperate to touch him. There was compassion in their eyes, love. I figured they must be his parents. Suddenly I felt a new and unusual emotion towards Jason Ramie. I felt sorry for him. I felt sadness for him. Somewhere along the line of his life, he had made some really terrible decisions and enormously cold-hearted mistakes, but he was once someone's little boy. The people behind him, his parents, looked broken.

Ugh. Unconditional love came with the highest of highs and the deepest, darkest, coldest, valleys of lows.

I tried hard to pay close attention to the proceedings, but my heartbeat was racing and my mind kept flittering to Porter and Mattie. Both the prosecution and defense teams gave their opening statements – short and sweet introductions as to how they were going to prove the other totally and completely wrong. There was lots of talk of alibis, testimonies, firearm ballistics, medical mistreatment, and circumstantial evidence.

After about an hour of listening to Detective Dillard talk about the bullet pulled from my shoulder and how it had matched the ballistic fingerprints from bullets fired from the gun found on Jason Ramie's person at the time of his arrest, Mr. Donaldson addressed the judge and called his next witness: me.

Porter

As far as I could tell, Mattie was possibly the easiest baby to take care of in the history of newborns. The morning passed calmly enough. No real crying or issues, and Mattie did well too. We were both torn up with concern about Ella and missed her terribly. Well, I might have noticed her absence more than the baby, but we'd never tell Ella that.

I was able to feed her a bottle and even though I loved every moment, every tiny little whimpering gulping sound Mattie made as she drank her bottle and gazed into my eyes, I told her not to get used to it and that Mommy would be back soon enough and these bottles would be long gone. Mattie's eyes drifted closed in what I took to understand as compliance.

Ella's parents showed up mid-morning letting me know Megan and Kalli were with Ella and that gave me some relief from the tension I had felt all morning. Guilt was weaving its way into my mind and taking root, but I tried to remind myself frequently that Ella was strong and could handle this on her own. Plus, I couldn't exactly promise myself that had I been in the same room with Jason Ramie he'd make it out of his own trial with his life.

Yes. It was better that I was here, calmly holding my daughter and just *looking* at her. She was beautiful, truly adorable. No one ever told me that when babies yawn, your whole heart sort of puddles around your feet. They yawn and stretch, arch their backs, and their tiny little bottoms push out making the whole thing too cute to stand. I watched her, enraptured by every wiggle, every sound, and every gurgle. I was interrupted when the door to her room opened and Dr. Edwards came in with more doctors in white coats flanking her sides.

"Hello, Mr. Masters. We've had a bit of juggling with schedules and procedures lately and it looks as though we'll be able to get Mattie in for her PICC line sooner than we had thought."

"Oh?" I asked, standing and placing Mattie in the crib.

"Yes. Is your wife here this morning?"

"No. She had to be at a trial this morning. She's downtown."

"Oh, well, that was probably difficult for her, but also good that she got out of this room. She's been so attentive, but one can only take so much confinement." Dr. Edwards gave me a smile that showed admiration.

"She's pretty stubborn," was all I could say as I laughed my reply.

"Well, be that as it may, she's done an excellent job." She looked over at Mattie. "We're going to take her now, if that's ok with you, and she should be back in about forty five minutes."

"Now?"

"Yes. We're ready for her."

"And I can't go with her?"

"Unfortunately, no. This isn't an invasive procedure, but it is important that it is done in a controlled environment. We will be using ultrasound machines to watch the catheter in her veins to make sure we get it placed correctly."

I paled at her words, feeling the blood drain from my face.

"You're not going to put her under, are you?" I became instantly panicked. Ella and I had talked about the procedure, but I was only given the information Ella provided me with, and obviously hadn't thought to ask any really important questions until this very moment when my pulse was racing and my protective instincts were trying to claw their way out of me like a caged bear.

"No, no, no. Mr. Masters, I am not trying to worry you." She patted my arm in an attempt to calm me, but I just wanted some answers. "We will simply be putting another line in her, just like her I.V., but it will be inserted in a different location – her elbow. Then we just watch it with the ultrasound as it makes its way up the vein and we place it right outside the heart. We do wrap the babies up very tight, leaving only the one arm available, just to keep them from wiggling, as they tend to do. But the procedure is relatively pain free, just like having an I.V. put in, and she doesn't need to be put under any anesthesia."

I breathed out a sigh of relief, then sucked another breath more urgent than the one before. "Wait," I rasped, suddenly terrified. "Could she... can this..." I couldn't even make myself say the words. I ran a hand down my face.

"Mr. Masters, please, take a seat."

I stumbled backwards and landed in the chair, putting my head in my hands between my knees. I felt Dr. Edwards kneel next to me.

"Mattie is going to be just fine. This is not an invasive procedure. We do them all the time, even on babies as tiny as her. I have never seen any real complications besides not being able to get the catheter in to begin with. The highest risk involved with this is infection." I lifted my head and looked at her, trying to take in her words and hear what she wasn't coming right out and saying.

Mattie wasn't going to die. This wasn't going to kill her.

"Well," I said as I shook my head and ran my hand through my hair, "that was a fun little breakdown."

"Mr. Masters, it can be very stressful having a child in the hospital, you're doing just fine. And hopefully, if everything goes well, you won't have to be here much longer."

I smiled at her and watched as one of her colleagues lifted Mattie from her crib and they took her away without really giving me a second glance. I collapsed back into the chair again, a new exhaustion coming over me. How had Ella dealt with all of this for a week? I didn't envy that Ella had been the one to take Mattie to the doctor to begin with, but now that I had a taste of the fear of not knowing what was going on with your child, I knew Ella had lived through something no one should ever have to.

I pulled out my phone to text her.

I have not given you enough credit for how strong and incredible you are. I love you madly, and Mattie is so lucky that you are her mother.

Also, they have taken Mattie to put in her PICC line. They say she should be back in about 45 minutes. How is everything going for you?

Ella

I could feel my hands shaking as I walked towards the chair where the bailiff was waiting to swear me in. He was big and burly. He also looked slightly unfriendly. He stood in front of me and made me promise I wouldn't lie. I, personally, didn't need the man to scare me into telling the truth, but understood the process and routine.

I took my oath and sat in the chair, smiling just a little at how full of uncomfortable chairs my life had been lately.

"Mrs. Masters, can you please tell the court where you were the night in question?"

I rubbed my hands on my thighs to wipe the dampness away and to try to tame the shaking.

"I drove back from the beach that night and came home to find my ex-boyfriend in our apartment, well, my apartment that we had previously shared. He wasn't supposed to be there. We had an altercation and I left. I then went to my store, Poppy, to wait for my boyfriend to come and pick me up."

"And how long were you at Poppy alone?"

"About an hour and a half. I fell asleep in the backroom."

"What woke you?"

"I heard a banging on the glass doors."

"What happened next?"

"I walked out of the backroom and saw a man standing outside the doors."

"Can you describe the man you saw?"

"Yes. He was tall, perhaps six foot five. He wore a dark hoodie and dark pants. Um," I stammered, trying to fight the nerves taking over. I also was trying not to look at Jason Ramie as I described him, Mr. Donaldson had warned me against that. "He had a defined chin, dark hair, light eyes, I think maybe blue? And his nose was crooked, as if it had been broken before."

"What happened next, Mrs. Masters?"

"He asked me for food, and I thought he was a transient so I told him through the glass that I didn't have any. Then he raised up his arm and was holding a gun." My voice wavered slightly, and I took a deep breath. I tried to push the memory out of my mind and my eyes found my sister and focused on her. She smiled at me and nodded. "The man," I continued, hoping I sounded a little more put together than I felt, "pulled the trigger on his gun and I was shot in the shoulder. The fall caused severe head trauma and I was taken to OHSU for treatment."

I exhaled, glad I had made it through the retelling of one of the most terrifying moments of my life.

"Mrs. Masters is it true that you identified your shooter in a line up at the Portland Police station?"

"Yes."

"Is the man you identified here today?"

"Yes."

"Can you point to him, please?"

I raised my arm, just as Jason Ramie had when he pointed a gun at me, and aimed my finger directly at him.

"That's him. The man who shot me."

"Thank you," he said to me. He then turned to the judge. "I have no further questions, Your Honor."

"Defense, the witness is yours to cross examine." The judge's voice was short, cold, and sharp. It made sense though. She was obviously impartial and not interested in anything except order. Jason Ramie's main attorney stood and buttoned his gray blazer, walking towards me with a slimy smile on his face.

"Good morning, Mrs. Masters, how are you today?"

Caught off guard by his question, not expecting to exchange pleasantries, it took me a moment longer than I would have liked to formulate my answer.

"I am anxious to put this all behind me. I have a brand new baby in the hospital waiting for me to come back to her. So if you wouldn't mind…" I tilted my head to the side, hoping my snark was coming across. I happened to catch Kalli grinning from her chair, so perhaps it was working.

"Right. We all want to get back to our lives, Mrs. Masters." He took a moment to let his comment sink in, and the meaning wasn't lost on me. I readjusted myself in my chair while he took his pregnant pause. "Tell me, what happened *after* you were shot?"

"I was taken to OHSU and treated."

"For what?"

"I had a gunshot to the shoulder and a sub-cranial bleed."

"But you recovered." It was a statement, not a question.

"Yes."

"But not entirely." Again, a statement.

"Objection, Your Honor. Counsel isn't cross examining the witness. He'd need to be asking questions to do so." Mr. Donaldson sounded exasperated. Being a lawyer took a lot of acting ability, I was learning.

"Your Honor, I am trying to make a point and if it pleases the court, I would like to continue."

After a few seconds the judge responded with, "Get to the point, Counselor."

"Mrs. Masters, you had some long-lasting effects from your unfortunate accident, didn't you?"

"A few. To which are you referring?"

"Memory loss, for one?"

"Yes. I suffered from retrograde amnesia."

"So, for a time, you couldn't remember the actual shooting in question or the shooter for that matter."

"That is true. But my memory returned about two months after the accident."

"Fully?"

"Mostly."

"Meaning?"

"There were a few things that were still fuzzy, and even now sometimes I have a hard time recalling things that happened in the six weeks of memory that I lost, but most of it comes to me fine."

"Was your shooter's face and identity part of the memory that came back easily?"

"As soon as my memory returned I remembered the shooting, but part of the shooter's face was blocked from me."

"And then, magically, while looking at a random line up of men, your memory returned and you conveniently remembered Mr. Ramie's face, is that true?"

"There was nothing magical or convenient about it, I assure you."

"Do you think it's medically possible for someone's memory to just return to them out of the blue?"

I was primed to answer the question with a resounding YES! Because that was exactly how it had happened, both times, but I was cut off by Mr. Donaldson's loud and angry voice.

"Your Honor, I object! Mrs. Masters is not a medical professional and can't possibly comment on the inner workings of the human brain."

"Sustained." The judge sounded a little upset with the defense too. "I think we all need a break. Court will recess for thirty minutes." She banged her gavel and everyone seemed to scatter. Jason Ramie was cuffed again and led back to wherever he had emerged from.

I pushed out a long and deep breath, releasing a lot of anxiety the last twenty minutes had created within me. I walked over to the girls to grab my pump.

"That man is a dipshit," Megan said, glaring at the defense lawyer, not bothering to keep her voice down. I was sure he heard her, but he made no motion to indicate it.

"Megan," I scolded. "This is not some bar where you can fling insults and get pushed out by a bouncer. In this bar, the bouncer is a bailiff and you don't get banned from the bar, you get taken to jail. So watch yourself."

"He's still a dipshit." She said, only this time much quieter. I nodded slightly, agreeing with her.

An intern working for my lawyer took the three of us to a private room that apparently was used solely for nursing moms. There was a little cartoonish sign on the door of a mom holding her baby and it only made me sad that I didn't have my baby with me. I was grateful for the space and the privacy though. I was also grateful for the break.

Once we were all situated and Kalli and Megan were discussing the defense team a little more openly now that we weren't in the courtroom, I pulled out my phone to check my messages.

I have not given you enough credit for how strong and incredible you are. I love you madly, and Mattie is so lucky that you are her mother.

Also, they have taken Mattie to put in her PICC line. They say she should be back in about 45 minutes. How is everything going for you?

Hey, Babe. Mattie came back sleeping peacefully, PICC line successfully implanted. It's actually pretty cool. And no more needle pokes so that's awesome. I hope everything is going well in court. Please text me when you get a chance. We miss you.

Reading his texts I was immediately struck by a multitude of emotions all at once. First I was panicked that she'd had the procedure done while I was away. I'd officially missed something important. The thought of not being there in case something terrible had happened made my chest ache and my breath caught in my throat.

Next came relief that everything seemed to have gone all right. Then came another wave of relief with the idea that she wouldn't need to have any more pokes to draw blood and no more I.V. shenanigans to be dealt with. I let the tension leave me with a sigh and typed my response.

I am so glad everything went smoothly. I miss you both too. Trial is, uh, interesting. I was on the stand and then they called a recess. Defense is trying to question my memory of his face.

I knew Porter would be upset by my update, but there wasn't anything I could do about it from across the city. A response from him was almost immediate.

Give 'em hell, Babe. Mattie and I will be waiting for you this evening. And by the way, she told me she didn't like the bottle. Hated it. Only drank it in protest.

I laughed out loud at his message, but my heart swelled in my chest at his words as well. He knew exactly what was most upsetting about this day and also knew exactly how to make it easier for me. I responded with a smile on my face.

I love you. Give Mattie some snuggles for me.

I'll try, but she keeps telling me that I'm not as comfortable to lay on as you are. She's pretty mouthy. ;)

Oh, and I love you too. Always.

Time passed too quickly and we found ourselves back in the courtroom and I was, once again, called to the stand to continue my testimony. The judge reminded me that I was still under oath, to which I gave her an understanding nod and a quiet, "Yes, Your Honor." The defense lawyer made his way towards me again, slowly, not making eye contact, reminding me of a snake in tall grass, slithering his way towards his prey. He tried to throw me off, intimidate me, but I wasn't having any of it. I could see him, plain as day, and refused to be anything but confident in that moment.

"Mrs. Masters, before the recess we were talking about your miraculous memory returning just in the nick of time to I.D. a random man in a line up."

"But he wasn't random. That was the man who was arrested and found to have a gun on him which matched the type of gun that shot me. That's not a coincidence."

"Your honor, this witness is not qualified to offer testimony as to what my client had on him when he was arrested or not. Please let her previous statement be stricken from the record."

"Sustained," the judge said. "Jury," she said, turning to address the group of people sitting to our left, "you will not allow the witness' previous statement alter or influence your final decision. It has been stricken from the record." The jurors all nodded and turned their faces back towards me.

"Mrs. Masters, let's try this again. Just tell me about how you saw Mr. Ramie in a line up, and identified him, if you couldn't remember his face."

I took a deep breath in and tried to sort out my thoughts before I spoke them aloud. "Up until the line-up at the police station, whenever I pictured the person who shot me, I could see everything except his face. His height, his build, his clothing. The only thing missing was the face." I took in another breath, letting it out slowly, looking to Kalli for a little strength. She gave me a small and tight smile, obviously nervous for me. "When I went in for the line up, I even told the detective I didn't remember anything. I assured him I wouldn't be of any help, but Detective Dillard insisted I try. I went in the room and I started at the beginning, looking at each man, trying to make desperately sure that I wasn't passing up the man who had shot a gun at me."

I finally looked the defense lawyer right in his eyes. "The first five men looked like strangers. I had no recognition of any of them. Nothing. But when I started looking at number six, everything started coming together, like a fog was lifting."

"A fog?" The lawyer smirked at me.

"Have you ever had amnesia?"

My question caught him off guard and he stumbled through a response, "Um, no."

"Then you have no idea what it feels like to have a memory return to you. It is an all-of-a-sudden occurrence. There's nothing slow and gradual about it. It's like having the answer to a question or the name of a song on the tip of your tongue. It seems like it's just *right there*, but it isn't, and it either comes or it goes. But when it does come, it's like a balloon popping. All at once and deafeningly loud. The memory screams at you to be remembered." My eyes roamed over to Jason Ramie and our glares met one another. He didn't look remorseful or contrite. He looked angry and annoyed. "Jason Ramie is the man who shot me and the fact that my memory returned when I saw his face is neither a coincidence nor a fallacy." I paused, looking back at the lawyer standing in front of me, his face painted with a look of shock, much like I might have just told him to kiss my ass. He looked baffled and disoriented as he tried to think of what to say next. "But I will let Dr. Bronson tell you about the medical side of amnesia, seeing as how I am not a medical professional."

The smile on my face probably looked bitchy. I most likely looked like the cat that ate the canary. But I felt wonderful. I'd finally gotten my chance to tell this small and secluded room of people what Jason Ramie had done to me. I'd looked him in the eye and told him that I knew who he was and what he'd done.

The rest of the trial dragged on. I might have been biased, but Mr. Donaldson was, in my opinion, a much better lawyer than Jason Ramie's. The prosecution pressed on after my testimony. Mr. Donaldson did a superb job of bringing witnesses to the stand that painted a picture of Jason Ramie's guilt. The jury heard about how the bullet pulled from my shoulder matched a bullet that had been shot out of the gun found on his person at his arrest. Detective Dillard did a wonderful job of talking about each gun's "fingerprint" and how the two bullets each had the same "fingerprint" on them and so they were both fired from the same gun – Jason Ramie's.

Dr. Bronson took the stand and spoke about my amnesia and, thankfully, backed up my testimony that memory loss was unpredictable and could reverse at any moment for any number of reasons. He also gave his professional opinion that I couldn't have involuntarily assigned a new memory. In layman's terms, I couldn't have forced myself to remember something unreal or untrue out of want or need. He also reiterated that memories can come back swiftly and in response to stimuli.

The prosecution rested around lunch time and I was in need of a break. I called Porter and learned that not only had Mattie gotten the PICC line, but that Dr. Edwards was also planning on getting her echocardiogram done soon. My head dropped and my eyes closed – another thing I would miss. Porter assured me that Mattie was open and vocal about her dislike for being with Daddy alone. He was doing everything he could to make me feel better about being away, and I loved him all the more for it.

After lunch break, the defense took control of the courtroom and I was surprised to find that even I, a fashionista with no background in law and criminal investigations, found their argument to be lacking. Jason Ramie's lawyers focused on the reliability of the testimony of the man who had exchanged information to lessen his own sentence. They tried to make it seem like the man who gave up Jason Ramie's name to begin with was unreliable and couldn't be trusted. This argument, to me at least, paled in comparison with the ballistics evidence presented by Detective Dillard.

The defense called me up to testify again and even though I was nervous to take the stand, my nerves quickly faded when I realized the defense was grasping at straws. His lawyer tried baiting me into talking about my mental health, attempting to argue that I had been struggling with depression and couldn't make a sound identification due to my mental status. Before I could even begin to tell him what kind of a ridiculous assessment that was Mr. Donaldson objected stating that the court had already established that I wasn't a medical professional and shouldn't be expected to comment on my own mental stability and should the defense want to explore it they should have subpoenaed my counselor.

I smiled at his smart assery.

Without much more to say about anything, the defense released me from the stand and shortly after rested their arguments. Closing arguments came and went, again, the prosecution taking one for the win. The judge turned her attention to the jury and started a long and in-depth speech about their next tasks, telling them they would be sequestered until they could come to a unanimous verdict. The jurors were led from the room by the bailiff and taken to their secret deliberation location, and Jason Ramie, again, was taken from the room, led off in handcuffs. The judge thanked the lawyers and stated that the court was in recess until the jury came to a decision.

I looked around at Megan and Kalli, and then at Mr. Donaldson who gave me a tired smile.

"So," I said quietly, looking around the room at everyone dispersing. "That's it then?"

"I'm afraid so. Now we just wait for the jury to come back with a verdict."

"And that could, in all seriousness, take days, right?"

He chuckled at me and laid a gentle and friendly hand on my shoulder. "Yes, there is always that chance. But realistically, I doubt the jury will have a hard time with this case. I wouldn't go far if I were you," he said with a wink. "But if you'll excuse me I will use the break to make some calls that are pressing." I nodded and stepped away, letting him pass and leave the courtroom.

We girls went back to our special nursing room and I could tell the girls were trying to keep my mind occupied on other topics because their conversations never touched on the trial or Mattie. They talked about Megan and Patrick's dilemma over where in Portland to buy a house, or Kalli's newest film she was working on. I let them have their conversation as I texted Porter to keep him in the loop. We'd had a good rhythm of texts going back and forth, but then suddenly his stopped and I didn't get a response from him.

"Why is your forehead all scrunched up, Fella? It's not good for wrinkles, you know," Megan asked, glancing at me and noticing my uptight state.

"Porter just stopped texting me. We were in the middle of a conversation and now there's nothing."

"Maybe he's feeding the baby?" Kalli supplied, trying to be helpful. I gave her a small smile.

We finished up and walked back to the lobby outside our courtroom. It felt weird to wait, especially since we had no idea for how long we'd be waiting. But to leave felt strange as well, like leaving the movie before the end, not knowing how it turned out, anticlimactic. So we waited. It was another half-hour before I received another text from Porter.

Hey. Sorry I disappeared. A lot happened in the last 30 minutes.

My breath exploded in my throat, catching, blocking any more air from coming in or getting out. I frantically typed out a response to his text.

What do you mean? Is Mattie ok?

I managed to force my lungs to work, taking in shaky breaths until I got his response.

"Ella, what's up?" Kalli asked. She must have noticed my shaky breathing and pale face.

"I'm not sure. Porter sent me a really cryptic text and hasn't explained himself yet. He said a lot has been happening at the hospital and that's why he couldn't text me back." My phone pinged with his response.

Babe, calm down. Everything is fine. Mattie had her echocardiogram, which was very cool, and the doctor said that everything looks fine. She thinks the murmur she heard in the emergency room might have just been something cause by stress of the infection.

I exhaled, but kind of wanted to slap Porter through the phone for causing me to lose years off my life from the sheer panic I had endured in his radio silence.

Well, that's good news.

Just as I'd hit send, Mr. Donaldson walked up to us with a smile on his face.

"The jury is done deliberating." His smile grew even wider as he said the words. "Court will resume in thirty minutes."

"Done already? It's been less than an hour."

"I'm not surprised, Mrs. Masters."

"Well, all right then." Just then my phone pinged again.

So, since she's got the PICC line, and her heart looks good, Dr. Edwards said there's no reason to keep her here any longer and she's discharged Mattie. We're just waiting to sign the paperwork and then we're free to go.

For the umpteenth time that day, I felt like a ping pong ball being tossed back and forth. Porter's words caused me to halt my steps, Kalli and Megan nearly ramming into me because of it. I was all over the emotional map. I was nervous about hearing the verdict of the jury, worried that such a short deliberation meant, surely, they'd found him innocent of the charges and I'd have to go back to living my life in fear of him again. Only now, since I'd so boldly taken a stand and publicly accused him of attempted aggravated murder, he had no reason to *not* hunt me down and finish the task he'd started last spring. On the other hand, I was gutted that my baby was being released from the hospital and I wasn't there to see she got home all right.

"What's up?" Megan asked, pulling me from the doorway as not to block anyone else entry into the courtroom.

"They're releasing Mattie."

"Oh my gosh, really? That's wonderful! That means she's healthy and ok?" Megan gave me a sideways hug as I still stared at the screen. Kalli smiled at me, waiting for me to say something.

"Yeah," I said, looking around, for what I wasn't sure. I suddenly felt very out of place. "Listen guys, I'm gonna go."

"Go?" Kalli asked. "Go where?"

"Home. To be with my husband and baby. I don't need to be here anymore."

"Don't you want to find out what happens?"

"It doesn't matter anymore." And it didn't. I'd done what I came here to do and said my piece. I'd done everything I could to put Jason Ramie behind bars, but now I refused to let him hijack anymore of my life. If my baby was going home, so was I.

"What do you mean it doesn't matter? Don't you want to see him convicted? Don't you want to watch them cuff him and haul him away?" Megan's voice was full of fury and she sounded like she was having a hard time believing I didn't want to stay and watch the circus she was describing.

"No. I don't need to see that. But if you want to stay, you could text me and tell me what happens, ok?"

"You want me to text you whether the man who tried to kill you gets convicted or not?"

"Um…Yes."

"Ella, it's almost time. It will only be a few minutes." Now Kalli was trying to reason with me.

"Look, guys, I appreciate your concern, really, but enough of my life has been disrupted by this asshole. There's nowhere else in the world I am supposed to be this evening than at home with my baby and husband. So," I said as I tossed my hands up in the air, daring either of them to argue with me. "Either stay and get the scoop for me, or go home. Either way, I'll find out about it somehow."

"We'll stay," Megan said as Kalli nodded.

"Great. Thank you. Text me," I said, kissing both of their cheeks before I broke into an all-out run, trying to make my way out of the courthouse with one thought at the front of my mind: I needed to get to my family.

Chapter Twenty

Porter

The last couple of hours at the hospital was somewhat of a whirlwind. The PICC line, the echo-cardiogram, the discharge – the hospital had been great to us, but in the end it was like they couldn't get us out of there fast enough. I smiled at the memory. Melody, the nurse Ella had mentioned many times and who I thought was, by far, the best nurse we'd had, fawning over Mattie, telling her to be good for her mommy who needed some good rest and relaxation. Melody smiled up at me, and looked as though she was contemplating something.

"What is it?" I asked her.

"Well, I don't want to overstep my bounds here, and I don't want to make anyone uncomfortable, but…"

"Melody," I laughed, "Spit it out."

"I just really liked getting to know Ella and I felt like we were becoming friends and I'm a little sad she isn't here for me to tell her goodbye. I guess I was hoping you could tell her goodbye for me? Just tell her I said good luck?"

I smiled at Melody and of course agreed, but also asked if I could give Ella her phone number. Of all the people on the planet, I understood how Ella could instantly put people at ease, make them feel important, and genuinely build relationships with people even in the worst of situations. I was not at all surprised that Ella had managed to befriend our nurse – she was so easily loved.

We made it home and even though Ella's parents offered to come back to our house with Mattie and me, I felt like it was important for us to be here alone. She'd done beautifully on the ride home, never fussing once, and as soon as we'd walked in the house I'd fed and changed her, then she fell peacefully back asleep.

The PICC line was hidden under her little shirt and unless you knew it was there, she looked like a normal four-week-old baby, well, as far as I could tell. She was the only baby I'd ever really been around. I'd made an appointment for the medical company to come out to the house tomorrow to show us how to hook her meds up to the port in the line, and Dr. Edwards assured me before we left that Ella and I were very capable of handling it.

I heard a car pull up the gravel drive and then listened as the car turned off and the door slammed. Not five seconds later the front door swung open and Ella came marching into the kitchen.

"Hey, Babe. You're just in time. Dinner's almost ready." I said, turning my head over my shoulder to talk to her as I stirred the simmering tomato sauce.

"Dinner?"

"Yes. Dinner. I figured you might appreciate something other than hospital food."

"Hospital food?"

I turned to her fully, turning the heat on the sauce down to low. "Are you ok? You're just repeating everything I'm saying."

"Where's Mattie?"

"She's asleep in her crib."

"Does she need to eat? Does she need a diaper change?" Ella moved to rush up the stairs, but I caught her around the waist before she made it past the kitchen island.

"Ella, she's fine. Why don't you take a minute and relax?" Her eyes darted back and forth between mine and I could imagine the thoughts bouncing around in her head. She was torn between trusting me that Mattie was fine and taken care of, sitting down and relaxing for a moment, and rushing right up those stairs to check on her. I would have been fine with either reaction, but I hoped for the former. She exhaled and relented, turning in my arms and placing her hands on my chest. "Hey," I said, leaning down and brushing my lips across hers.

"Hey to you too." She let me walk her backwards until she plopped into a kitchen chair. I knelt down in front of her and placed my hands on her thighs.

"Tell me about the trial."

"It kind of went exactly as I thought it would, although it didn't last very long at all. I was really surprised when it ended."

"Are you ok?" She knew what I was asking. She knew I was worried about her having to go through with the testimony without me, having to sit in a room with him, look him in the eye, and walk through her pain again. Her hand came up and brushed down the side of my face gently.

"I am ok." She sat up a little straighter. "I'm more than ok, actually. I thought it was going to be really hard. I had built it up in my head to be something really draining and emotionally tumultuous. But you know what? It was really, kind of, liberating. He seemed really smug and not at all affected by my testimony, but I sort of enjoyed sitting there and airing his dirty laundry." She paused for a moment, smiling to herself. "His attorney was the biggest asshole though. I think he knew he didn't have a good case so he was just trying to make me falter by baiting me." She shook her head.

Both of our heads turned towards the monitor when we heard Mattie squawking. Ella's eyes closed as if hearing her baby's voice could heal any ailment she might have had. She opened her eyes again and looked at me.

"Do you mind if I go up? Can we postpone dinner for a little while?"

"I'm ok with that, as long as I can come up with you."

She leaned forward and kissed me gently. "Of course you can come up with me." We walked up the stairs, hand in hand, and found Mattie in her crib, cooing up at the stars dangling from her mobile.

"Hey there, Pretty Girl," Ella said as she bent down to pick Mattie up. "Mommy missed you today." I watched as Ella nuzzled into the baby's neck, taking her time soaking up the baby scent that even I could admit was totally intoxicating. Nothing smelled as good or as calming as baby. A calm came over the room as mother and daughter sat in the corner, in the rocking chair we spent so much time picking out before our baby was even born, imagining moments just like this.

From downstairs we both heard Ella's phone ping and she looked up at me with pleading eyes. "Would you mind going downstairs to get my phone for me?"

"Of course not."

When I made my way back upstairs Ella was nursing Mattie with a dreamy smile. She was floating somewhere on a baby high, drunk off her love for her daughter. It was breathtaking to see and filled every tiny empty crevice within me to the brim with love. She held Mattie's tiny hand in hers and brought it up to her mouth for a kiss, making silly faces at her, asking the baby about her adventurous day, filling in the blanks, not waiting for her to miraculously talk and respond.

"You've got a text," I said to her quietly, not trying to interrupt their moment.

"What does it say?" She whispered to me without taking her eyes off the baby, her voice floating over the darkness of the room like a shimmering light.

"Guilty."

I looked over at her and she was smiling at Mattie, her fingers trailing over the plumpness of her cheeks, feathering over her small ear, brushing through the hair on her head that I knew felt just like silk.

"Did you hear that Mattie? Every single thing in the world is ok now."

Epilogue

Ella

Mattie's First Birthday

"I don't think we could have gotten more beautiful weather," Tilly said, placing one of her cheesecakes on the picnic table outside. We were busy decorating for Mattie's party, but I took a very long and hard look at her cheesecake. It had been a while since I'd tasted it and my mind wandered to the last time. I felt the blush come over my face and I turned away from Tilly not wanting her to see me thinking about her son in compromising situations.

"Very true. You never know what the weather's going to be like on the Oregon Coast." Usually, Lincoln City in August was a pretty safe bet, but we did luck out with the cloudless blue skies and no wind – which was key. We couldn't have all our pink and purple princess decorations flying away.

"Birthday girl is up from her nap." I heard Porter's voice from behind me as he came from the house. Just his voice was enough to send shivers of desire coursing through me, but when I turned and saw him holding my world in his arms, it was like sex personified. His muscled arms encircling our baby was nearly enough to make my ovaries implode.

"Hey, Sweet Girl," I said as they walked up to me. She reached her chubby arms for me saying loudly 'Ama! Ama!' which was Mattie's baby version of Momma. Porter was Ada and we didn't argue with her about it. As he passed her to me, I felt his mouth caress the shell of my ear with a whisper.

"Is that cheesecake?" His words against my ear caused me to moan quietly and then I felt his lips against the sensitive skin of my neck.

"Mmmhmmm." It was all I could respond with. He gave me a playful yet promising slap on my rear and then picked up the cheesecake and started back towards the house. "Where are you taking that?"

"I'm hiding it in the very back of our refrigerator for later," he said, waggling his eyebrows at me. I laughed and tried to stop him but got caught up by the cars arriving in the driveway and immediately moved into party-host mode.

Today was one of those days when I really had to steal a moment to take in how lucky and blessed Porter and I were. Mattie was happy and healthy, completely recovered from all her health scares and hadn't been sick a day since she was released from the hospital so many months ago. Our families continued to be incredibly supportive and really took immense joy in all things Mattie. Our parents couldn't get enough of her and we always had a plethora of people ready and willing to babysit. Even Megan and Patrick took joys in spending evenings and weekend afternoons with her. They weren't ready to start their own family yet, but took great pride in being the best aunt and uncle ever.

Kalli came to celebrate and even brought the man who I was convinced was going to make her the happiest person alive – if only she'd let him. He loved her, anyone within ten feet of them could tell, but she was still trying to allow herself to be loved. To me though, she was the best friend I had ever had. I missed her when she was away, but treasured the time she spent with us when she managed to make it to Portland. That was just another reason I wanted her to wake up and see the man in front of her for what he was offering. Perhaps letting herself be happy would bring her closer to being settled, and if I was lucky, she would settle somewhere close to me.

I watched as Joy and Faith chased Mattie around the yard, Brook and Matt chatting with Porter, all of them watching our girls and laughing at their silly games.

"Hey, Ella, sorry I'm late. You know how it goes."

I turned to see Melody walking towards us, a big purple gift bag with a plume of balloons in her hands.

"Mel! I am so glad you could make it!" Of all the stress and heartache that came from Mattie's hospitalization, I was so happy that we gained a friend from the whole ordeal. Melody was bright, honest, funny, and sweet. After Mattie was back to her normal self, Melody and I started meeting for coffee every week and eventually she was just as much a staple in our lives as Megan or Kalli. The best part? Mattie *loved* Mel. They'd formed a bond in the hospital that really touched me. And just as much as Mattie loved Mel, you could tell that Mel loved my baby just as much. All our lives were enriched by her presence.

"Lell! Lell! Oons!" We all laughed as Mattie ran up to Mel and jumped up and down at all the balloons she was holding. She leaned down and tied one on to Mattie's wrist and then followed suit when the other two girls requested their balloon bracelets as well.

"You're a big hit with the balloons, Mel," I said laughing.

"What can I say? I know what my girl likes."

"Let's get you something to drink," Porter said from behind me, taking Mel to the table filled with food and beverages.

For the rest of the afternoon and well into the evening the adults sat around laughing and talking, watching the children play. We opened presents, we grilled hamburgers and hot dogs, we even lit off a few fireworks we had saved from the Fourth of July. Porter and I helped Mattie open her presents and spent an hour reminding her to say 'Thank You', which in the end sounded a lot like "Ank Ooo," but it would do. We watched her tentatively eat her very first piece of cake, waiting for either her father or me to take it away, confused when we encouraged her to eat it. We took pictures, we laughed, and more than once I caught Porter watching me. His stares always made my blood boil with the heat of his love, but today I understood his gazes to be more than just appreciative and lust filled. Today he looked at me like he was thankful. I tried to return the meaningful looks whenever I caught him giving them to me, but made a few mental notes to properly thank him for everything important in my life later in the evening.

When it became obvious that Mattie had hit her limit of fun for one day, we changed her into her pajamas and kissed her goodnight, placing her in the car seat that had a permanent place in the back of my parent's car. Their gift to us for her birthday was an evening alone. At first I was not happy with the idea of spending the night of her birthday away from her, but eventually I was convinced by my husband who told me stories of how she would never even remember us sending her away and would likely sleep the entire night away regardless of where she was. I couldn't really argue with him about it and a whole night alone did sound fabulous. Eventually we both agreed and now watched as my parents drove away with my *toddler* in their car.

"I can't believe she isn't a baby anymore," I whispered quietly, trying to wipe away the single tear that had managed to escape before I could stop it. Porter's hands wrapped around my waist from behind and his chin rested on my shoulder.

"No, I guess she isn't, is she? But she's a beautiful and smart little one-year-old. She has to grow up, Ella. Think of all the fun experiences that are still in store for us."

Perhaps dads just lacked the gene that made mother's ache at the thought of their baby not being a baby anymore. No one ever warned me that birthdays were tough business for moms. I'd spent the day remembering her birth, thinking about the tiny baby that I had held in my arms just one year ago today, and comparing that image to the chubby, smiley, happy child that roamed around our yard all day. She'd eaten cake for goodness sake. She'd soon have her last bottle. Where did it stop? I needed a distraction from my sad yet happy thoughts so I moved to clear the food from the table.

Everyone stayed and helped clean up and then said their goodbyes, leaving Porter and I on the porch, waving to our friends as they left us to enjoy the rest of our evening. I leaned up against the railing, watching the taillights of our family and friends drift away when I felt him come up behind me, his arms caging me in, his mouth hot against my neck again.

"Want some cheesecake?" He rasped against me.

"Is that code for something?" I grinned.

"Nope. I really want some cheesecake." He pushed away from me and walked back into the house. I rolled my eyes with a smile, but followed him into the house anyway. I noticed some of Mattie's toys hadn't quite made it back into the toy box and started picking them up absentmindedly.

"Babe, stop it. Don't start cleaning. Why don't you go upstairs and get in some comfy pajamas and I'll bring up enough cheesecake for both of us?"

"Now *that's* an offer I'll take you up on," I said, dropping the toys on the floor at my feet with a smile. "Bring some wine too."

"What kind of a man brings his wife cheesecake with no wine?"

"Not my man," I said with a laugh and walked towards the stairs. When I walked into the bedroom my eyes grew wide with shock and my hand came to my chest to hold in the breath I felt escaping from me.

The bedroom was bathed in candlelight and there were vases with all different kinds of flowers scattered around the room. Hanging on the door to the bathroom was a hanger on which hung a new and very expensive piece of lingerie. I walked over to it, fingering the soft silk, trying to think of when Porter had enough time to orchestrate this without me knowing anything about it.

I took the silk and lace off the hanger and went into the bathroom. If he'd gone to all the trouble of setting this up, the man sure as hell was going to see me in a sexy piece of lingerie. The fabric felt wonderful against my skin and I made a note to myself that I needed to wear sexier things to bed more often. Just having the silk trailing against my thighs made me instantly feel sexier. I should try not to wear the flannel nightgown *all* the time.

When I came out of the bathroom I was met with the sight of my husband carrying a tray with plates of cheesecake and wine glasses. He stopped as soon as he saw me and I watched his throat constrict as he swallowed, his eyes roaming all the way from my head, down to my feet, and back up. His eyes lingered on my breasts and between my legs longer than any other area and I felt the heat pooling there, as if his eyes made it happen.

"You found my gift," he said, his voice low and gravelly, his eyes still roaming over my body.

"I love it," I whispered softly. He finally found his senses and set the tray down on the dresser. He turned back to me and my heart rate picked up as he slowly stalked towards me.

"You look..." he paused and I stopped, waiting for him to find his words. "Beautiful." He took another step towards me. "Perfect."

I was lucky in that Porter never seemed dissatisfied with my body after having a baby, but that didn't stop the insecurity from seeping in from time to time. My body was different than it use to be – not worse or better – just different. And even though we never had a problem being intimate, having a child in the house changed things between us. When before we would make love throughout an entire night, now we were lucky if by the time we were done we hadn't woken the baby. The frequency of sex and the ability to really let ourselves enjoy one another, gave way to naptimes and trying to be quiet so that we could get some sleep afterwards.

We were parents. I wouldn't trade it for the world, but life was different now.

When he was just inches from me, I held my breath and closed my eyes, anticipating his touch. I could feel his eyes on me and I knew he was enjoying looking at me as much as I enjoyed having his gaze burn over my skin. I slowly let out a sigh when his hand finally landed on the curve of my hip, and I leaned into his hand when I felt it gently cup my cheek. His thumb grazed over my cheek and I worried my bottom lip between my teeth.

"God, Ella, you have one sexy mouth."

Before I had a chance to respond, his mouth was on mine, covering it, melding to my lips. A soft moan escaped me and I wound my hands up behind his neck, running my fingers through the hair at the nape of his neck that had grown long in the summer months. I pulled him into me, used my tongue to beg him to let me in. His hands both found my face and he angled me perfectly against him and took everything. The kiss went from tentative to scorching in one instant and I was more than willing to risk being singed from getting too close to the flame.

There was nothing between us – no space, no air, no fear. Whatever he was, I was that too. We were the same in that moment. He walked me backwards until my legs bumped up against the mattress. I sat down, breaking our kiss, only to peel away his belt and pants, shoving them to the ground around his ankles, needing him to be free of any obstacles. I needed access. I needed connection.

My hands slid up his chest, fingers rippling over hard muscle as I pushed his shirt up, urging him to remove it. He was free of all his clothes quickly, crawling over me with a growl. His mouth chased mine all the way to the head of the bed where his lips finally caught me, kissing and breathing and taking everything from me. His hands were everywhere, skimming over my thighs, moving around to grasp at the swell of my bottom, covering my breasts, palming them, thumbs brushing over my nipples, causing me to cry out.

My body woke up, no longer submissive to his seduction. My hands wandered over his arms, my leg hiked itself over his calf, my hips rolled up to find him.

He placed wet kisses along my collar bone, moving in towards the valley between my breasts. I felt him pull the silk and lace away from my body as he continued down, his mouth capturing my breast, taking my nipple in his mouth hungrily.

"Oh, Yes. God, Porter..." My hands were in his hair, hips still grinding upwards, trying to connect. "Don't stop," I cried. His tongue flicked over one nipple while his fingers started tugging gently on the other.

"You taste fantastic," he said around my breast. His words registered but I couldn't respond, couldn't find the words. His mouth and hand moved away from me and I heard myself moan at his absence. He grabbed the hem of the nighty I wore and started pushing it up and over my head, leaving me only in the lace thong that came with the ensemble. Once I was free of the garment his mouth began its pilgrimage down my body again, gifting my skin with his tongue and lips. When he made it to the thong I felt his laugh rumble in his chest.

"These look rather flimsy." Without another word he wrapped the lace around his hands and pulled it apart slowly, his eyes never leaving mine. Eventually, the panties gave way and I was left bare and trembling.

"I hope those weren't expensive," I managed through a shaky breath.

"Only the best for my wife."

Without further conversation his mouth descended upon me and I gasped as his tongue caressed me, parting me, and only adding fuel to the heat he'd already built there. His tongue worked quickly, first just gliding up and down but then I felt him deeper and I lost the ability to keep my eyes open or my mouth closed.

"Yes, Ella." He rasped against my most sensitive skin. "Give me all of your sexy sounds. I want to hear you whimper. I want to hear you scream." He moved his mouth to my clit and my hands moved into his hair. He worked me like he was starved, relentlessly swiping his tongue against me, kissing and sucking until my back was arched and my hands gripped his hair tightly, holding him against me.

"More…" I managed. The pressure was maddening. I was just a fragment away from breaking to pieces. His tongue and lips and mouth had sent me skyrocketing into bliss and I wanted so desperately to crash back down on a wave of ecstasy. "Oh God, just a little more…" I begged. I felt him shift and gasped when his fingers entered me. He pumped in and out, matching the rhythm of his tongue, and the pleasure became almost too much to bear.

"No, no, I can't...please..."

All the muscles in my body were coiled, tightened, ready to snap. My head shook back and forth, my voice pleading for the orgasm that would surely end me. Porter responded by growling against me, the vibrations pushing me that much higher, his fingers becoming more aggressive, and his other hand reaching up and palming my breast. I mewled and thrashed, experiencing the universe's most brutal and beautiful build up in the history of orgasms, and all it took to send me over the edge were his eyes. I looked down, wanting to watch him work my body into hysterics. Our eyes met and all I could see in the chocolaty pools was love. His eyes pleaded with me to come, to give him everything I had, to offer myself to him in that way.

And then I fell.

I crashed.

I burst.

I was still in the middle of the most exquisite orgasm I'd ever experienced when he slowly entered me. Shaking and trembling, my hands found his face and pulled him down to me. I didn't have the wherewithal to kiss him, I just held his mouth against mine, breathing him in, still coming down, still floating back to earth.

He slowly pumped in and out of me, prolonging my superb orgasm, expertly building me towards another one before I'd even landed from the first.

"You're all I'll ever want, Ella," he said, suddenly changing the mood of our lovemaking from scorching and hot to heart wrenching and beautiful. "I'll never need anything as long as I've got you." His words touched me and his mouth splayed tiny kisses along my neck and he continued to move inside me.

Tears pricked my eyes and I gently kissed his shoulder, wrapping my arms around his back, pulling him even closer to me.

"You're my everything," I whispered against his sweat-slicked skin.

"Tell me you're mine." His hips picked up speed and he began thrusting quicker, his hands roaming my body as if he couldn't get enough of me.

"I've never been anything but yours," was my answer, and the truest words I would ever say.

"Forever."

"Always."

He'd had enough words and I felt his primal side take over again as he leaned up and away from me, his hands moving to my ass, lifting my hips up and driving deeper and deeper into me. My hands gripped the sheets beneath me and I watched with true rapture as my husband lost himself in me. I loved giving him my body and nothing was hotter than watching him enjoy me. He moved me how he wanted, manipulated me to bring himself bliss, and I aimed to be anything and everything he needed in that moment.

I wrapped my legs around him, bringing him in deeper, hearing him groan with pleasure. I moved my hips in time with his, loving the idea of giving him everything, but also bringing myself back up, building another orgasm. He grabbed one of my ankles and placed it over his shoulder, his hand caressing my calf and thigh as it trailed back down to my waist. He pumped faster, the new angle adding depth, and my mouth opened with a moan.

"Oh, God…" I mewled.

"Yes," he rasped. "Fuck. You're so wet."

I couldn't answer him. I couldn't form words. All I could do was let him use me, let him bring me higher all over again.

I knew he was close. His hips moved faster and his hands were grasping me wherever they could find purchase: my hips, my waist, my shoulders. He desperately tried to begin and end inside me and I wanted him there more than anything. I hung on the precipice, just waiting for him to take me with him.

One of his hands grasped the curve between my shoulder and neck and held on as he pumped in and out quickly, and his other hand reached down and caressed me where our bodies met.

"Together," he breathed.

And together we fell.

An hour later I was sprawled across Porter's body, his arm behind me, my leg draped over his, my head laying on his chest. The hand he had behind me ran through my hair, his fingers trailing through my tresses as we lay quietly with each other. On his stomach lay a plate with a piece of cheesecake and I watched as he lifted a bite to his mouth.

"Oh, God. That's good." His voice was rough, sleepy, and sated. I smiled as he scooped up another forkful and brought it to my mouth. I wrapped my lips around the cake and sighed in contentment as it melted against my tongue.

"Nothing in the world beats the taste of your mother's cheesecake," I said between swallowing and licking my lips.

"Hmmm." He responded around another bite.

My mind, still high and elated from being with my husband, made its rounds through the random and happy thoughts flitting around my brain. I thought about Mattie's party, how happy she looked surrounded by family and friends. I thought about my husband, playing with our daughter, making her laugh and making her smile. I was instantly filled to the brim with love and feel the familiar pang as tears start to well in my eyes.

I moved to wipe one away and took a deep breath to halt any others from falling.

"Hey," Porter whispered, his finger wiping away the wetness from my cheek. "What's this about?"

I tilted my head up to his face and smiled at him.

"I was just thinking about our day, and our life, and our family, and I realized that I am so incredibly happy. You've made me so happy, Porter."

He pressed a kiss to my forehead and continued to glide his fingers through my hair.

"I promise you," he whispered against my hair. "Whatever you're feeling, it doesn't come close to how I feel. There's no way to measure the joy you've given me."

I sighed and met my husband's eyes. He always looked at me with love, but in that instant I also saw wonder and contentment and fulfillment and peace. My hand found its way to his cheek and I loved the feeling of his stubble against my skin. My thumb grazed gently against his cheek.

"Did you ever, in your whole life, think you'd be this ridiculously happy?"

His mouth quirked in a small smile and he leaned down, brushing the tip of his nose against mine, softly and gently.

"Never."

The End

I hope you'll all look forward to Kalli's story.

Never Standing Still

Coming 2015

Acknowledgements

To all my beta readers who helped me mold my story, I appreciate you so much! Becca, Kara, Andrea, Lynn, Kelly, Kim, and Lesley, thank you so much for all the time you spent on my book, I appreciate the help so much!

To all the blogs that have supported me, Thank You. There are so many who do so much for me, and I could name them all but we'd be here a while. I would, however, like to shout out to Once Upon a Crush Book Blog, Prisoners of Print, Two Book Pushers, A Literary Perusal, and Reading Amore for their overwhelming support and unending kindness. Big loves to you guys.

To all my ladies in the Indie Round Table – I am forever grateful for all your support and *help*. I know I can always go to you with questions and when I need advice. It is more valuable to me than you realize. Thank you.

Jen Andrews, I am so glad to have found a friend in you over the last couple of months. You've been an ear for me, someone I can ask my dumb questions, and someone I feel like I can trust implicitly. Thank you for your help with this book.

Brook and Krysta, as always, thank you both for your hard work and for being so supportive the last year and a half. I couldn't have done it without you. Krysta, thank you for being with me at my first signing. I probably didn't tell you how much it meant to me to have you with me, but it was huge. Thank you.

To my family, thank you for the unwavering support, traveling with me, Mom, and helping me spread my wings in this new and exciting job. Demian, you're the best husband I've ever had. Honest. Thanks for watching me leave the house every Saturday morning and not giving me a hard time about it.

Most importantly, to the READERS! Oh my gosh, thank you so so so so so so much for being the most awesome group of readers I could ever ask for. EVER. *EVER.* You guys are the reason I do what I do and I love all of you. Even if I've never spoken to you, even if I talk to you all the time, and even if you fall somewhere in between those two poles: I wouldn't get to do this fantastic job if you didn't read my books and tell other book lovers about them. I can't wait for you all to see what I come up with next!

How to find me, because I love talking to readers:

Email: anie.michaels@gmail.com

Facebook: http://www.facebook.com/AuthorAnieMichaels

Blog: http://aniemichaels.blogspot.com